The
Trial
of
Lotta Rae

The
Trial
of
Lotta Rae

SIOBHAN MACGOWAN

WELBECK

Published in 2022 by Welbeck Fiction Limited,
an imprint of Welbeck Publishing Group
Based in London and Sydney.
www.welbeckpublishing.com

A CIP catalogue record for this book is available from the
British Library

Hardback ISBN: 978-1-78739-731-6
Trade paperback ISBN: 978-1-78739-782-8

Printed and bound by CPI Group (UK) Ltd., Croydon, CR0 4YY

10 9 8 7 6 5 4 3 2 1

In memory of my darling mother

Therese Mary MacGowan

And still we're cloaked in her love and magical spirit.

GIBSON SQUARE, LONDON, OCTOBER 16TH, 1919

William Linden laid his wig and gown on the rosewood dining table. Stroking the gown's black silk one last time, the wig's coarse horsehair, its looped tail, he smiled ruefully, remembering both the itch and ceremony when first he'd worn it. The wig of a judge. Yet whatever pride he had felt, even then, had been tainted. So badly tainted. He fixed it on his head, looking in the ornate mirror above the fireplace.

I pronounce you guilty.

Yes.

The familiar clutch at his gut. Agitated, he opened the trunk sitting at the hearth, tossing in both wig and gown, before snapping it shut. At the clatter of hooves on the darkened street, he looked up, catching his reflection in the long balcony window; that strained, old face. He closed the shutters, wanting to chase away that expression: haunted, startled. To pretend, for one moment, that the hansom cab on the square did not wait for him. He listened for the knocker at the hall door, breathing in those last precious seconds.

'It's here, sir.' The maid's voice behind him. She left quickly as he nodded.

He cast a last look at the trunk, his initials embossed there in gold. *WJL*. Lifting his eyes to the piano, he closed them to the ring of music, lure of long-ago tunes, the echo of laughter at the dining table. A bright fire in the grate. He opened his eyes to the charred coals, the ghosts disappeared.

Gone, all gone. Now he too could take his leave. Without glancing back, he left the room to descend the stairs. The maid hovered by the hall door.

'When shall we expect you back, sir?'

He didn't answer, but smiled. She took the prompt, unlatching the hall door, closing it softly behind him.

In the cold of the street, under the gaslight, he arranged his fur collar. The horse's breath made mist in the air, the smell of the nag pungent.

'Where now, sir?'

He noted the irony. The airy question. The weight of his answer.

'Old Jewry, in the City. But we must make a stop. At Chiswell Street. I'll knock when we get there.'

'Very good, sir.'

He hesitated before he climbed the step. He would grant himself a moment. Before he must face who he knew waited within. At last, he hauled himself up, closed the door, sat rigid against the black leather. She was there.

As the carriage lurched, he stared out the window, his face turned from his unwelcome companion. He had hoped, his decision made, she would allow him travel alone. But no. A vain hope. She had too long shared his prison. Too long had they been shackled together by fate.

He could not banish her on this, his final journey. She must bear witness to his end.

1

I too will stare from the window, William, stay turned from you. But I could not let you travel alone. Not this night. This night when it seems we will reach the end of our story. Perhaps this night, when it is done, I will leave you in peace. Perhaps I will no longer be a curse, a trouble to you. But you know why I must stay close, William. For you know by what secret we have been bound.

For too many years, you have condemned me. Thought me guilty of a deception. But you know the truth in your heart. As I know the truth in mine. And tonight you will hear my testimony. It will be no trouble to you, for you are a man versed in the weighing of testament, the measuring of guilt. You have witnessed many trials. I have witnessed just one. I have seen my name become notorious. Lotta Rae. The talk of all London. There was talk, much talk for sure. But was there truth? Was there justice?

Justice. Long ago, Pap taught me the seven ancient gates of this city I was born to. I knew young the terror of Newgate and the scourge that was Newgate Prison. But they ground those fetid walls with dead men's bones beneath and rose upon that unholy sod all they proclaimed good and mighty, the baptised stone of the Old Bailey. And crowned it with a hallowed dome. A noble beacon: the Golden Lady.

High, high the Golden Lady stood, so high she kept watch over all the children of London; she bid them, *come.* For she would deliver them justice.

She bid me come, William. And I believed her promise. Pap too. For, just like myself then, he was a simple soul. Bowed to his betters, teaching me to do the same. I trusted fine gentlemen such as you. Thought they could do no wrong. My father trusted in man, my mother in God. But I have seen what one can do, and what the other will allow in this world. And I trust in neither.

But I think too on my blessings. A child I'd run in from rolling the hoop, swiping cherries and roasted nuts on the market streets of Spitalfields, to eat bread and treacle at our comfortable fire. 'We're the lucky ones,' Mam would say, hanging washing at the hearth, I listening, dismayed, to her tales of the rookeries.

Mam and Pap were no strangers to those slums, remembering the swell and stink of Rose Lane before it was gutted and came pouring from its belly the broad sweep of Commercial Street and Peabody House, the fine lodgings the kindly Mr Peabody donated to the likes of us, the respectable working class. I know you will scoff, but we were that. Respectable. Pap a proud working man at the Whitbread brewery on Chiswell Street.

Some days I would excitedly carry Pap his lunch, stopping at the arch to let the hefty dray horses pass, dodging the cartloads of barrels in the courtyard. Below, in the cellars, by the troughs of stinking white foam, Pap and the men would tease me with the tale of some poor soul who'd been found long ago floating dead in one of those very same troughs, or so they claimed. When I asked what misfortune he had suffered, they said it was no human hand had delivered his end, it had been ruled that he had 'died by the visitation of God'.

But what horror was to befall me there, in that place, nine years later, was no visitation of some such spiteful deity. But the visitation of man. One man. Him.

And you.

2

His pores stiffened at the coldness of her silence. Above, the driver cursed an omnibus, the motorcars that were infesting the streets, choking all breathable air out of London. They were a menace. William had never travelled in one, nor would he.

It struck him that he might never again be afforded the chance. He felt the rise of panic. For a moment he thought of raising his cane, rapping the roof, ordering the driver to turn. But he stopped short. His eyes flitted towards his silent companion. *Justice.* He turned back to the window, wearily.

It seemed an age ago. When the flame of justice had truly lit his heart. A barrister at the razing of Newgate, he'd watched in awe the mounting of the Grecian columns, the regal dome of the court risen in its place. Never had he been more sure of his calling than at the sight of that golden vision. Arms in perfect symmetry, steady hand arbiter of the scales, sword of both protector and punisher glorious against the sky, promising to strike swift and true. For this was the mistress of whom he was servant. Lady Justice.

Yet what short time it had taken for him to betray her. Barely a year. Enchanted as he'd been by the Golden Lady, he could hardly fathom it now, the depth of that betrayal. For he had held himself a worthy bearer of her sword: *Protector. Punisher.* Never would he have doubted it.

Punishment. His mind lingered there. Eyes closed, he punished himself with a guarded memory. He'd taken Raff to see the court before it was complete. He allowed a wan smile. *Raff.* He'd been called Ralph, after his grandfather, but as a child had only ever been able say Raff. They'd called him that ever after. How old had Raff been then? Perhaps sixteen. Yes, for it had been a misty November, November 1906.

He recalled his son's wonder at the palatial mosaic arches and lobby, his footsteps echoing on the Sicilian marble floor. Afterwards, they'd strolled home through Gibson Gardens to Gibson Square, Raff chasing off to the morning room where Margaret liked to write her letters, to tell his mamma all he'd seen.

'Well, that sounds fine,' Margaret had said, smiling. He could see her now, turning from the writing desk, her cherished spider plant curling over its shelves. A tendril of her ash-brown hair had fallen from where it was tied loosely at the nape of her neck. He could see again her soft, hazel eyes, the mellow sun on her white lace dress, the mole she hated, but he loved, on her collarbone. Raff had leaped onto the chaise longue before her. She'd leaned to touch their son's eager face, smooth back his black curls. 'Perhaps one day your voice will ring out in those very courtrooms. You will sound your oratory just like your papa and grandfather. Imagine, three generations of barristers all from this house.'

Raff had grown serious.

'But Papa prosecutes for the Crown, Mamma.' For a moment, he'd looked almost shamed. 'If I'm to be a barrister I think I'd like to help people. I think I'd like to defend.'

Margaret had looked surprised, glancing over the boy's head, to catch his own eye.

'Well,' he'd said, walking over to ruffle Raff's hair, 'that is a noble enough calling. Each man is entitled to a good defence. That is the very basis of our profession.'

'Each man and each *woman*,' Margaret had said, chiding him.

'Indeed.' He'd smiled, conceding to his wife's affinity, if not his own, with the thorny cause of women's suffrage.

'There are so many people that need help. So many poor people. Don't you think, Mamma?'

He'd been taken aback at his son's sensibility. He couldn't recall possessing any like sentiment at Raff's age. Perhaps at any age.

'Papa helps people too, Raff,' Margaret said. 'There are so many who have been victims of awful crimes, who seek solace in justice.' She'd stroked his hair. 'But when you're grown, you will be whatever you wish.

It's a new century, Raff, a new world. And it belongs to you.'

His smile disappeared. He opened his eyes.

* * *

You are remembering, William. And I know the torment of it. That, I know only too well.

3

In autumn 1906 I was nineteen years old and employed at the Whitbread brewery. Finishing my schooling at thirteen, I'd worked a while at Flossie Bradshaw's grocery in Spitalfields, but, praised for my reading, writing and arithmetic, when I turned seventeen, Pap had a word with Penny Peter who found me a place in the busy office. They called him Penny Peter for he ran the accounts with a whip; they said he was so mean that, with all the fuss in the courtyard, he would scour the paving for dropped farthings. But that was uncharitable, for he was a kind man.

Before long, Archie, one of the clerks, had taught me to type and I'd sit at my green typewriter with bundles of invoices and taverns' orders. I was the only girl in the office and dearly loved my work, and how the men would tease me. Especially when Albert Townsend had cause to visit my desk after deliveries. For it's true, I was taken with him. They called him Blushing Bertie for his face would redden when he handed me the delivery docket and I fear mine did too.

Bertie and I started to court. If his cart was back at lunchtime, we'd cross to Whitecross Street market, push through the bustle, and he would pick me out a knick-knack. If the weather was clement we'd sit in the courtyard and steal from each other's lunchboxes. As time passed, he grew braver, walking me back to Spitalfields, where Mam and Pap welcomed him into our home, even as Pap warned him to take care around his girl.

'You treat her like the queen she is,' Pap said, while I begged him stop.

Those days were sweet. When I think on them now, they appear in rays of rich golden light. Bertie sharing a meal with us at Spitalfields, Pap in his braces, breaking bread, eyeing Bertie as if to make sure of him, Mam slapping his arm, telling him to leave the boy alone. Boating with Bertie in Victoria Park, supping tea with him at the pavilion there, riding the carousel with him at the fair.

But when I think of him, I see the shadow. I have tried to remember when first I saw him. But only know I had been a year or more at Whitbread when he started to frequent the office. He would pass through with the gaffers, explaining to him the workings and doings of the brewery. He was a trim enough man, but broad and tall. Big bones, Mam would have said. He had dark hair, speckled with grey, but was beginning to bald under his topper. He wore a coat of the finest black cashmere with velvet trim and, like you, always carried a cane. But this you know well, just as you know his name: Henry Allen Griffiths.

We would all show reverence when he and the gaffers passed through, although we lashed them rightly when they'd gone. The visitor wasn't well liked as he was pompous and proud with a loud way of talking. But Penny Peter cautioned us be courteous, as the man was an investor and close friend of the Whitbreads, so had their ear. Even then, as he passed my desk, his eye and the way it would settle on me would make me ill at ease. But, in truth, I paid him little mind. Albert was all then that occupied my thoughts.

If I cannot remember my first sighting of him, I recall only too well our first real encounter. I'd finished work and was rushing to meet Bertie. As I hurried through the sheltered passageway beside the barrel stacks in the yard, I spied him ahead. As we met, he put out his cane to halt me.

'Where are you rushing to, you pretty little thing? Lotta, isn't it? Well, Lotta, have you time to stop and talk to a gentleman?'

I stiffened, for I did not know what to say. I was daunted by his domineering stare, his hefty frame, grand coat and fur collar. The way he had drawn down his cane had startled me. I could not fathom why he would wish to talk with the likes of me.

'I am just on my way to meet my friend Albert, sir.'

'Ah, your friend. Is he your sweetheart? Do you walk out together?'

I reddened at his questioning, knowing it too familiar. But I answered him.

'Yes, sir. We are courting.'

'Well, isn't he a lucky fellow? Tell me, what kind of things do you do together? I'm sure your kisses taste sweet.'

He was smiling, but I felt it the smile of a snake. I knew he shouldn't talk to me so. I said nothing, and he said, 'Off you go, then. Don't keep your young lad waiting. I'm sure he will be eager for you.'

I didn't tell Bertie what had happened. Somehow the exchange had made me feel shamed, as if I were wrong to allow such talk. I also knew Bertie would be riled by it, and I wanted no trouble. And I didn't care to waste our precious time together on one such as him.

But, from then, I dreaded his visits to the office, his habit of lifting his hat to me, making a special point of lingering by my desk, or fixing his eyes on mine too long. Always he would pass some remark about my hair or dress, in a way that a proper gentleman would not. The others noticed and Archie made comment.

'I think Mr Henry has taken a fancy to our Lotta. Well, young one, you've captured the eye of a toff. But don't get too keen. You know he has a wife.'

I was vexed, unsettled by his banter. 'You think I would ever bother myself with the likes of *him*. Stop with your nonsense, Archie, get away from my desk.' I stared crossly at my typewriter while Archie just laughed.

I do not know exactly when it happened between me and Bertie. Whether it was before or after that encounter in the passageway. But I do know it was not as they said. Not as they said in court. There, their words had no warmth, no soft tones but were sounded harshly in black and white. Making it seem something cold and stark. Something sordid, something shameful. It was not like that. In truth, if it is truth you finally seek, we hardly knew what we were doing.

Bertie had lodgings near Chiswell Street. His landlady allowed no evening visitors but I had gone there one afternoon. It must have been a Sunday for we were both free of work. It was a bright day: I remember the sun streaming through the window, reflecting on the cast iron of the narrow bed. There was little else to sit on in that tiny room and we both sat there on its edge. Bertie started tickling me and my foot shot up, kicking over the basin on the washstand and we laughed as we fell back against the pillow. And he kissed me softly and I pulled him to me. And in the fever of that moment we went further in our caresses than we ever had before or ever did again. But we were so young. Then, I was not even sure we had done what they said we did. I trusted him.

Just as I trusted you.

* * *

The carriage hit a hump in the road, jolting him from his daze. He turned to look out at the passing street, ladies making fast their hats, men turning up their collars on this cold, blustery evening. He rested his head back on the seat.

Cheapside. It had been to an inn near Cheapside he'd been summoned that December night in 1906. The inn was within walking distance of his chambers, but was not one the lawyers would normally frequent. He'd been surprised at the place, perturbed by the invitation. It had come from on high: King's Counsel, a trio at the highest ranks of Crown Prosecution, those close to Lord Desart, Director of Public Prosecutions. Those who would not typically concern themselves with any not of their standing. Especially not him. Not then.

He tried to remember the workings of his mind. To justify now what had come of that night. His certainty then of what the summons signalled. He recalled the pitying looks he'd endured over many months in chambers, from his fellow barristers, worse still, the clerks.

'Just a bad run, that's all,' Hedley, a colleague, had pronounced cheerfully, an encouraging hand placed on his shoulder as he'd returned from another appalling showing, his fourth consecutive defeat in court. He'd murmured some nonsense in reply, shut himself in his office.

He was a forty-six-year-old man. One who should be at the peak of his career. But he was failing. Failing badly. It was clear the losses had affected his colleagues' attitude towards him. They'd become patronising, like Hedley. Feeling sympathy for him, not respect. Avoiding him in court corridors, no longer so willing to engage in pleasantries, excluding him from the witty repartee that took place after wins. His pride had been shattered. He was a disappointment. There had been much expected of him; his father a highly respected Queen's Counsel. Now he imagined his father shamed, peering from some heavenly cloud to cast damning judgement on his only son.

But, truly, it had not been the pride. But the fear.

The fear that had hounded him those sleepless nights. The tangle of thoughts that kept him restless and wakeful. He would turn to watch Margaret peacefully in slumber, unaware of his carefully hidden torment. The cases were drying up, the clerks now loath to award him briefs. Daily he sat at his desk in an attempt to appear busy while, in truth, he had very little to occupy him.

He'd suffered panic those nights. The wife and son he loved beyond measure relied solely upon him. If what he feared came to pass, that he be discreetly asked to stand down, he would no longer be in a position to provide adequately for them. Provide for them at all.

His sweat would run cold as he recalled a former middle-aged prosecutor in chambers: Frederick Asherton. He then a youth, devilling for a senior barrister, he'd never been clear what had caused the man to lose his position. Was it drink? Some other vice? Whatever it was, the consequences had been dire. He remembered he'd been filing papers just beyond his master's closed door when the door had opened and Asherton had exited. He'd caught sight of Asherton's face: his expression wretched, the unmistakable tears in his eyes, his pitiful efforts to stymie them. William had felt a bolt of shock. He had never witnessed a man cry. And that had been the last time he'd seen him. Asherton had disappeared from chambers and the whispers had begun. He'd listened horrified. The man had first lost his servants, then his home, had ended up in a debtors' prison. There'd been talk of the workhouse for his family.

It had had a great effect on him, that horror. He'd learned what incompetency might cost.

He'd thought of Margaret, so accustomed to genteel living. The astronomical expense of running Gibson Square. What if she were forced to leave that home? He'd thought too of Raff, still only sixteen. His school. The fees. If he had to be removed from that school, the consequences for his son's future. What position could he hope to hold in society without the benefit of the right education?

The legal world was small. His inadequacy would become well known. Even if he were to change allegiance, seek placement in a defence chambers, he would have to go begging and probably to no avail. The thought was unbearable. He could see no way through.

Plagued by these thoughts, when the invitation arrived he'd been quite sure what it indicated. It had not come by telephone, but with a clerk bearing a note. He'd read it at his desk, then looked up to the messenger.

'Yes, of course.' His restraint masked the grip of desperation. 'Please tell the good sirs I'd be delighted to accept.'

With clammy fingertips he'd slid the note back and forth over the mahogany. So this was it. The reckoning. A polite meeting to inform him his career was over, his services to the Crown no longer required.

Two nights later, he'd stumbled more than walked the broad streets of Cheapside to the inn. Clarence Neville KC was being served by the landlord at a dim corner table when he'd arrived.

Neville turned to see him. 'William! Welcome! Welcome to the Ward of Cheap. It suits me greatly as I, myself, am exceptionally so.' He rattled his glass on the table before the waiting publican. 'Landlord, I demand your finest ale for a penny!'

Cecil Dudley and Thomas Herbert laughed at their companion's banter, met by the landlord's wry smile. Mind fixed on the very worst, he'd been bemused at their good spirits.

'Sit down, sit down,' Neville said. 'What will you have?'

Sitting, he'd requested a glass of port and, as the landlord went to fetch it, he'd gazed uncertainly at the candle's flame, the glasses of liquor lit in a mellow glow. Neville had cradled his whisky, then leaned across the table.

'Well, I'm sure you're curious as to why we asked you here tonight. We have a proposition for you. Something we believe you might find of interest. It's a case, obviously. One that will garner much attention, but tricky. We were wondering if you might consider accepting the brief.'

4

Pap called it the Night of the Wandering Souls. A child, I would nestle into him on the chair by the hearth, as he whispered to me of those poor spirits lost and restless. Ghosts holy and unholy come to roam an earth lit by the glow of the coldest moon. This he would say of All Hallows' Eve: the night it happened. But it was not the dead I had to fear that night.

Each Halloween a party was held. One hosted by the Whitbread gaffers for the workers. Every year there would be much excitement at the prospect of our mingling masters, tongues made merry by drink, the courtyard lit with flaming torches, each reveller masked as an animal. When young, I would watch Mam make Pap's mask, longing to wear one. Now I had my own. That year Mam made me the mask of a black cat, sewing on it colourful beads and buttons, fashioning two ears and whiskers of felt. I paraded in it around the kitchen, whacking Pap as he mimicked me, strutting in his lion's mask, a shredded hessian sack from the market for the mane.

I recall the thrill as, Pap linking my arm, we entered the torchlit courtyard. Pap stopped to joke with his workmates, but eager to find Bertie I hurried him on. 'Come on, Pap, stop your quacking.'

The hall surrounded us like a grim carnival; blood-red paper chains strung overhead, tall candles casting shadows and flickering light upon the hobgoblins, witches and fairies strewn in every corner. Beside the Jack-o'-lanterns on the tables were bowls of roasted nuts, syrup apples, and our own bottled beer aplenty. Musicians stamped their feet, belting out piano and fiddle, the music growing wilder as the night went on, as we danced and played our games.

I remember Bertie and I had just finished dancing when I saw him there in the hall. He was joining in bobbing for apples. I recognised him even before he lifted his mask, clasping his hands behind his back to dip his face in the bowl of water. He wore the mask of a white horse, but that could not disguise his burly frame, nor his jarring voice. He ducked his face in, thrashing about to bring out an apple. He shook it in his teeth, then let it loose with a roar of laughter, the gaffers by his side laughing along. I tried to spy the wife I'd heard of, but it seemed she was not there. I supposed a do such as this not the place for a lady.

It was later, while playing these games, that Bertie and I argued. He was cross I had taken part in one where I must peel an apple then look in the great hall mirror where I might see the face of my future husband. He grabbed my arm, angered that I should care to look for my future husband when I had him.

I spat at him. 'You're a buffoon, Bertie, a big bumbling ape.' Shaking off his arm, I marched outside, away from him in temper.

I don't know the time, for I didn't glance at the brewhouse clock, but I was walking the torchlit, sheltered passageway when I heard footsteps behind. I recognised the voice calling after me. 'Hold up. Hold up, little lady, wait.'

My mask torn off in vexation, I had frustrated tears in my eyes as I turned to face him. The man of the white horse mask. Henry Allen Griffiths.

'Well, well, well.' His mask hanging around his neck, I noticed his eyes had the strangest appearance: bulging, rightly round, red-rimmed with a wide stare. 'What are these? Tears?' He went to stroke my cheek with his big thumb and I flinched. 'Will you not let me dry them? Is it that young lad of yours upsetting you?'

I did not want to answer him. If I were to take comfort from anyone it would not be from him.

'There, there.' He removed a green silk handkerchief from his breast pocket and offered it to me. Although I did not want to, I took it, not wishing to seem impolite. 'Come,' he said. 'Let us walk awhile. The courtyard is quite beautiful under torchlight, don't you think?'

Even though my stomach seized against his company, I found myself walking by his side. He took my arm, linking it tight. I froze inside, but was too petrified to pull away. Ahead, I saw Jack Cooper and Tom

Hawkins chatting, laughing, masks in hands, ambling towards us. They looked up, surprised to see us strolling there. I tried to send them a message with my eyes that this jaunt was far from what I wanted. I was terrified they would tell Bertie I was walking with a man in the yard. But they only looked sheepishly away as they passed. I looked back to see them leaning against a window ledge, Tom lighting Jack's cigarette for him.

We reached the end of the passageway, below the looming brewery chimney. Beside us was the alleyway that ran into the south yard where the horses were stabled.

'What lies up ahead? The stables?' He was peering through the alley arch. 'Perhaps we might find some privacy there.'

'Nothing, sir, nothing. There is nothing up there.' I was frightened now. Frightened enough to find my voice. I tried to pull away my arm but he gripped it tight.

'Come, come,' he said. 'Don't be coy. It will suit us well to find some peace and quiet. It is so noisy inside, don't you think? Perhaps you would care to confide in me your troubles. Unburden them to an older, wiser ear. Perhaps I might be of some service.'

'No, sir, please,' I began to plead. 'I should get back to Bertie. To Pap.' I wanted to remind him my father was near.

'Come on, Lotta.' His voice was low, mean, spiteful now. His grip grew hard and painful on my arm as he hustled me through the arch, pushing me roughly against the damp alley wall. 'Don't tease a man.' I could smell the mould in the stone, as I recoiled, turning my face from his close to mine, the reek of beer on his breath.

His hand was fixing my shoulder to the wall, as the other started to lift my skirts.

'No!' I shouted. 'No! Stop!'

'Shut up!' He slapped me hard around the face. I was stunned, the shock so great that, in my daze, I did not feel him tug at my drawers until the cold air bit my bare thighs.

'That's it,' he said, his voice more mellow. 'There's a good girl. Just do as you're told.'

I will not shame myself by telling it to you now, as I had to in court. Only know that, still, to this day, I can smell his breath, feel the lick of his tongue, his slobber on my neck. Still I feel his brutish hands forcing down my shift, the agony as he twisted and kneaded at my bosom as if it were dough. But worst are the sounds. I can hear them still, his grunts like a pig, mixed with my whimpering, my tears. If I had not been sure that Bertie and I had committed an act such as this, I was certain at that moment. At every thrust I felt I might vomit. All I did was wait for it to be over. *Please, please*, I begged silently, *let it be over. Please. Let it be over.*

I felt his body go limp, slump heavily against mine. He lolled there just a moment then, slowly, straightened up. 'There,' he said. He fumbled with the buttons on his trousers, brushed down his jacket. 'There now.' Although I could hardly bear look at him, I could see his eyes no longer held their mad stare but were drooping. He seemed almost as if in a stupor, as if talking to himself. He wobbled as he stepped back. 'Off you go, now. Off you go.' And he stumbled, out of the alleyway, and away.

Quickly I pulled up my drawers, rubbed his stinking spit from my neck. I leaned my head back against the wall, raised my eyes to the heavens, and cried. My sobs must have carried, for I was groping about for the shoulder of my dress, trying to cover the welts I could feel, when Jack and Tom came running.

'Lotta, Lotta, what is it?' Tom said. 'We've seen the toff going off on his own. A right state he's in. What's happened?' They stared dumbfounded at my own state of dishevelment. 'What happened, Lotta?'

I slid down the wall, sank to my knees. Put my head in my hands and wept. Tom and Jack crouched down beside me, Tom touching my shoulder, and I screamed. He sprang back.

'I'm sorry, Lotta. We only want to help. Tell us what's happened.'

I shook my head silently, face in my hands, still moaning, sobbing.

'I'll go for your father,' Tom said.

'No!' I cried out. 'No, don't get Pap, please.'

'All right. All right, Lotta. Then get up, please. Get up and come with us.'

Slowly I rose, still struggling with my dress, wiping my eyes. My cat mask and his handkerchief were at my feet. I kicked them away, letting Tom and Jack take my arms.

'Where will we take you?' Jack said.

'Take me home,' I murmured. 'Take me home to Mam.'

Mam's mouth opened as if to scream when she saw me. But she made no sound, only leaped up from her nap at the hearth, rushing to me. She shook Tom and Jack's hands off my arms, clutching them herself, eyes bewildered.

'Lotta! Love, what is it?'

At her loving face, I crumpled. I fell sobbing into her arms where she held me tight, urging Tom and Jack to tell her what had happened. I could hear them, nonplussed, telling her they did not know. At last, my sobs subsiding, she led me to sit at the hearth chair.

'We'll go now, Mrs Rae,' Tom said. 'Now Lotta's home safe.'

Mam nodded, thanking them. As the door closed, she pulled in a chair, close to me, gripping my hand.

'Now, love, you're going to tell me what's happened. Has Bertie done something, is that it?'

I shook my head, choking. 'No, Mam, no.'

'Then, what?' she implored me.

It seemed there were no words for what I must tell. So innocent I was, I was unsure what name to give the crime that had been committed against me. I did not have the trickery of tongue. Your legal wizardry that magicked the gore, the troublesome mess away, to render all neat and clean. Then, I only knew that evil had been visited upon me. A repulsive, repugnant deed. A crime against all the love and goodness I had ever known, all that felt natural and right. My voice broke as I began to tell her. The shame was so great I thought I would die. I wanted to crawl away into the black crevice there in the hearth, curl there, never to be seen, heard of, spoken of again. But Mam made me speak on until I had told her all. All I could bear to tell. She started to shake, her hand trembling over mine.

'Oh, Lotta, Lotta. No.'

My stomach churned at her cry, the noise of a wounded animal.

'Oh, why did you go walking with him?'

'But he was a *gentleman*,' I wailed. 'Not a ruffian, Mam, a gentleman.' My shame grew even greater for bringing her such trouble, such sorrow. 'I'm sorry, Mam.' I started again to cry, causing her own tears to spill as she shook her head, taking me once more in her arms.

'No, love. You have nothing to be sorry for, nothing.'

We stayed like that for the longest time, she cradling me as that eve of All Hallows turned and the Day of All Saints dawned. The day, each year, that Mam took to her knees to pray.

You see, Mam had never cared for Halloween. She thought it ungodly, profane to be flirting with the spirits, dabbling with ghouls and goblins. She believed All Hallows' Eve a sacred feast, one heralding All Saints and All Souls. She said if there were any spirits come to dwell amongst us it would be only those dear to us. Our own beloved souls now departed. She held there were no evil spirits to fear. But I knew differently. For it was no ghost holy or beloved that found me that Night of the Wandering Souls. But the devil himself had come for me that night.

5

'What nature of brief?' He'd been trying to absorb it, order his scattered thoughts. This was far from what he had been expecting.

Clarence Neville had taken a sip of his drink, leaned back in his chair.

'Sexual offence. A rape. Alleged to have taken place on the night of Halloween, in an alleyway at the Whitbread brewery on Chiswell Street – you know it? One of their workers, a young woman named Charlotte Rae, has made the claim.'

He'd nodded briskly, an effort to appear composed. 'And the alleged perpetrator?'

Clarence had held his eyes for a moment.

'There's the thing. It's a man named Henry Allen Griffiths. Do you know of him?'

He'd frowned in thought. 'The family name is familiar.'

'They're a very influential clan,' Thomas Herbert said, at his side. 'A lot of money there. Griffiths' grandfather made his fortune in mills up north. He's a business partner of the Whitbreads and an extremely powerful lobbyist in Parliament.'

In the momentary lull, Clarence had studied his glass. 'The biggest problem is there are two witnesses, two men, both workers at Whitbread, who found the girl in an awful state.'

'Problem?' He hadn't understood. Corroborating witnesses could only be of advantage.

His three companions had exchanged glances, before Cecil Dudley, beside him, spoke. 'May we be frank, William? There's great disquiet in the inner circles about this charge. A man's reputation stands to be ruined. A lot of big noises in the City and around Parliament are declaring the girl's claim utter balderdash. And it could be. Griffiths maintains that he came upon the girl outside and was simply comforting her after an argument with her gentleman friend. He holds that she was very drunk, upset, and he let her link his arm to steady her. She led him to the quiet of the alleyway, saying she wished to confide in him. And there she started to make advances. He insists that if there was any rough play at all, it was because he had to take her by the shoulders to calm her, to stop her hysterical clawing of him. He believes now, she attempted seduction to spite her beau, and, as well as feeling spurned, is touting this story to account for her state of disarray. Which is what these two witnesses saw.'

The monologue allowed him time regain his senses. 'What exactly do the witnesses say?'

Clarence Neville leaned in. 'They're friends of both the girl and her father and they're sticking hard to their story.

Saying she was very upset, that she seemed frightened. Acting as if she'd been hurt. And the father himself is a big problem, insisting on bringing the charge. He's creating a right hullabaloo, shouting the odds everywhere. Between him, and the boys spreading the story, the rumours are rife. It seems the hacks in Fleet Street have got wind of it and have Griffiths' name. It's all the talk as they swipe their ale at the Old Bell. Only a matter of time before every street-seller in London knows it. Desart says we have no option but to prosecute. Justice, as we know, must be seen to be done.'

Any clarity was lost. 'And you want *me* to prosecute?'

It was unfathomable. Just an hour before, he'd been certain he was finished. Yet now he was being asked to prosecute a case that would surely be the talk of all London. His unspoken question lingered between them: why?

*　*　*

Pap came home in the wee hours that Halloween night, the lamp still lighting in the kitchen, but no sign of me and Mam. He went hunting and found Mam sitting by my bed, watching over my fitful sleep. Mam put her finger to her lips to hush him, led him through the door, out to the kitchen.

My dreams were full of lumbering dark men in outlandish toppers lunging at me, slapping my head hard against stone, my jaw squeezed, an iron bar ramming between my legs. It did not take much to rouse me from my broken sleep.

'No, no, Moll, what are you saying?' Pap's voice, pleading, strangled, like I had never heard it, caused me to wake with a start. I let out a whimper at its strangeness, bit on my lip, creeping from my bed to the door to see Pap standing in the kitchen, Mam gripping his arm, begging him be quiet.

'But I thought she had gone home. She disappeared from the party, Bertie too, I thought he had walked her back. Oh God, Moll, what's happened, what's happened?'

He fell. Fell straight down on his knees before Mam, began to sob as she held his head against her skirt. Great wracking sobs, that split open my heart. I fled from the sound, its eeriness sickening my stomach, buried myself in my blankets. Hearing Pap cry, he who was the measure of my world, who I'd counted on, always, to be solid and strong, made it seem the whole earth was shifting beneath me, that everything I had ever believed certain had been ripped away, leaving me flailing with no hand to steady me, or guide me to sanctuary. I covered my mouth to muffle my moans; I did not want Mam or Pap to hear.

I drifted in and out of fretful sleep. It was light when I heard Mam and Pap stirring in the kitchen. I wanted to stay there hidden in my bed, but Mam came to fetch me. She helped me gently up, wrapped a blanket around my shoulders, and we both went in to where my father sat at the table. His face was ashen and drawn.

'Lotta.' He just managed say my name before his face crumpled, and I ran to him, flung my arms around his neck.

'Pap, don't cry, please,' I begged, my own throat thick with tears.

'What did he do to you? What did he do?' He was mumbling, moaning over and over. 'There'll be hell to pay over this, *hell*.'

I drew back at his fury, stared at him, dismayed.

'Pap, no, please. You mustn't do anything. I don't want anyone to know.'

'The whole world will know by the time I'm finished. Will know exactly what kind of man – of abomination – he is.'

'Mattie, no.' Mam sat at the table to face him. 'We can't do that. Think of the shame.'

'Shame!' Pap was shouting. 'Whose shame? His and his alone. Let his pretty wife find out what kind of monster she's married to. The bosses at Whitbread see who they do business with. Then we'll see who's shamed.'

Mam reached her hand across the table to hold mine. She understood what horror I felt, the humiliation I feared. That far from more trouble, I only yearned for the trouble to disappear. But Pap was adamant; our pleas went unheard. He walked that very morning to Wood Street police station, demanded he be seen right away.

That afternoon a peeler came to Peabody House. Mam and Pap were in the kitchen with me, where I sat by the stove, with a blanket. No matter how many clothes I put on, I shivered, for I could not seem to get warm.

Introducing himself as Constable Rudd, he eyed me from the door before coming to stand over me at the hearth. Although Mam offered him a chair, he refused. Him standing there, in his helmet, a hefty, older man looming over me, made his presence all the more threatening.

'You are Miss Charlotte Rae? And I understand you wish to make a complaint against a . . .' He looked at his notebook. 'Mr Henry Allen Griffiths. Is that correct?'

I nodded lamely. I was not sure I wanted make any complaint at all. I only knew Pap wished it.

'And that you bring against him an accusation of rape.' The constable reddened. 'That is the carnal knowledge of you forcibly and against your will.'

My face and eyes burned. I murmured. 'Yes.'

'Well then, I must make some notes.'

Thankfully, at last he took off his helmet and sat. He suggested first, that perhaps Mam might like to leave the room, but Mam held my hand tightly, determined to stay. Then he asked me every question there could be to ask. Where I had first met the Man. How long I had known him. How well did I know him. How did I come to be walking in the passageway last night. Had the Man forced me walk with him.

'No,' I said. 'Not exactly.'

'Not exactly?' He lifted the pencil from his notebook. 'What do you mean by that?'

'I felt I had to. I did not want to but felt I had to.'

'He did not make any threats to your person? Did not physically compel you to walk with him?'

I shook my head. 'But he pushed me into the alley. He pushed me in there.'

Then came the worst of it. Pap was sitting on our battered couch, his head in his hands, Mam sitting by me, her hand rubbing my back as he made me tell all that had happened in the alleyway. His questions were brutal, near as shocking as the slap to my face the night before. He pressed me on every act. Made me conjure up for him the tugging down of my shift, my drawers. Where the Man had touched me. How. With what. To recount this with Pap listening was agonising. My stomach felt as if a snake were crawling in it.

'And you did not encourage or desire, in any way, this man's attentions?'

Pap leaped to his feet. 'What do you mean by asking that? Of course she didn't!' He came storming over to me, tore away the blanket, pulled back the shoulder of my dress. 'Look at the marks here. You can see how he forced her. Look!'

The constable stood over me, inspecting me as if I were an insect he had captured under glass. I withered under his gaze as he noted each bruise in his book.

'Very well.' At last he was finished.

That night, in the kitchen, as Mam petted me, soothed me with cups of hot milk, Pap sat silently at the table. I looked at his lost face, and for a moment he glanced up. He gave a watery smile but, in those seconds our eyes met, I knew. Knew that Pap would never see me in the same way again.

A memory came to me. Of how, a child, I'd made for Pap a rhyme of the seven ancient London gates he'd taught me. How I'd stood so often before him at that very table, sang for him my song:

Run Aldersgate to Smithfield, mind, no fat! St Paul's at Ludgate, doff your hat. Scarper from Newgate away from the rats. St Giles at Cripplegate, bend your knee. Leap Moorgate to Bishopsgate, you'll meet me!

I'd cackle at his wincing as I banged out a rhythm that made his cup jump. Bending my knee, doffing an imaginary cap, I'd make claws of my hands, moons of my eyes for the finish: *But stray Aldgate to the Tower, then you're meat!* With a flourish I'd slice my neck and fall, basking in his choking laugh, Mam's smile.

Now I knew my father would no longer see his daughter, full of life, joy and girlish hope, but see instead a stain where that bursting heart had been. Something dark, tainted, creeping slowly through her body, like worm rot through wood. Something that had come to savage, make invisible to him that little girl who had sung for him her songs.

That was the day the light left Pap's eyes. I felt as if I had destroyed him.

Not him, Henry Allen Griffiths.

But me.

6

My days at Whitbread were over. Nothing could coax me back, and no one tried. I fretted at first that the loss of my wage would cause us hardship, but Pap assured me: he had kept us and kept us well all the while I was growing. And he would again. I was so greatly relieved. To know myself the talk of the brewery, to imagine those once fond faces marred by pity or scorn, tortured me. The very thought of being near the place it had happened caused me to retch.

Pap had no such misgivings. To him, right on our side, we had nothing to fear nor any reason to be ashamed. The wagging tongues at the brewery only inflamed him, stoked his desperation for truth and justice. From my room I heard him telling Mam of the gossipers skulking by the barrels.

'If your tongues are only brave enough to wag behind barrels, you'd be better holding them!' he'd shouted at them. 'Or come stand before me. Come say what you have to me, Mattie Rae.'

I listened to Mam, always more canny, more shrewd than Pap, warning him: 'Be careful, Mattie. The bosses are not going to like this. Keep up this rumpus and they'll want rid of you.'

And so it was. One we called Haughty Harry summoned Pap to his plush office where he and his cronies tried to cajole Pap into abandoning his pursuit of Henry Allen Griffiths. But Pap was unwavering.

'And if it was your daughter, sir, would you do what you ask of me? Would you allow the monster that savaged her go free? I will no more abandon my chase of that demon than I would abandon my daughter. Any father worth the name would do the same.'

You see, Pap believed in truth. That the truth he held like a beacon before him would prevail, would protect him. His fellow workers did not have such faith. Although most secretly supported him, rallied him, they did so over smokes in dim corners for fear of losing their jobs.

I saw Bertie just once more. Once more, before I saw him next in court. He came to visit me in Peabody House, sheepish as he bent his lanky frame through the door, and when Mam offered him tea he would not accept it. Even as he sat before me at the stove, told me he had left the party to look for me that night, but had given it up and gone home, I noticed he would not meet my eyes.

'It's guilt, love,' Mam said, afterwards. 'He feels he should have been there to protect you. Like Pap does.'

But I knew it to be more than guilt. Our bond was somehow broken. It was as if what had happened had dried the flow of ink from a pen. That without any words, any need to justify or explain, our courtship was over. It was quite certain in my mind, as soon as I saw him. It seemed all from my life before, every simple thing that had once brought me joy, was dashed. Lay shattered like a spinning-top thrown to the floor. As if I had been childish, foolish ever to believe in such innocent delight. I simply did not feel the same for him. Although he hung his head, his eyes peering through his fringe in a way that would once have warmed my heart, I registered it only coldly as what had once been. Nothing could make me reach over the gulf now between us.

And Bertie felt it also. I knew him only there from a sense of duty. In truth, he could hardly hide his eagerness to leave. Although we did not discuss it, I was sure he believed Pap's account of that night, but, even so, I was altered in his eyes. Not the same girl – his girl – anymore. I was his Lotta morphed into some cursed creature. Defiled.

Bertie told me he had given a statement to the police. I had given my own statement at Wood Street police station, to two policeman in a tiny, whitewashed room, Pap by my side. 'Don't interrupt, Mr Rae,' they kept warning Pap as he tried make certain I revealed every horror. Although they were stern, somehow, in that cold, impersonal room it felt easier to speak of such obscenity. In my own home, those words had seemed an abomination. Something diseased amongst the familiar warmth and comfort. The station room felt as stark and bleak as what I must tell.

The trek to Wood Street was to be my only outing those November and December months. I spent my days huddled in bed or by the hearth with Mam, Pap relentless, pestering the police while I just allowed myself be cradled in Mam's arms. I felt so hopeless. So worthless. As if I had nothing to offer now. Only a burden to Mam and Pap. A weakling they must tend to. For I could see no way before me. I no longer knew my place in the world. How I should behave. What I should think. What I should *be*. For everything I had ever believed right and true had been shown to be a lie.

It was near Christmas when Pap came home with the news we'd been appointed a barrister. News that made startlingly real all I'd been desperate to ignore. It was as if the world I'd denied now hammered at my door. But Pap was so pleased, I bit back my dread. For it seemed the only thing that buoyed him, brought back the light to his eyes, was his cause.

'You'll meet him in the new year, pet,' Pap said, delighted. 'It won't be long now till we see justice done.'

He told me the barrister's name.

A William John Linden.

* * *

He remembered the meeting well. He sat now, in the carriage, picturing that January afternoon in his chambers, standing at the sash window, gazing on the street below, flicking specks off the leaves of the rubber plant as he'd waited for her to arrive.

He'd been surprised when he'd turned to see her. He'd been expecting perhaps a slight thing, a typical working girl, mousy, unremarkable. But when she walked through the door she had a presence. She was tall, seeming long-limbed under her olive gaberdine coat, somewhat striking. Thick dark hair, rolled loosely under her hat. Well-defined eyebrows over green eyes that, even lowered in shyness, he suspected capable of fire. Her cheek bones were strong. If it had not been for the spray of freckles on her nose, she could be considered a beauty. She stood hesitantly by the door. He ushered her over, urged her to sit.

As he sat to face her across the mahogany desk, watching her remove her gloves, he noticed a ray of harsh winter sun fall on her hands. She rubbed them nervously. He'd smiled, tried to put her at ease.

'Well, Miss Rae, thank you for coming to see me today.'

'Lotta,' she'd said. 'Everyone calls me Lotta.'

'Lotta,' he'd repeated. 'Charming. And I'd be very glad if you would call me William.' He'd smiled again. She'd managed a slight smile in return.

He'd leaned over his desk, studied his file of papers. Looked up to meet her eyes.

'I realise this is going to be somewhat difficult for you. But I would be most grateful if we might go through some of the details of that night. You understand it is necessary I ask you questions so I get the fullest grasp of the facts. So I can best serve you.'

She'd nodded quietly. He'd leafed through his papers, settled on a page.

'Now, on the night in question, you were attending a Halloween party at the Whitbread brewery. May I ask – over the course of that evening, did you consume much alcohol?'

'No.' She shook her head. 'I don't like the taste of beer. I tried a bit because Bertie was teasing me, saying I was a misery not drinking. But I only took a few sips from his bottle.'

'Bertie. That is . . .' He looked at his notes. 'Mr Albert Townsend, your gentleman friend?' She nodded. 'So you would not consider yourself to have been at all intoxicated, as the accused, Mr Henry Allen Griffiths, has claimed?'

'No. No, I was not.'

'And at some point in the evening – we believe, from Mr Townsend's statement, to be just before ten o'clock – you were walking alone in the sheltered passageway that runs through the Whitbread main yard. Is that correct?'

'Yes.'

'Would you tell me how you came to be there? Mr Allen Griffiths maintains that you had argued with Mr Townsend. Mr Townsend has confirmed this in his statement. Is that so?'

She'd nodded. 'Yes. I'd had a row with Bertie and I went outside to get some air. I just wanted some time alone. To calm myself, I suppose.'

'And that is when you happened upon Mr Allen Griffiths?'

'He shouted from behind, called out for me to stop. I think he must have been watching us. Me and Bertie. I'm almost certain he followed me out.'

'I see.' He looked up from his notes. 'That is important, of course, because if, indeed, he did follow you, that could show intent on his part. That he followed you with the intention of meeting you.'

'Yes, I think so.'

'He holds that you were upset and he tried to comfort you. Is that so?'

'He gave me his handkerchief. I was crying.'

'And then you asked him to walk with you? Or he asked you?'

'He asked me. He made me.'

'Made you? What do you mean by that? That is important. Did he force you?'

She flushed. 'No. But it felt like I must. He linked my arm.'

'He linked your arm? Not you his? That is a point of contention, for he claims you were upset, unsteady from drink, and linked his arm, urging him to walk to with you.'

'No. No, he said we should walk and he linked my arm.'

'But you did not try to remove your arm?'

'No. I was too frightened.'

'In what way?'

She thought for a moment, fiddling with her fingers. 'That I might offend him.'

He met her eyes. 'The reason I ask this, is that, in many cases of this kind, if it is shown that the woman in question has walked willingly with a man, it is very difficult to obtain a conviction. That is why I must labour the point. I hope you understand.'

She nodded. 'Yes.'

'You walked as far as the brewery chimney, that is correct?' He looked again at his notes. 'The defendant claims you suggested walking through the alleyway to the stables, saying you wished a peaceful place to confide in him. Is that so?'

'No.' Agitated, she reddened. 'No. He pushed me into the alley. I said I wanted to go back. To Pap. To Bertie.'

'You made it quite clear you wished to return to the party?'

'Yes. I wanted to go back. I told him. But he pushed me in. Pushed me in and up against the wall.' Her voice was anguished.

He leaned forward. 'I am so sorry, Lotta. So sorry to press you on this. But I must be certain of the details of that night. Only then can we present our best case.'

She lowered her eyes, drew a handkerchief from her coat pocket.

'And now, I'm afraid, I must ask you what happened in that alleyway.'

He probed her gently to build a picture in his mind, noted her words on the page before him. She'd been

46

compelling. Utterly sincere in her distress. There was no doubt in his mind she was telling the truth.

'You understand he alleges that you made advances to him?' he'd said, at last, in the quietness when she'd finished. 'He purports that you wished to spite Mr Townsend after your row. And that is how the bruises came to be on your shoulder. That he held you there in an attempt to ward you off.'

Even as he said it he didn't believe it. A case could be made for it, certainly. But this woman was not some vixen, some spiteful cat. As she protested, he shook his head. He did not need to hear her denial. He believed her entirely.

'Now, Lotta, that's over.' He smiled at her. 'From this moment on, you must think of me as your friend. Your ally. For I will be your advocate. Your champion in court.' He'd reached over to lightly touch her hands where they clutched her handkerchief on the desk. 'You must trust me as you have never trusted another before.'

7

We became friends, didn't we, William? In those weeks following, those months before the trial. Mam and Pap were grateful, surprised by your attentions. Pap thought it most kind of you to give of your time so generously. You assured us it was not only your pleasure, but important you come to know me well, that we grow at ease in each other's company, before our days in court. For it was then, you said, you would be most compelling. It would enable you to bring me alive in the jury's mind, allow them to see my true nature, know me as you knew me. You said you wanted to make the jury as certain of me as you were.

You invited me and Mam to tea at the Lyon's teahouse in Piccadilly. Still unnerved by the outside world, I was reluctant to accept, but was more than glad I did. For Mam was so happy that afternoon, looked fine in her best hat and coat, relishing her Madeira cake and the luxury of the delicate china, the tiny forks and silver pot of tea as you poured for her. You were so charming. You made us laugh, as we had not laughed in the longest time. I am not too shy to say that, over those months, you brought some pleasure back into our lives. In February, with the early signs of spring, we strolled once or twice in Victoria Park. Beside you, I felt safe. Protected. As if I were the ward of the warmest, most able guardian. I saw you as a knight by my side. You restored a little of my faith in gentlemen.

Always you encouraged me to confide in you. One afternoon in your chambers, you told me that the Man had retained the finest lawyers, ones who would be ruthless in defence of their client. You warned me if there were anything unsavoury in my present or hidden in my past, they would uncover it. You asked me about Tom and Jack.

'I need to be sure before I put Tom Hawkins and Jack Cooper on the stand. Are they completely reliable witnesses? Or is there anything that might suggest a flaw in their characters? Anything the defence could use against us?'

I wavered before I told you. About Jack. It was well known around the brewery that Jack had been carrying on with a woman who held a stall in Whitecross Street, Ivy Bullock. Jack was married, father to three young children, his wife just borne the third. Ivy Bullock was married also. All of us in Whitbread knew it. He would go to see Ivy every lunchtime and some evenings he would tell his wife he was working late to get a delivery out. You saw my hesitation.

'Be honest now, Lotta,' you said, gently. 'It's vital we're not surprised in court. If there's anything, anything at all, please tell me so I am prepared.'

So I told you. You smiled, patted my hand across the desk. Told me it was good you knew, so you might counteract it.

But what preyed on my mind that February was not Jack and his dalliances, but something other. Something that had worried me after my fumblings with Bertie. Something that disturbed me far more now. I was robbed of sleep, plagued by a terrible fear. What if the Man had left me with child, infected me with his spawn? I did not even know if it was possible I could conceive from an act of such horror. In our long talks, I had asked Mam, but she did not know.

It was during our second stroll in Victoria Park, sitting on the bench by the bathing pond, amongst the newly sprung daffodils, that you sensed something at play on my mind. You turned to me, pressed me gently.

'What is it, Lotta? Is there something troubling you? You know you may ask me anything.'

I wrapped my scarf tighter round my neck. Thought for a time before I spoke.

'William. Could it be . . . Is it possible . . .'

'Go on. Please.'

I was too ashamed to look at you. But I made myself say the words. 'Is it possible that I could be . . .' I touched my belly. 'Because of what happened. Could I be carrying?'

For a moment, you looked confused, then smiled so kindly, laughed a gentle laugh. But you grew serious to reassure me, rested your hand on mine. 'No, Lotta, you mustn't worry. The very best advice we have is that it's highly improbable. Doctors have long testified it unlikely for pregnancy to occur in truly forcible circumstances. The woman would have to consent in some way for the conditions to conceive.'

I was so relieved. When you asked me if I'd had any indication, in that I was not truthful. For there had been no sign of my monthly, but Mam consoled me, saying it was the shock. After our conversation, I didn't worry for I was full sure one such as you would know the answer. Yet, it seemed you didn't, William. For you did not see me those last days of February.

You did not see me as I screamed, writhed in my bed, terrified, for I had never known my monthly be like this. Only Mam saw me then.

'What's happening, Mam?' I wailed as she stripped away the bloody sheets, did not even try to save them but burned them in the stove while Pap was at work.

'It's all right, love, all right,' she said as she bundled towels beneath me. Mam knew this was no monthly. It was then I discovered she had suffered miscarriages of her own. She wanted to fetch the doctor but I begged her, 'No, Mam, no,' because of what you had told me. That I must have consented to conceive. All of this, we hid from Pap. Mam told him I had caught a chill, covered me up when he came to my room.

'Poor pet,' he said. 'Just keep wrapped up. You'll be right and dandy soon.'

At his face so trusting, so innocent of the truth we kept from him, I wanted to cry. We never told Pap of it. Afterwards, I never told you I had been with child. For it would have made of me a liar.

* * *

The last days of February. It had been in those very days that the court had opened. This modern wonder, the new Old Bailey, finally risen, magnificent in the early spring sunshine. He remembered the pride of all the barristers, justices and dignitaries gathered in the palatial entrance hall for the ceremony. How they had dined, afterwards, on smoked salmon, cheeses and olives in the judges' dining room, drunk champagne.

Clarence Neville had been there, of course, as well as Cecil Dudley and Thomas Herbert. Neville had approached him, glass of champagne in hand.

'Well, William, not long till your first case in this fine establishment. I trust you are well prepared?' He'd raised his eyebrow as he'd sipped his drink.

A grip at his navel, he'd given a grim nod. 'Everything will be in place.'

'Good, good,' Neville had said. 'We must make sure it is a success.'

Stomach churning from the conversation, he'd scoured the room for Margaret, suddenly craving her company. She stood by the tall arched window, chatting with some of the barristers' wives. He'd gone to her.

'So exciting,' she'd said to him, flushed from champagne. 'Such a beautiful place. So impressive. You will do good work here, William, good work.' She'd smiled, touched his arm. He'd forced himself to smile back.

The knot in his stomach had only tightened the six weeks following. Six weeks he had spent assuring Lotta, preparing her for her day on the stand. At odds with his nausea, the scent of spring, that peculiar smell of freshness, promise, had charged the air that April Monday. April fifteenth, 1907. First day of the trial. He would never forget the date. The fledgling sun shone weakly upon the narrow street, as he'd approached, on foot, the court door: adorned with the imposing stone figurines on which he refused dwell. The Recording Angel. And the Angel of Truth.

Already, the Fleet Street hounds were milling outside with their notebooks and cameras. They'd been rousing the readers of their rags with the upcoming case for weeks. Their efforts had had the desired effect, crowds flocking to the side steps leading to the public gallery, jostling for positions in the queue.

Thankfully, they were some distance from the court's main entrance. Stepping inside, he'd climbed the marble steps to the seclusion of the private room reserved for barristers. He'd laid his papers on the desk, eyed his gown hanging on the closet door, before sitting for a moment, quietly, staring down at his papers.

He'd been overtaken by an urge to flee. To feign an illness. Anything that would give him time. Some time to think. But his clerk had knocked, peering around the door, to inform him of the timings. The court would be punctual, sitting at ten o'clock. The Rae family had arrived. They were in the witness room. As the clerk left, he'd eased himself from the chair, taken down his gown from the door, removed his wig from its case inside the closet.

Robed, he'd walked heavily to the nearby witness room where the Raes waited. They sat in a line along the bench, Tom Hawkins beside them. There was no sign yet of Jack Cooper or Albert Townsend.

Matthew Rae had risen immediately to greet him, robustly shaking his hand.

'Will any of his lot be in here?' he'd asked, anxiously. 'Any of his witnesses?'

He'd shaken his head reassuringly. 'They will be in a different room.' He didn't tell him the reason. That there was a separate room for the supposedly better class of witnesses, those who would testify as to Allen Griffiths' good character.

Moll Rae attempted a smile, Lotta beside her, eyes cast downwards. She had seemed ravaged by nerves, tapping her feet, biting her lip.

'Lotta?' He'd smiled down at her.

He'd been taken aback by her reaction. She'd sprung suddenly to her feet, flinging her arms around him, clinging to him. He'd been astounded. He'd patted her back, awkwardly.

'There, there. Don't fret, Lotta, don't fret. It will be all right.'

Her father had nodded at them encouragingly, her mother looking on, pained. Lotta had stepped back from him, cheeks puce. Her eyes looked sore from lack of sleep or crying.

He'd clasped her by the shoulders, spoken to her gently.

'Just tell the truth, Lotta. Tell the truth.'

8

Closing his eyes in the trundling carriage, he stepped, once more, into that courtroom. He could smell again the newly crafted oak, hear the unsettled wood creak beneath his feet; look up from the barristers' table to the vast arches, the regal line of chairs for the justices. At either side of the judges' podium the witness stand, pews for witnesses and family, to the rear of the courtroom the dock low, so all might greedily eye the accused. Above, the curving public gallery where, that day, the press and public leaned eagerly over the balcony, the artists busy sketching the impressive surroundings.

He'd turned to the nearby pew where Lotta sat alone, her father with her mother in the witness room where Moll Rae must remain until she had given her evidence. Matthew Rae had wanted be in the courtroom, but Lotta had begged him stay with her mother. It was clear she did not relish the thought of further hurting her father through her testimony. Relieved of that anxiety, she believed she would stand stronger. He'd tapped the pew railing, smiled, attempted what little comfort he could with his eyes.

His clerk beside him, he'd nodded over at the defence lawyers. He'd known them, of course. Edmund Holford KC and his junior, Laurence Green. Murmurs in the public gallery, amongst the lawyers, he'd glanced up from his papers at a hush as the doors swung open, the accused being led by a bailiff into the courtroom. The hacks and artists had started to scribble furiously as Henry Allen Griffiths climbed to the dock. Dressed finely in charcoal morning coat, crisp white shirt and cravat, he looked disgruntled, his steps laboured. He made an indignant noise, marked in the silence, as he sat heavily.

From the barristers' table, he'd turned to measure Lotta's reaction. Her head hung low, she was anxiously wringing her hands. He'd tried to meet her eyes but she refused to raise them. He'd turned back at the court clerk's hammer. 'All be uprising.'

The court rose as the judge stepped onto the podium. He and the other barristers bowed their heads. Although not personally, he knew of this judge: Justice of His Majesty's High Court, the Honourable Sir Charles Grantham. The judge flicked out his robes to sit.

'The court may be seated.' The judge turned to the jurors. 'Gentlemen of the jury, please remain upstanding so you might swear your oath.'

Turning from the judge, he'd studied the jury as the court clerk swore them in. All was as normal. Twelve men of property and good standing. The clerk requested the jury sit as, in the dock, a bailiff ordered Henry Allen Griffiths to stand. He did so, gruffly.

'In the Crown versus Henry Allen Griffiths: a charge of sexual offence: rape. How do you plead?' the clerk called from the podium.

'Not guilty, your Lordship,' Henry Allen Griffiths spoke with a dry croak.

The judge signalled him to sit, then viewed the court. 'Before we commence, I must make an order. Due to the nature of this case I require that all women – children, if any – be removed from the public gallery. Bailiffs.' He nodded to the bailiffs at the side of the courtroom to perform the deed.

There were gasps of disappointment, sounds of discord and dismay as bailiffs escorted the protesting women from the balcony. At last, after much scuffling, only men remained.

'And to the gentlemen of the press.' The judge addressed the gallery. 'You will bear in mind that the court will not tolerate publication of any material that might be seen as an affront to common decency. Therefore, you will be circumspect in your reporting of this case.'

Amongst mumblings from above, the clerk hammered at the podium. 'The Crown calls on Mr William Linden to deliver his opening statement.'

Notes in hand, he'd risen, smoothed his gown and walked to the jury box. He'd paused before he'd spoken, glanced at each juror, in an attempt to engage them.

'Gentlemen of the jury. You are called on today to deliberate, to cast judgement on one of society's most heinous crimes. Where we are required, as gentlemen, to protect and cherish those most gentle of creatures, the women trusted to our care, you will hear instead of the betrayal of that duty, of the defiling of one of nature's most tender creations. You will hear of the wholly despicable act committed upon Miss Charlotte Rae, a woman of modesty, of exemplary character, hailing from a good, respectable working family, who, on the night of Halloween just passed, had stolen from her surely the most precious of things. That virtue which every woman of good fame holds most dear. Her virginity.

'It is often proposed that if a woman be acquainted with a man, if she willingly walks with him, no carnal act that takes place thereafter can truly be without consent. But you will hear, through Miss Rae's own testimony, that acquainted with Henry Allen Griffiths, she placed her trust, as she might, in the honour of a gentleman, and went walking with him that Halloween night only to be most cruelly disappointed. You will hear, from witnesses, of her distress. You will hear from the police of the marks of violence upon her. We will prove to you that the defendant, far from being a gentleman, took from Miss Rae, that awful night, surely all hope of that very thing for which all young women yearn. For in the robbing of her chastity it is probable he robbed from her, also, any hope of the noble institution of marriage. On October thirty-first 1906, Henry Allen Griffiths, more likely than not, deprived Miss Charlotte Rae of her rightful expectation to marry. The Crown asks that your verdict attests to your harshest condemnation of this most vile of crimes.'

He walked from the jury box, nodded at the defence as the clerk called for Edmund Holford KC. Holford took to his feet, to stand before the jury box.

'Gentlemen of the jury. You see before you in the dock a fellow gentleman. A gentleman of the highest standing. Mr Henry Allen Griffiths. Mr Griffiths is a married man, a man of great means, successful in business, a philanthropist, well respected by his peers, indeed counting amongst them many members of our own Parliament. Through his business dealings with the Whitbread Company he became acquainted with one of their workers, the alleged victim, Charlotte Rae. It was on Halloween night, at a social gathering in the Whitbread brewery, that he encountered the girl in the courtyard, intoxicated and weeping after an argument with her gentleman friend. There he attempted, as any gentleman might, to comfort her. You will hear how the girl, in an effort to steady herself, linked his arm and walked willingly with Mr Allen Griffiths. Even the prosecution cannot disclaim this. There was no force, no compulsion involved. You will hear how the girl, knowing the brewery well, coaxed Mr Allen Griffiths into a quiet alleyway and there made drunken advances towards him, we contend in an attempt to spite her gentleman friend. It was during Mr Allen Griffiths' efforts to restrain her, to ward off her advances, that her shoulder came to be bruised. We assert that she fabricated this appalling story to account for her slovenly state to two witnesses who happened upon her once Mr Griffiths had escaped her. It is a sorry state of affairs that, while being chivalrous as his breeding would warrant, Mr Griffiths now finds himself victim to a vicious attack on his impeccable character and reputation. Gentlemen of the jury, we ask that in delivering your verdict you restore this reputation to him.'

Holford sat. The judge spoke from the podium. 'Mr Linden, you may call your first witness.'

He'd stood. 'The Crown calls Constable Rudd, Your Lordship.'

From the table he'd watched as Constable Rudd climbed to the witness stand and took his oath. He spoke: 'Constable Rudd. On November first of last year, 1906, you were summoned to an address at Spitalfields to where a Miss Charlotte Rae resided. There, in the company of her parents, you did take a statement from Miss Rae, is that correct?'

Constable Rudd nodded. 'Yes, sir.'

'And in that statement she did make charge that the defendant, Henry Allen Griffiths, had the previous evening – on the night of Halloween, October thirty-first 1906 – committed an unlawful act upon her. That is, the carnal knowledge of her against her will. Is that so?'

'Yes, sir.'

'How would you describe Miss Rae's state of mind on that day? What was her demeanour?'

'Upset. Very upset, sir.'

'Was she coherent, however, in her statement?'

'Yes, sir. She gave it with some difficulty though. It seemed hard for her to talk about.'

'I see. So it would seem to you, then, that this was not a woman who was being manipulative, or one who was practised in her statement. Who had calmly concocted a story to deliver to you?'

Holford rose to his feet. 'Objection. Calls for conjecture, my lord.'

'Objection denied,' said the judge. 'As you, yourself, in your opening statement, Mr Holford, have proposed that the alleged victim is manipulating the facts, I find this question goes to the point and is pertinent.' The judge turned to the constable. 'You may answer the question.'

'No, sir, it did not seem to me that the lady was practised in any way. As I said, she seemed very upset and it was hard for her to get the words out.'

'And during that visit to Spitalfields, did you examine Miss Rae for any injuries to her person?'

'Yes, I did, sir.'

'And what did you see?'

Constable Rudd consulted his notebook. 'I saw deep-purple bruising on her right shoulder, sir.'

From the barristers' table, he'd looked meaningfully at the jury. 'Thank you. That is all.'

As he sat, Edmund Holford rose.

'Constable Rudd. You have stated that the alleged victim seemed upset and . . .' he read from his notes, '"found it hard to get the words out."'

'Yes, sir.'

'Could this not also be interpreted as one who is not sure of their story? Who is trying to think of what they might say? In other words, manufacturing a story?'

'Objection, my lord.' He'd risen from his own table to his feet. 'Calls for far too much conjecture.'

'No, I'll allow it,' the judge said, turning to the constable. 'You may answer the question.'

'I could not say, sir.'

'Yet, it is possible?'

'I suppose so, sir. Yes, it is possible.'

'And during the course of that visit you saw . . .' Holford again consulted his notes. ' . . . deep-purple bruising on her right shoulder. Is it possible that such bruising could occur from someone trying to restrain her?'

'Objection, my lord.' He'd risen again. 'The constable is not a physician.'

'Objection granted,' said the judge. 'Mr Holford, the good constable, no doubt, is a man of many skills but he is not, as Mr Linden has pointed out, a physician. I will disallow the question.'

Edmund Holford bowed to the judge. 'That is all, Constable. Thank you.'

As the constable left the witness stand, he'd stood:

'The Crown calls Miss Charlotte Rae.'

9

I feared my legs would not carry me as I crossed that courtroom. My skin prickled under the scrutiny of a hundred men, their eyes probing me in sordid fascination. Even though I did not raise my head, I could sense the Man's dark presence, was certain of his venomous stare from the dock.

When the bailiff placed the Bible in my hand, my mouth had gone dry. I did not think I'd be able to speak, but, somehow, through swallowing, I swore my oath. My hand trembling as I held the Bible, I did not want any to see. I hoped to seem strong and sure, did not want him to see me shiver before him. I was sorely relieved when you left the table and came to stand close by me, in front of the stand. You looked up at me kindly, with a gentle smile.

'Miss Rae.' I tried to meet your eyes, but it seemed the effort made my lips quiver. 'I understand how difficult it is for you to be here today. But remember, all we require of you in this courtroom is that you answer each question truthfully.'

You tried to put me at my ease. You did as you'd said, went about painting a picture of me in the jury's mind. My life in Spitalfields with Mam and Pap, how we'd held solid lodgings in Peabody House, how Pap had been gainfully employed all his working life at Whitbread. You drew from me that I had done well in my schooling and so secured a respectable position in the brewery office. You coaxed me speak of my steady courtship with Bertie.

'And so, on the night of October thirty-first 1906, content in your work, having formed a comradery with your fellow workers, you were looking forward to a social evening at the Whitbread brewery to celebrate Halloween?'

My nerves somewhat soothed, I remembered to speak up. 'Yes. I was.'

'And who did you attend the party with?'

'Pap, sir. My father.'

'And you were to meet your gentlemen friend, Mr Albert Townsend, there?'

'Yes, sir.'

'Would you tell us a little of that evening whilst at the party? Were your spirits good?'

'Yes, sir. I was enjoying it very much. I was dancing with Bertie – Albert. And we were playing games.'

'At any point during the evening, did you see the defendant, Henry Allen Griffiths, in the hall?'

'Yes, sir, I did. He was playing one of the games. Apple bobbing.'

'And did yourself and the defendant, at any point in the hall, exchange words?'

'No, sir. We didn't talk at all.'

'Did you drink much alcohol that evening?'

'No, sir, I just took a few sips of Albert's beer.'

'So you were not in any way intoxicated?'

'No, sir.'

'And yet, at some point in the evening, you argued with Mr Townsend?'

'Yes. Albert was annoyed that I had taken part in one of the games.'

'Would you call it a serious argument?'

'No, sir, it was a silly row. I'm sorry for it now.'

I bit my lip at the regret, the threat of tears.

'Of course,' you said quietly, before going on. 'So, after this argument, which you have described as silly, did you wish in any way to spite Mr Townsend?'

'No, sir. Not at all. I only wished to take some air, then return to him and the party.'

'So, it was as a consequence of that argument – we believe the time to be just before ten o'clock – that you went outside and began to walk the sheltered passageway that runs through the Whitbread courtyard, is that so?'

'Yes.'

'Please tell me what happened then.'

'I was walking and I heard him calling behind me . . .'

'Him? Might you clarify for the court to whom you are referring?'

I felt spikes of anxiety. 'Henry Allen Griffiths.' His name in my mouth tasted foul. 'I heard him call me from behind. Telling me to wait.'

'He specifically asked you to wait for him?'

'Yes. So I waited and he caught up with me.'

You pressed me then as you had in chambers. Ensured the jury hear that after he had given me his handkerchief it was he had asked me walk, not I him, he that linked my arm, not I his. That it was he who had suggested we seek privacy at the stables through the alleyway, not I. How I had wanted to turn back.

'So, you made it quite clear that you wished to return to the party?'

'Yes, sir.'

'And what happened then?'

'He grabbed at me, sir. Pulled me into the alleyway. He pushed me up against the wall. I shouted out, no. Stop. But he slapped my face. He slapped my face hard.'

'He slapped your face.'

'Yes, sir. I was so shocked I hardly knew what was happening. I felt him then, tugging at my drawers. He was holding me against the wall, tugging at them.'

I did not want to falter. I tried keep my voice steady. Tried not to feel his stare from the dock. You looked at the jury.

'And did he pull them down?'

'Yes, sir.'

You spoke softly. 'And what happened then, Miss Rae?'

I struggled to master my tremor. 'He forced his hand down the front of my dress. Then he bunched up my skirts and pushed himself against me. His whole body right up against me.' I welled with shame – but said what I knew I must. 'And in me.'

'In you.' You looked again at the jury. 'This is important, Miss Rae. Are you saying to the jury that the defendant, Henry Allen Griffiths, wholly and against your will forced his male member into your female person?'

I could hear the shocked murmurs above in the gallery.

'Yes, sir.' My voice was breaking. I gritted my teeth, squeezed my palms hard against the stand, to strengthen it.

'And did you resist, Miss Rae?'

Did I resist, William? Yes, I resisted. With all my heart, my very soul. Everything within me cried out for him to stop. But it seemed my wits had fled, my mind journeyed to a place where the solid earth had ruptured and I was scrambling hopelessly in water, trying not to drown. I was stunned. Horrified. Unable to believe what was happening. Mam said afterwards, it was the shock. When you asked me this question in chambers, you said it would look badly for me unless I was seen to have resisted. You said the defence would raise the issue, so you must raise it first. When I told you that, in my daze, I had not hit him or tried fight him off, you told me not to worry, for we had the bruises, the marks of violence. You told me what I should say.

'I tried to resist. But he had me so tightly in his grip I could not move.'

'And how long did you have to endure this attack?'

'I cannot say, sir. It seemed like the longest time. But at last he stopped. He fell against me and stayed there a moment. And then he left.'

'He simply left?'

'Yes, sir.'

'And what did you do?'

'I fell to my knees, sir, and cried. Tom and Jack must have heard me because they came running.'

'And did you tell them what had happened?'

'No, sir. I just asked them to take me home to Mam. I told her.'

'Thank you, Miss Rae.'

You sat down. It was then Edmund Holford rose to his feet. He glanced down at his notes, then walked towards me at the stand. He wore a smile, more like a smirk, a glint in his eyes as they caught mine. At his scathing amusement I felt a rush of panic: my throat choked, my chest felt as if it was crushed under rock. I clenched my stomach at a swell of nausea, gripped the stand.

The judge spoke from the podium. 'Miss Rae, are you all right?'

I looked up at him. 'I don't know, sir. I don't feel well.' Above, I could see the artists peering over the balcony, studying me as they drew, the hacks hungry for my every word. Before me, Edmund Holford his mouth ugly, contorted in scorn. I wanted to go on, show no fear, but I felt light-headed as if the courtroom were growing dark, smaller, the walls drawing in.

You stood. 'My lord. If it pleases the court, might I suggest that Miss Rae has a brief respite before her cross-examination?'

The judge nodded. 'Yes. Indeed. That would be a good idea.' He eyed the pocket watch on his robe. 'I think in the interests of expediency we will continue with your witnesses, Mr Linden, and then, when Miss Rae has recovered, perhaps after lunch, she might return for cross-examination.'

'Thank you, my lord,' you said.

I started down from the witness box. A bailiff took my arm to escort me back to the witness room, to Mam and Pap. I did not glance up at the Man as I passed the dock but I could feel every ounce of his contempt.

10

Tom Hawkins had proven a sound witness. Short, youthfully chubby, dark hair combed carefully, he had succeeded in a smart appearance. On direct examination he'd been clear, concise. Questioning him from the barristers' table, he had led Hawkins to the point in the evening he'd passed Lotta and Henry Allen Griffiths in the passageway. He'd asked of his impression of the two as they'd walked.

'I was surprised to see her walking with him, to be honest, sir. To be truthful, I didn't think she liked him.'

'Why would you say that?'

'Just from talk around the brewery, sir. There was a joke that he'd taken a fancy to her.'

'Taken a fancy to her.' He'd looked at the jury. 'And this feeling, as far as you know, was not reciprocated?'

'No, sir. That's what I mean. We used to laugh that she was always having to fend him off. That Bertie – Albert Townsend – might have to challenge him to a duel.'

'And was Albert Townsend aware of these jokes about Miss Rae and Henry Allen Griffiths?'

'Oh, no, sir. We never joked about it when Albert was around. I don't think he knew anything about it.'

'So that night you were surprised to see them walking together. How would you describe Miss Rae's demeanour as you passed?'

'Serious, sir. A bit dour. She looked a bit red-eyed when she looked up at me.'

'And Henry Allen Griffiths' demeanour. How was that?'

'He seemed happy, sir. Chatty.'

'I see. So, of the two, would you say that it was Henry Allen Griffiths who seemed more happy to be walking than Miss Rae?'

'Yes, definitely, sir.'

'After you'd passed, did you see Henry Allen Griffiths and Miss Rae enter the alleyway?

'No, sir. I was having a smoke with Jack. We weren't paying any mind.'

'And did you hear anything?'

'No, sir. Not a sound. The first we knew was when Henry Allen Griffiths came back down the passageway. He looked a bit wild-eyed and in a state. That's when we first thought something might be wrong – and then we heard Lotta – Charlotte – cry.'

'Cry? Cry out or weeping?'

'A sort of weeping. More like a howl.'

'And what did you do?'

'Me and Jack looked at each other, then ran up to the alleyway where we'd heard it. She was there on the ground, tugging at her dress, trying to pull it up at the shoulder. We were talking to her but she hardly seemed to know we were there. She wouldn't talk to us or let us come near her. She was just crying – heaving crying. We wanted to get her father but she wouldn't let us.'

'So might you describe her as distraught?'

'Yes, sir. Distraught. She just wanted to go home to her mother.'

'And as she allowed you to escort her home, did she say anything at all of what had happened?'

'No, sir. She didn't say a word.'

'Thank you.'

As he'd sat, Edmund Holford had risen.

'Mr Hawkins.' Hands on the table, Holford looked down to consult his notes. 'You have said that Charlotte Rae looked "serious, dour. A bit red-eyed," as you passed her in the passageway. Is it possible that her red eyes came not only from frustrated and angry tears over her argument with Mr Townsend, but also from too much alcohol consumed? In other words, that as well as angry, she was drunk?'

'I don't know, sir. She seemed steady. I don't think she was drunk.'

'Yet it is a possibility.' Holford walked from the table to the stand. 'Also, you have described Mr Griffiths' demeanour as "happy, chatty". Would that not seem the demeanour of one who was trying his best to cheer and rally his companion?'

'Possibly, sir.'

73

'So Mr Griffiths displayed a pleasant demeanour.' He turned to look at the jury. 'Not the demeanour of one who would seem to be plotting an act most foul upon his companion?'

'I don't know, sir.'

He turned back to Hawkins. 'But you do agree that his demeanour was pleasant?'

'Yes, sir.'

'Yet Miss Rae's demeanour was dour, serious. More likely then, of the two, to have something somewhat sinister on her mind?'

'Objection, my lord.' He'd risen from his own table. 'Conjecture. And leading.'

The judge spoke. 'Granted. Mr Holford, you should know better.'

'Apologies, my lord. I'll withdraw.' Holford paused. 'Mr Hawkins, yourself and Jack Cooper sat quite near to the alleyway in question? Near enough to later hear what you have called a "howl" from Miss Rae?'

'Yes, sir. Quite near.'

'And yet, during the time the alleged attack is said to have occurred, you did not hear any cry from Miss Rae? Or any sound at all?'

'No, sir.'

Holford glanced at the jury. 'Your next encounter, then, with Mr Griffiths was when you saw him returning towards you in the passageway. You have described him as being "a bit wild-eyed and in a state". In what way do you mean a state?'

'He looked dishevelled, sir. He was brushing himself off. Almost as if he'd been in a fight.'

'A fight.' Holford looked keenly at the jury. 'Almost as if he'd been fighting someone off, perhaps?'

Tom Hawkins remained silent, clearly realising what he'd said.

Holford continued. 'And then, despite having heard not a sound earlier, you heard this "howl" coming from the alleyway. Is that correct?'

'Yes, sir.'

'Is it possible that, rather than a howl of distress, the sound you heard could have been a howl of frustration? Or rage? Of one whose plans had been thwarted? Of one who had been spurned?'

'I don't know, sir. All I know is that Lotta – Charlotte Rae – was in a terrible state when we got to her. She was just as I said earlier. Distraught.'

Holford returned to the table to sit. 'I won't contest that she was in a state that evening, Mr Hawkins. Thank you.'

The judge checked his pocket watch. 'Mr Linden, if you have no further questions of Mr Hawkins, I believe there is just enough time before lunch for a direct examination of your next witness.'

He'd stood, bowed to the judge. 'Thank you, Mr Hawkins, that is all. The Crown calls Mr Jack Cooper.'

Tom Hawkins left the stand, passing Jack Cooper as he entered the courtroom. Jack Cooper, a wiry man, who had obviously done his best to tame his straw hair and present himself neatly in a checked jacket, climbed into the witness box and swore his oath.

'Mr Cooper.' He'd directed his questions from the barristers' table. 'You were in the company of Tom Hawkins on Halloween night last, around ten o'clock at the Whitbread brewery, when the two of you came upon Miss Charlotte Rae and Henry Allen Griffiths walking in the courtyard passageway. Is that correct?'

'Yes, sir.'

'Would you please tell the jury your impression of Miss Rae's demeanour and that of Henry Allen Griffiths as you passed?'

Jack Cooper had reddened. 'They seemed happy, sir.'

'Happy?' He'd looked urgently at his clerk, who quickly began leafing through his file. 'You are saying to the court that both Miss Rae and Henry Allen Griffiths looked "happy"?'

Jack Cooper's lips were pursed. 'Yes, sir.'

'In what way, exactly, did Miss Rae look happy?'

'She was smiling, sir. Smiling up at him – Henry Allen Griffiths.'

'And yet in your statement to the police,' he'd taken a paper from his clerk, 'you stated that . . . "Charlotte Rae looked sad, almost as if she'd been crying". Yet, now, you say she looked happy?'

'He was making her smile, sir. Henry Allen Griffiths. She did look sad, but he was making her smile.'

'And yet you neglected to mention this in your statement to the police?'

'I didn't realise how important it was, sir. Every smile, every laugh. I just gave my impressions of Lotta as I saw them. It was true, she did seem sad, but he was cheering her up. I didn't know that was important.'

'I see.' He'd paused, ordered his notes before turning his attention again to Cooper. 'So, having passed Miss Rae and Henry Allen Griffiths in the passageway, yourself and Tom Hawkins sat on a nearby window ledge to smoke a cigarette, is that correct?'

'Yes, sir.'

'And did you see Miss Rae and Henry Allen Griffiths enter the alleyway?'

'No, sir. But I heard her laugh.'

'You heard Miss Rae laugh?'

'Yes, sir. After they'd passed, while we were lighting the cigarettes I heard her laugh.'

'Again – you did not mention this in your statement to the police.'

'No, sir. But as I said – it's only now I'm realising the importance. Of mentioning everything. I'm sorry, sir. I should have said it before.'

From the table, he'd raised his eyebrows meaningfully. 'And while you were seated on the window ledge, near the alleyway, did you hear any sound?'

'No, sir.'

'So your next sighting of Henry Allen Griffiths was when you saw him returning towards you in the passageway, is that correct?'

'Yes, sir.'

'Would you describe for the jury Henry Allen Griffiths' demeanour at that point?'

'He seemed mad, sir. Mad to get away.'

'Mad to get away? As if he were running away? Attempting to avoid apprehension?'

'Running away from someone, sir. Wanting to get away. That's how it seemed to me.'

'How can you possibly know that, Mr Cooper?'

'That's just how it seemed to me, sir.' Cooper's lips were set tight.

He'd shaken his head, in an exasperated fashion. 'And what happened then, Mr Cooper?'

'We heard a screech, sir. A sort of screeching coming from the alleyway. So me and Tom ran up there and found her – Charlotte Rae – kneeling in the alleyway. She was crying, sir. It seemed almost in a fit of anger. A sort of rage. She wouldn't let me or Tom come near her. And she wouldn't let us get her father. She just wanted to go home.'

'So, you are saying that Miss Rae was displaying anger rather than distress?' His tone was incredulous.

'She might have been distressed, sir. I'm not saying that. But she was definitely angry. It was like she was lashing out at us.'

He'd given a weary shake of his head as he sat. 'Again, Mr Cooper. Not a detail you included in your statement to the police. Thank you. That is all.'

As Jack Cooper left the stand and the judge dismissed the court for lunch, he'd glanced across the table at his fellow barrister.

Holford had made no attempt to disguise his delight.

11

I knew something was wrong by your face: so serious as you came into the witness room where I was sitting with Mam and Pap. Bertie was there too. You took my arm at the bench, drew me up, saying you must speak with me. You did not smile, your voice was not comforting, soft as it would normally be. You led me out into the bright, curving corridor, our footsteps echoing on the marble floor. We stood at the window, through which I could see, it seemed, every roof in London. There, you whispered to me of Jack, of what he had said. I shook my head in rage and disbelief.

'*Lies,* it's all *lies*!' I shouted as you tried hush me. I could not fathom why Jack would say such things. How he could betray me so. There was no sight of him, but I felt a compulsion to run. To run, straight away, to find him, challenge him. But you held my wrist, stopped me.

'He's not yet finished his evidence, Lotta. If you're seen to be interfering with a witness, you will be in contempt of court.'

80

At my distress, you became yourself again. Heartening, soothing me. We still had a strong case, you said. I must try not to worry. You would make it right.

* * *

In the carriage, he turned to look out the window. They were still far from the City. He thought now of Holford's unbridled glee when Cooper had returned after lunch to take the stand. Jack Cooper turned from gift to the prosecution to a bounty for the defence. Holford had made Cooper reiterate his words, repeat them so there would be no misunderstanding. Miss Rae had been smiling. Miss Rae had laughed. Could it be seen that Miss Rae had been flirting? He'd risen to his feet: *Objection*. Objection denied. Denied. Granted. It had been of no matter. The jury had heard it. The poisonous word.

He had not re-examined his witness. It was pointless. Best practice to let him fade from the jury's mind. So that he had done. Dismissed Jack Cooper from the court.

* * *

I saw him. I was waiting outside the courtroom, surprised him, grabbed his arm as he came through the doors. I hissed at him.

'What did you say, Jack? What did you say?'

I had his arm tight in my grip. Alarmed, he struggled to shake free.

'I'm sorry, Lotta. I'm sorry.' As he broke away, his eyes told me that indeed he was. He was sincere. I could hear the regret in his voice.

'But why?' I called after him as he turned to hurry away. 'Why, Jack?'

I could see him shaking his head, refusing to hear my pleas as he disappeared down the corridor. He would not turn. I looked after him, hopeless.

And then I heard my name called.

The hours passed had not improved your learned friend's features. His eyes still glistened like a night rat you might spy by gaslight, his mouth as if struck by palsy, frozen in its sneer.

'Miss Rae.' He approached me, notes in hand. 'I trust you are quite recovered?'

'Yes.' I would not grace him with a thank you. Although I was trembling from my altercation with Jack, I tried my best to face him. To meet his eyes.

'Very good. In that case, perhaps we might go straight to the events of the night in question.' He lifted his notes to consult them. 'Now, whilst in the hall that Hallow-een evening – as you have testified, enjoying yourself dancing and playing games with Albert Townsend – did you consume much alcohol?'

'No. I did not.'

'You did not.' He glanced down at his notes. 'Yet, you have said you took sips of Albert Townsend's beer. Is that correct?'

'Yes. Just sips.'

'How many sips, Miss Rae?'

I faltered at his absurd question. 'I don't know how many sips, not exactly. But it wasn't many. I don't like the taste of beer.'

'You don't like the taste of beer?' He looked at me. 'Do you care for alcohol in general, Miss Rae?'

'No.'

'No.' He paused. 'So would it be fair to say that you are not accustomed to drinking alcohol?'

I frowned, frustrated by his talk of drink. 'No. I mean yes. I'm not used to drinking alcohol.'

He studied me. 'In that case, would it not be fair to assume that any amount might have an effect upon you? Make you a little giddy perhaps?'

'No.' I was resolute. 'No. Well, I wasn't giddy that evening anyway.'

'Well, that can be the trouble with alcohol, Miss Rae.' He turned with his smirk to the jury. 'One often doesn't realise when one has had too much.'

I flushed, irked at the sound of titters above in the gallery.

He turned back to me. 'Now, later in the evening, we believe to be just before ten o'clock, yourself and Mr Townsend had an argument. Is that so?'

'Yes.'

'An argument you have described as,' he glanced once more at his notes, '"silly". Yet it was a serious enough argument that you walked away in temper?'

'Yes. I was annoyed.'

'Annoyed, Miss Rae, or angry?'

'Annoyed. Just annoyed.'

'Yet, you were crying?'

'Yes.'

'So it would seem that you were greatly upset.'

'I was upset, yes. But not greatly.'

'Mmm.' Letting out a doubtful murmur, he paced slowly before the stand. 'So, having left the party in temper, upset and annoyed, you were walking the courtyard passageway when you came upon Mr Allen Griffiths?'

'He called me. He called me from behind.'

'So Mr Allen Griffiths recognised you there in the passageway and greeted you. What happened then?'

'He came over to me and saw that I was crying. He gave me his handkerchief.'

'He kindly offered you his handkerchief which you accepted?'

'Yes.' I baulked inwardly at *kindly*.

'And then, still upset, you wished to walk?'

'I . . . I wished to walk, but not with him.'

'You did not wish to walk with him?'

'No.'

'Then why did you link his arm?'

'I didn't. I didn't link his arm. He linked mine.'

He raised his eyebrows. 'He forced his arm into yours?'

'No. He—'

'He offered his arm?'

'Yes. Yes, he offered his arm but—'

'And you accepted it?'

'Yes . . .'

'So, what Mr Allen Griffiths asserts is correct? That he came upon you, upset, in the passageway and that, unsteady, you linked his arm, expressing a wish to walk.'

'No. That's not what happened. I wasn't unsteady and I didn't wish to walk with him.'

He strolled, as if jaded, towards the jury. 'Come, come, Miss Rae. Are you asking the jury to believe that Mr Allen Griffiths, against your will, dragged you along the passageway? Did he force or physically compel you in any way to walk with him?'

'No . . .'

'Let us move on.' He walked back towards the stand, hands and notes clasped behind his back. 'You have now linked Mr Allen Griffiths' arm, and you are walking along the passageway. Whereupon, you encounter two of your acquaintances, Tom Hawkins and Jack Cooper. If you were feeling in any way threatened by Mr Allen Griffiths, why did you not call upon their aid?'

'I didn't. I didn't feel threatened. Not exactly. Not then . . .'

'No.' He stood still to face me. 'You didn't feel threatened. For, is it not true that Mr Allen Griffiths, in his manner, was only pleasant and kind?'

'Yes, then. He was then.'

'So pleasant, in fact, that you started to smile and laugh.'

'No. I did not.' I was adamant.

He turned back to the jury. 'And yet Mr Jack Cooper has sworn to that very fact, today, in this court.'

'That's a *lie*.' I said it fiercely.

'Ah.' He smiled wryly at the jury. 'A lie. Yet another person you claim is lying, Miss Rae. Of course, it is not you that is telling lies, but another.' He began his pace again. 'Now, you reached the brewery chimney by an alleyway that leads to the stables beyond. Would you say that you know the brewery well?'

'Yes.'

'Better than Mr Allen Griffiths?'

'I don't know.'

He looked at me. 'I would think it safe to assume that one who had been working two years at the brewery would know it better than an occasional visitor. You knew very well that the stables lay beyond the alleyway. A place where you might enjoy some peace and quiet, did you not?'

'No.'

'You did not know of the stables?'

'Yes, I did. But I did not want peace and quiet. He wanted it.'

'So you claim.' Again, he paced. 'In any case, there is no dispute that yourself and Mr Allen Griffiths entered the alleyway. However, you would say, and would have the jury believe, that with dazzling swiftness, morphing, as if through sorcery, from gentleman to demon, Mr Allen Griffiths . . .' he stood still to lift his notes, read from them in a mocking tone, '"grabbed" you, "pulled" you into the alleyway, and "pushed" you up against the wall.'

'Yes.'

He dropped his notes to stare at me. 'Yet the only sound that has been testified to, in this court, is that of your laugh. Certainly no cry was heard. Why did you not cry out?'

'I did. I think I did.' I cursed my confusion. 'I did make a sound, I'm sure. But I was so shocked, terrified. I did not understand fully what was happening.'

'You did not understand what was happening?' His voice was incredulous as he held his stare. 'You were unclear that Mr Allen Griffiths was grabbing you, pulling you into the alleyway?'

'Yes, I was aware but I . . . I had no time to react.'

He paused, turning with a dubious eye to the jury. 'So, without warning, you were grabbed and pulled into the alleyway. Yet you made not an audible sound. You say Mr Allen Griffiths then pushed you up against the wall. Does this really seem like the act of a gentleman?'

'No.'

'And, you say, when you cried out for him to stop –
a cry unheard by Tom Hawkins or Jack Cooper – he
slapped your face hard. Again – does this sound like
the action of a gentleman?'

'No . . .' I could feel my voice tiring under his
tirade.

'You say then, Mr Allen Griffiths was,' he lifted his
notes, '"tugging at my drawers". Did you tell him again
to stop?'

'I don't . . . I don't know. I might have . . . I was so
shocked . . .'

'Ah, yes.' He turned once more to the jury. 'This
famous shock that seems to have rendered you both
senseless and speechless. If you had truly wanted him
to stop during this alleged attack, why not hit or push
him away?'

I rallied, remembering what I should say. 'He had
me too tight in his grip.'

'Too tight in his grip?' He turned from the jury to fix
me with that stare. 'But, surely, you had one free hand?
If this attack took place, as you say, with Mr Allen
Griffiths' left hand holding your right shoulder, why
not hit him or push him away with your free hand?
Your left hand? You could have beaten him with it, yet
you say you did not?'

I was flummoxed. Speechless. I had no answer.

'Miss Rae.' His voice was now weary. 'Is not the truth
of this whole sorry affair that on that Halloween night,
upset and angry, you were flattered by the kind attentions

of a successful, wealthy man of high social standing, and took your chance to spite Albert Townsend, and make drunken advances towards him. That, once rejected, feeling spurned, you concocted a story that would account for your slovenly state witnessed by Tom Hawkins and Jack Cooper. You knew very well that what they had witnessed would carry to both your father and Albert Townsend. And so you fabricated this story to satisfy your father and Albert Townsend of your innocence.'

'No!' I shouted, through tears of exhaustion.

He observed me coldly, saying nothing for the longest time. The courtroom was silent.

'Miss Rae.' He spoke calmly, slowly. 'You have claimed that Mr Allen Griffiths committed a diabolical act. The act of pushing himself up against you and *in* you. In other words, that he forcibly penetrated you. How would you know, Miss Rae?'

I could hear the shocked murmurs all about the courtroom as I shook my head. I did not understand the question.

'How would you know if Mr Allen Griffiths had penetrated you?'

I was struggling to find the words, as he sprung on me like a hawk. 'Is it not true that you would be all too aware of how it feels to be penetrated by a man, as you are no stranger to it?'

There were gasps in the pews, in the gallery. I stood dumbfounded.

'Miss Rae. Are you a stranger to penetration?'

'I . . .' My tongue locked in my mouth.

'Is it not the truth that you are no stranger to matters of the carnal kind? That, in fact, you are practised in such matters. For, is it not a fact that yourself and Albert Townsend have indulged in carnal acts?'

I gripped the stand.

'Is that not a fact, Miss Rae? And, therefore, is it not a fact that you are far, far from what the prosecution has claimed – a woman of good fame.'

12

A woman of good fame. I did not understand then, how fateful was that moment, William. I only knew the heat and horror of humiliation; the shame flushing through my every pore. As I stood before that sombre room of men, it felt every eye suddenly stripped me, my flesh shockingly revealed, as if pockmarked, repulsing them. I wished, at that moment, for Mam's god to strike me dead.

You were only too aware of the portent of that moment. Quickly, you rose, said softly, 'That is all, Miss Rae.' I was so stunned, I hardly heard you. You repeated it, but still I did not stir. A bailiff had to come take my arm before I understood I should leave. So stupefied I was, I did not see any face before me as the bailiff led me across that silent courtroom, barely thought, even, of the Man there in the dock. You told me afterwards that you had acted swiftly to release me, for my stupor was clear. You'd doubted I had the faculty to speak, or the wits to give any good account of myself or my actions. Instead, you said, you were compelled to call your next witness. Bertie.

I had no chance, nor time, to warn him, to beg him not to tell, as we crossed paths in the courtroom, a bailiff both at his side and mine. I looked at him desperately, but knew he did not understand. All I could do was return to the witness room, to Mam and Pap. Mam, when she saw my bloodless face, leaped from the bench, Pap rushing to my side.

'What's wrong, love?' Mam urged me.

But I could not tell them. This misery I had brought upon them, against my will, was enough. I could not destroy them again through revealing my own wilful deeds. Perhaps they would even start to think their girl no innocent, be suspicious of what had happened in that alleyway. I knew Pap would rage against Bertie and I could not bear the uproar.

And so I simply sat, shaking my head, fending off their questions by saying Holford's quizzing of me had been gruelling, my mind occupied with just one thought: who had Bertie told? Who had he *told*?

* * *

Albert Townsend, a gangly lad, had held himself awkwardly in the stand. He had seemed ill at ease and lost in those grand surroundings. He remembered how he'd felt somewhat fatherly towards the boy as he'd gently led him through the events of that night: his and Lotta's enjoyment of the party before their argument, how she had not drunk much, she never drank, how after she had left he'd gone looking for her but could not find her.

Again, he'd employed best practice. Set about the task of restoring Lotta as a woman of repute in the jury's mind. He'd stood before Albert at the stand.

'So, Mr Townsend, after your nearly two-year-long courtship of Miss Rae, would you describe her as a woman of good character?'

Albert had nodded vigorously. 'Yes, sir. Oh, yes.'

'Have you ever known her to lie or to act in bad faith?'

'No, sir. Never.'

He'd looked towards the jury. 'And knowing Miss Rae as you do, would you describe her as a woman of honour and virtue?'

'Yes, sir. Definitely.'

He'd turned back to Albert. 'And, that being the case, during your courtship, have you cherished Miss Rae's virtue? Have your intentions towards her always been honourable?'

'Yes, sir. Indeed they have.'

'Thank you, Mr Townsend. That is all.'

He'd returned to the table to sit, Holford rising to approach the stand.

'Mr Townsend.' Holford stood square before the witness box. 'You have told us of your nearly two-year courtship of Charlotte Rae. During that time, what kind of things might you do together?'

Albert hesitated, his eyes raised in thought. 'Lots, sir. We'd always have our lunch together at the brewery. I'd go to her home for meals. We'd go to Victoria Park, maybe boating. We've been to the fair, out to tea. Lots of things, sir.'

'I see.' Holford's hands were clasped behind his back. 'So would you say yourself and Miss Rae know each other very well?'

'Yes, sir. I like to think so.'

'Intimately, in fact?'

Albert had faltered. 'We know each other well, sir.'

Holford paced before the stand. 'Now, you live alone at lodgings in Moor Lane, near the Whitbread brewery in Chiswell Street where you are employed, do you not?'

'Yes, sir.'

'And, during your courtship, did Miss Rae ever visit you at your lodgings in Moor Lane?'

'Yes, sir.'

'How often might Miss Rae visit you there?'

Albert had looked uncertain. 'I can't say, sir. But she called on me there several times, I'm sure.'

Holford continued to pace. 'And on any of these occasions might Miss Rae stay with you awhile alone in your lodgings?'

'Not often, sir. It's very small. Most times she would call and we would go out.'

Holford stood still, to face Albert. 'But not always, Mr Townsend?'

Albert had looked confused.

'Have there been occasions when Miss Rae might tarry awhile with you there?' Holford clarified. 'When you might enjoy some time alone?'

'I . . . sometimes, sir.'

Holford remained facing Albert. 'And on those occasions, when Miss Rae and yourself were enjoying time alone in your lodgings, what might you do?'

Albert flushed. 'We would talk, sir.'

'Talk. Yes.' Holford began to pace. 'But perhaps as a courting couple you might take advantage of the time alone to embrace?'

'Objection, my lord.' He'd risen from the table. 'Leading.'

The judge had nodded. 'Granted. Mr Holford, do not lead the witness.'

Holford had bowed to the judge. 'Apologies, my lord. I'll rephrase. Mr Townsend. During your times alone in your lodgings with Charlotte Rae, did you ever embrace?'

Albert reddened. 'Yes, sir.'

Holford still paced. 'And how would you describe the nature of these embraces?'

Albert's mouth had opened, unsure.

'Would you describe them as chaste?' Holford stopped to face the stand. 'Or, would they lead on occasion to something more? Would they ever lead, for instance, to the touching of skin?'

Albert said nothing.

The judge spoke. 'Mr Townsend. Please answer the question.'

Albert was hesitant. 'I . . . yes, sir. I suppose so.'

'You suppose so?' Holford's voice rose in surprise. 'Mr Townsend, have you touched the skin of

Charlotte Rae? Have you touched, for instance, her hand?'

'Yes, sir.'

'Where else have you touched Charlotte Rae, Mr Townsend?'

There were murmurs in the courtroom, Albert shaking his head, as if nonplussed.

'Her neck? Her shoulders?' Holford stared at Albert. 'Or her intimate parts?'

The murmurs rose as Albert sat silent. The judge prompted him. 'You must answer the question, Mr Townsend.'

Albert spoke timidly. 'I have touched her . . .'

'On her intimate parts, Mr Townsend?' Holford said, quickly.

Albert's face puce, his voice a croak. 'Yes.'

'Please speak up, Mr Townsend,' Holford said. 'Did you say you have touched Charlotte Rae on her intimate parts?'

'Yes.'

Whispers abounded in the pews and the gallery.

'Have you touched Charlotte Rae on her bosom, Mr Townsend?'

'Yes.' Albert's eyes were cast down.

'And her other intimate parts?'

Albert said nothing. The judge was leaning from the podium, to instruct him to answer, when he said, hastily, 'Yes.' His voice was deep with shame.

'With what, Mr Townsend?' Holford stared fiercely. 'Your hands? Or something other?'

Albert shook his head as if he could not answer.

'Your hands or something other, Mr Townsend?'

'Other.' Albert's voice was barely audible.

'Other.' Turning to the jury, Holford reiterated it. He turned back to Albert. 'Mr Townsend. Have you had carnal knowledge of Charlotte Rae?'

Albert, eyes still cast down, was silent.

'Mr Townsend?' Holford urged.

'Yes.' Albert spoke suddenly, in a burst. 'But only for a moment, sir. I only . . . just for a moment.'

Holford sharply raised his voice, turning to the jury. 'You have had full and intimate knowledge – carnal knowledge – of Charlotte Rae. Is that correct?'

'Yes.' Albert's voice was defeated.

Amongst the rising murmurs in the courtroom, Holford returned to the table.

'And yet you describe Charlotte Rae as a woman of good character, honour and virtue.' He flicked out his gown and took his seat. 'Thank you, Mr Townsend. That is all.'

* * *

I paced outside the courtroom, waiting for Bertie. At the sight of his face, my stomach plummeted. I knew, but still I rushed to ask: 'Did you tell?'

When he nodded, with those hapless eyes, I wailed. 'How did they know, Bertie? Who have you told? Tell me.'

'No one, Lotta, I promise you, no one,' he said, his voice anguished.

But I let out an embittered cry and walked away. I did not believe him.

13

Bertie was the last witness for the day. The court dismissed, I searched for you before we left, but could not find you. Your clerk said you'd been summoned to the judges' chamber. When Mam, Pap and I walked out into the sunshine, a gaggle of Fleet Street hacks were waiting, squawking like geese:

'Miss Rae, Miss Rae, have you a word for us?'

We guessed rightly they'd been hounding our neighbours in Spitalfields for some of them called me Lotta. 'Lotta, Lotta, have you anything to say?' One with a camera tried to take my picture but I moved too quickly for him. I could feel the heat of them, their breath on my neck as they chased us, Pap shouting at them: 'Get back, you vultures, keep away from my daughter. Go back!' But they stayed on our trail to Spitalfields, swarming around Peabody House.

Once safe inside, Mam put the kettle on the stove, Pap sat by the hearth, I at the kitchen table. We spoke little, exhausted by our day. As we supped our tea, Mam looked at my face so subdued and said, 'What's wrong, Lotta? I know there's something.'

You had advised me not to tell Pap about Jack's treachery while we were still in court, for fear of the rumpus he would make. But I told them now. Pap leaped up.

'What the hell?' He stormed across the room. 'What in hell's name did he mean by saying that? I'm going to the bastard's house now. I'll throttle him.'

Without coat or cap, he made for the door, but Mam jumped up from the table to stop him.

'No, Mattie,' she said, clutching his arm. 'Not now. You'll see him at the brewery soon enough. We need to be here now with Lotta. No more trouble tonight, Mattie, please.'

Knowing Mam was fretting about giving evidence next morning, needed no more strain, Pap reluctantly did her bidding, but although I knew Mam craved peace I also knew I must tell them about me and Bertie. For, once Mam had given her testimony, both she and Pap would be in court and bound to hear it.

It was so hard to say it. To see their shocked faces. As I told it, Pap who had been standing sank back into the hearth chair, Mam just staring at me across the table. I saw the well of disappointment in her eyes, almost more painful to me than any other thing. But Pap surprised me. I'd been dreading his fury, but after sitting oddly still and silent in his chair, he just said, quietly:

'It won't look well for us in court. I don't think it will look well.'

We sat there in that strange hush, and after a while Mam simply began to go about her tasks, peeling potatoes for the pot and clearing the table. Helping her, I felt such relief. It seemed with all the strife we could bear no more.

Early next morning, I found you in the barristers' room. I was distraught over what the court had heard of me and Bertie, terrified that all of London would hear it now. As I cried, you placed your arm around me.

'I'm sorry, so sorry,' I mumbled into your shoulder. 'I've never told anyone. It's Bertie must have told.'

You soothed me. Told me all would be well. Soothed me even as you knew what I could not.

I dreaded sitting again within sight of the Man, but was determined to be in court for Mam. Pap clutched my hand in the pew, constantly eyeing the dock, while I did not allow my own eyes to stray, but settled them on Mam. I had no need to worry about her. She was staunch as she told you of my distress, my bruises, bore witness to how I had cried in her arms. When Holford rose, I felt as a tiger. As if he attacked Mam, I would spring from the pew to maul him. But he was airy, amused, dismissive. When she told of my disarray, he said he did not doubt it, for my story was an attempt to explain that disarray away. But Mam was not shaken by him.

'No, sir. I brought my girl into the world, have watched her grow to be the fine woman she is now. I know my daughter. And I know what I saw.'

As she left the stand I was proud of her, hopeful that the jury would be swayed. The prosecution resting with Mam, now came the defence. I left the courtroom swiftly with Mam, I did not want to see the Man testify. But Pap stayed. He wanted to be there to hear his every word. To meet his eyes.

* * *

Henry Allen Griffiths had an imposing presence. A man with dark, iron eyebrows, tall in stature, heavy in bone. He'd moved slowly across the courtroom, as if time belonged to no other but him. His air had been calm, his voice assured, as he'd held the Bible to swear his oath. Although perfectly able, at Holford's request, he'd been granted permission to sit in the witness box. Griffiths had nodded his appreciation to the Judge.

From the barristers' table he'd observed Holford's manner, his tone change. No longer bumptious, but respectful, he'd led Griffiths through the history of his family's northern mills, the employment of many at his present textile factory in Lancashire, his connections in Parliament, his benevolence through various charitable works. All the while, a poised Griffiths had answered authoritatively. Holford had left the table to approach the stand. 'And your wife assists with your philan-thropic works, does she not, Mr Griffiths?'

Griffiths had nodded. 'Indeed she does.'

'You have been married for over twenty years?'

'Twenty-four years this summer.' His voice was throaty, almost a growl.

'And would you describe your marriage as happy?'

'Very much so. My wife is the bedrock of all my endeavours.'

Holford began a slow pace. 'Now, it was through your business dealings with Whitbread that you came to be at the brewery's Halloween party on the evening of October thirty-first, last. Did your wife accompany you there?'

'No.' His tone was sardonic. 'It would not be a suitable occasion for a lady.'

'Would you tell us a little of that night whilst in the hall?'

Griffiths settled back in his chair. 'Well, it was an interesting little affair. A party they throw annually for the workers. I attended purely to show good manners and a willing spirit.'

'And were you enjoying the evening?'

'Yes, in a fashion.' He sounded offhand. 'They were playing all manner of games. I was doing my best to join in.'

Holford continued his pace. 'Now, at around ten o'clock, you came to be in the courtyard, in the passage-way. Will you tell the court how you came to be there?'

Griffiths spoke casually. 'I had just stepped outside to take some air. The music was rather loud and the night was cold. I was already wearing my coat so I was thinking of going home. Perhaps of hailing a cab. Then I saw the girl in the passageway, crying.'

'You saw Charlotte Rae?'

'Yes. Charlotte Rae.'

'You knew Charlotte Rae from your visits to Whitbread?'

'Yes.' His tone was cursory. 'I would see her in the office when I was there on business. And I had passed the time of day with her perhaps once or twice.'

Holford stood to face the stand. 'Now, the court has heard a claim by a Whitbread employee, Tom Hawkins, that you had "taken a fancy" to Charlotte Rae. Is there any truth in that statement?'

Griffiths had bristled. 'Certainly not. I am a married man. And married to a woman of great propriety and grace. I most certainly had not taken, as you say, any fancy to an office girl.'

'Have you any idea why Tom Hawkins would make that statement?'

Griffiths' mouth was tight, his answer clipped. 'Yes. Because workers like to gossip. You know those types. They hold all sorts of notions and like to entertain themselves with stories and rumours. But I can assure you there is no truth in that statement whatsoever.'

Holford returned to his slow pace. 'So when you saw Charlotte Rae in the passageway that evening, what did you do?'

'Well, I saw that she was crying. So, naturally, I went to see if I could assist.'

'And you offered her your handkerchief?'

'Yes. Of course.'

'Indeed. What happened then, Mr Griffiths?'

His tone was blasé. 'I could see that she was greatly distressed and I thought from her manner she was drunk. She was very unsteady on her feet, so I offered my arm. She took it and said she would like to walk.'

'She asked you to walk with her?'

'Yes. It didn't really suit me – as I said, I was thinking of going home – but I could not leave her there in a state of distress, so I did as she asked. I intended only to walk as far as the end of the passageway, then turn back.'

'And during your walk did Charlotte Rae's spirits improve?'

'Yes. I did my best to cheer her. She started to smile and laugh. In fact, she seemed almost giddy.'

'She seemed giddy.' Holford turned to the jury. 'What happened when you reached the end of the passageway?'

His manner was composed. 'As I say, I wanted to turn back. But she made mention of the stables that lay beyond an alleyway next to us. It seemed she wished to walk there. I gathered she wished to confide in me. To find some peace and quiet.'

'She said to you she desired peace and quiet?'

'Yes. Again, it did not suit me, but I felt that at least I should try to calm the girl and then escort her safely back to the party. So I entered the alleyway with her.'

'You did not "grab" her or "pull" her into the alleyway?'

'Certainly not.'

'Or, once within, push her up against the wall?'

'No, certainly not.' He straightened in his chair, emphatic. 'It was she who turned from girl to banshee, to something demonic. Not I.'

'Will you explain what you mean by that, Mr Griffiths?'

He spoke as if both bemused and repelled. 'She dropped my arm and stopped there in the alley. Leaned back up against the wall. I was confused, attempting to proceed along the alley, but she grabbed at me, tried to pull me to her. When I resisted, she leaped upon me, began smothering my face with kisses, clawing at me like an alley cat. I could feel her tongue. It was disgusting.'

'And what did you do?'

His air was apologetic. 'Well, there, perhaps I acted badly, I'll admit. I pushed her back, away from me, against the wall. She was laughing in a manic way, like we were playing a game, and came at me again. That was when I used force to push her back, my hand holding her left shoulder hard against the wall. Perhaps I was too rough. I regret that now. But I had to stop her clawing of me. She was like a thing gone wild.'

'And then what happened, Mr Griffiths?'

He seemed perturbed. 'I started to walk from the alleyway and she came at me again. I pushed her back again and got away. I then started down the passageway. All I could think of was that I wanted to get home. Home to my wife.'

'You were shaken by the incident?'

'Badly shaken. I have never witnessed behaviour like it. And hope never to again. I went straight away out onto Chiswell Street and hailed a cab.'

'And went home to your wife?'

'Yes. She was in bed, asleep, when I got home.'

'And you did not tell her of what had happened? The next morning, perhaps?'

He replied ruefully. 'No. I would not want to disturb her with something so debased. I thought the girl so drunk or crazed she would remember little of her actions. I wished only for the whole thing to be forgotten. The first my wife knew of it was when the police came knocking on our door.'

'And has your wife been greatly upset by this incident?'

'Yes.' His expression was full of remorse. 'That is my greatest regret. That an act of misplaced kindness has led to my wife's distress and brought our family name into disrepute. Has made us the subject of such sordid speculation.'

Holford bowed his head. 'Thank you, Mr Griffiths. That is all.'

* * *

Often, over those coming years, I wished that Pap had not stayed that day in the courtroom. For it was when he returned to Mam and I in the witness room, that I first saw it. There was an absence in his eyes, a sort of haunting. It were as if what he had heard he could not, would not share. He never told us what the Man had said, and I did not ask, for I did not want to hear.

Yet, I thought afterwards that I should have done more to release Pap of his burden. That I could somehow have stopped what came to pass. Ever after I cursed the taunts, whatever lies he had heard in the courtroom. For I think it was in those very moments that we lost Pap. It was in those days, those weeks after, that I would catch his eyes as if fixed on some distant place. Another world that only he could see.

And now every step would lead him surely towards it.

14

The carriage rocked, a blustery rain spattering the window. He rested his head there, to gaze at the drops. The day that Henry Allen Griffiths had testified, Raff had arrived unexpectedly at the court. He'd found his son waiting for him in the barristers' room after his cross-examination of Griffiths. Raff had donned a stray gown and sat playacting at the mahogany table, his expression sombre as he prepared to pass judgement. His own heart, heavy, had revelled in his boyish antics, felt his joyful laugh as a balm. Yet now he rued the moment Raff had climbed the court steps.

He closed his eyes, wondering at the ifs. If the school had not had a free afternoon. If Raff had not had the fleeting thought to surprise him. Then all that came after would most certainly not have been. For, it was in that moment Raff chose to turn from home to the court that the remainder of his life unfurled like a rich Persian carpet to reveal its weave. Those few heedless steps that had led him to his fate. He opened his leaden eyes to the spitting rain.

Raff, of course, had wanted to watch him that afternoon from the gallery. He'd told him only adults were permitted due to the nature of the case. And he was glad of it. He did not want his son's eyes on him. Not on this day. Not during this sorry case.

He thought of his cross-examination of Griffiths. In many aspects he had done as required. Had challenged Griffiths' claims of who had asked whom to walk, who had suggested the stables to whom, who had assailed whom in the alleyway. But it had been in what he did not say. Little matter. The die had long since been cast.

He'd stood with Raff in the corridor that day, as he bid him goodbye. Standing at the window, behind his son, he'd nestled him in his arms, buried his face in Raff's black curls, smelled his hair. He'd yearned for the softness of him, the comfort of home.

Now, he could hardly believe it possible. That from that act – that one small act – would spring his son's destiny. This past year, he'd struggled to comprehend: could it be each fate not ordained, but random? No masterful design, but patched together with mere moments. That we were victims or victors of chance, nothing more?

Oblivious to it then, he'd had little to occupy him that afternoon as Holford called upon the mighty of London to bear witness to Henry Allen Griffiths' upstanding character. Cross-examination was neither appropriate nor necessary. The myriad witnesses from businesses and houses of good works had droned on to the end of session, the interminable parade allowing him time to reflect on his next morning's task. His closing argument.

* * *

I was proud of you that morning, William. The closing arguments on the third and last day of trial. Mam, Pap and I, showing strong together in the pew, watched you, clear and commanding as you strode before the jury, addressing the solemn rows of men.

You told them I was a lady who had no like of alcohol and, as Albert had sworn, had not been intoxicated that night. That the argument between myself and Bertie had been trivial, too petty to warrant my avenging it through some sordid act. You told them that although, true, I had walked with the Man, this had been purely through politeness, not wishing to offend. That I had assumed, as a gentleman, I might trust him. You said that despite Jack testifying to seeing me smile, hearing me laugh, he had not initially stated this to the police. Tom Hawkins had been firm I'd looked unhappy.

You reminded them of Mam's testimony as to my distress, saying that surely as a mother she would know me best. Of Constable Rudd's opinion that I had not been practised in my statement, but sincere. And then, your voice passionate, you asked the jury to consider: why on earth would I invent such a tale? Of a crime so abominable, sure only to bring shame upon me. One that would tarnish me in the eyes of society.

At your words, Mam, Pap and I smiled at one another. Mam squeezed my hand. You nodded at us, smiled too, as you took your place back at the table.

* * *

Holford had been caustic. Across the courtroom, he'd observed his opponent, his studied disdain, his slow pace before the jury.

'Gentlemen, we have heard much from the prosecution of Charlotte Rae's good breeding. They would have you believe her a woman so pure, that even in the throes of a raucous night, at a brewery party to wit, she touched hardly a drop of alcohol, but there can be no doubt that she was under the influence of at least some alcohol that evening. Despite her protests, there is no credible contest that she walked willingly through the passageway with Mr Allen Griffiths. As she herself has testified, at the time of walking, she felt no threat, and did not call upon either Tom Hawkins or Jack Cooper to intervene when she had the chance to do so.

'Tom Hawkins has testified to her being dour and red-eyed when they passed, indicating that the argument between herself and Albert Townsend had not been "silly" as she has claimed but serious enough to severely upset her. Jack Hawkins has testified to her smiles, her laugh before entering the alleyway. Charlotte Rae knew well, much better than Mr Allen Griffiths, of the stables that lay beyond and therefore seems much more likely to have suggested they walk there. Neither Hawkins nor Cooper heard any sound when Mr Allen Griffiths supposedly "grabbed" and "pulled" Charlotte Rae into the alleyway. And the slap.' Holford paused to eye the jurors. 'You must ask yourselves if that is probable. Does that really sound like the act of a gentleman? Or more likely to be the fancy of a working girl?'

He continued his pace. 'I come, now, to the matter of resistance. I am afraid that Charlotte Rae, in her fevered imaginings, has not schemed well enough. Her lies have undone her on the stand. Within her own version of the incident, she had one free hand with which to strike her supposed assailant, yet she did not.' He stood solid before the jury. 'Charlotte Rae made no attempt to resist during this alleged attack. She made not an audible sound. Yet her howl once Mr Allen Griffiths had departed was loud enough for Hawkins and Cooper to hear. How are we to explain this?' He settled his gaze upon the twelve men. 'I invite you to look upon Charlotte Rae. She is a young woman, perfectly able. Of sound mind, in no way physically impaired. So, ask yourselves, gentlemen. Is it credible? That such a woman would put up no resistance against her attacker? Would not fight with all her strength permitted to protect her honour? Just as any virtuous woman would if that honour were at stake.'

He paused before walking the length of the jury box. 'And then we have the bruises. The prosecution has offered the bruises upon Charlotte Rae as evidence of an attack. But these bruises are easily explained by Mr Allen Griffiths' own account of the struggle that took place between them. His attempts to fend her off.'

He turned once more to face the jury. 'I will finish with this. My learned friend has posed the question: why would Charlotte Rae concoct such a story? Why raise the vile spectre of rape, a thing so odious it would only bring shame upon her? The answer is twofold.

'You must remember that Charlotte Rae, unhinged by drink, rage and panic, feared what story Hawkins and Cooper would carry to Albert Townsend. Feared greatly that her betrayal, her wanton deeds would find her out. So, hastily, she fabricated a tale that would render her not perpetrator of a debauched, lustful act, but a victim. But she had not counted on her father. He, ensnared by her lies, went immediately to the police. Her tricks had outdone her. She had woven a deceit she could not untangle.

'But more. Crucially. You must now cast aside any thought of the ladies in your lives – your mothers, wives, sisters and daughters – or any lady of your acquaintance. For Charlotte Rae is not like they.

'The stark fact is that Charlotte Rae is not the woman the prosecution would have you believe. She is not a woman of modesty or propriety. Not chaste, but well practised in the art of seduction. You have heard the testimony of Albert Townsend, of the immoral nature of their relations. Therefore, it is clear – Charlotte Rae does not measure herself, or her standing in society, as a lady might.'

Holford looked towards him at the barristers' table. 'In my learned friend's opening statement he spoke of that virtue which every woman of good fame holds most dear: their virginity.' He turned back to the twelve men. 'Charlotte Rae is not such a woman. For, that which each lady of honour holds dear, Charlotte Rae does not. Far from valuing that most precious of things, she has given of her favours freely. Charlotte Rae has no concern of what shame this tale might bring upon her.

'Charlotte Rae knows no shame.'

* * *

Charlotte Rae knows no shame. Those words sounded across the courtroom to sting me, stun me. Afterwards, in the witness room, Mam sat holding me close on the bench as we waited for afternoon session while Pap, incensed, would not sit.

'What kind of a man is he?' Mam kept muttering about Holford, while I was mute, shocked at hearing myself described so. I wondered in those moments if it was true. Was I shameless? I searched for the answer in Mam's eyes, seeking any of the disappointment I had seen before, but all I found there was fury. As she gripped my shoulder tightly, I knew whatever she had thought then, she did not think it now.

Pap stopped his pacing, coming to stand over us. 'It's of no matter. You'll see, all of no matter. The jury will look beyond that vermin's poison to the truth.'

You see, Pap had not yet lost his faith in men.

At two o'clock, the judge took his seat at the podium. Gravely, he turned to the jury. He said now came the time for them to weigh the evidence. To determine which witnesses they found credible, whom they believed where evidence was conflicting. But he must instruct them on matters of law, would direct them before they began their deliberations.

He said for a charge of rape to be proven the jury must be wholly satisfied that the act of penetration – *vaginal* penetration – without consent had occurred. I recoiled at the vulgarity. Before my talks with you, I had never heard that word, did not know what it meant. Now, knowing only too well, I imagined the picture vivid in each man's mind.

He talked of the evidence of physical injury, the bruises upon me. He said it was for the jury to decide if they believed the Man's or my account of how these bruises came to be.

He said that learned counsel, Mr Holford, in his closing argument had addressed the issue of resistance. It was right for the jury to ask themselves why, in this case, the alleged victim had not resisted. That was a matter for them to ponder.

And then he came to his last point. He talked of the eminent Lord Matthew Hale. How his wisdom had guided the courts on the charge of rape for centuries. He said a pillar of Lord Hale's doctrine stood on the matter of good fame. The woman's moral character. Whether she was chaste, or unchaste. Had known carnal acts outside of marriage. On this question the jury must think most carefully and must decide if they were convinced by Albert Townsend's testimony. If they believed his account that carnal relations had taken place between himself and Miss Rae they must then consider how much weight could be given to her testimony. Must ask if the word of a woman who had consented previously to such relations, who had showed herself willing to engage in immoral acts, could be relied upon. He urged them to give this point the utmost deliberation.

Then he nodded his assent for the jury to rise.

I was not certain I had understood. The jury risen, as we sat in the pew I looked at Mam and Pap's faces. I think Pap's nerves were so heightened he did not grasp it. But Mam did. Her face stony, she wrung her hands in her lap.

'Mam . . .' I touched her hand, urging her to speak, to tell me I had not heard rightly.

She brusquely shook her head, tugged my arm to pull me up as she stood. Sharply, she told Pap to come.

I wanted to speak to you, to hear your assurances I had misunderstood, but I caught only a glimpse of your gown as you disappeared through the door behind the podium. We returned to the witness room where I stood over Mam sitting stiff and strained, Pap pacing again.

'I hope they'll be speedy, now, hope they'll hurry on,' he said, fretfully.

Mam snapped at him. 'For heaven's sake, Mattie, sit down. Did you not hear what the judge said?'

I sat down beside Mam. 'Mam. Did he say . . .?'

Her words burst from her. 'He said if the jury believe what Bertie told them . . . about . . . they're not to trust a word Lotta says. He all but told them that.'

'What?' Pap stopped still, staring down at Mam. 'What do you mean?'

'That's what the judge said, Mattie. That's just what he said.'

I felt my face drain of blood. 'But why, Mam?' I wailed it, implored her as if she held every answer. 'How does what Bertie said change what that man did to me? How?'

'It doesn't, love,' Mam said, gripping my hand.

You came to us then. Pap rushed over to you at the door. 'What the hell is going on? What's going on, William? What did the judge say?'

You took his arm, sat with Pap beside us on the bench, your face concerned as you consoled us. 'I am so sorry. We've been badly hindered by Albert

Townsend's testimony. The judge's direction was inevitable. In a rape charge, where an unmarried woman has been seen to engage in a previous intimate relationship with a man, the courts will cast doubt on the reliability of her word. Even infer that if the woman has given consent once, she is likely to have done so again. They are not supposed to draw the inference, but often do.'

Pap, livid, leaped up to rail over you. 'You're telling me because my daughter shares a little tenderness with one man, the law believes she'll welcome the attentions of every other?'

'But, I don't understand.' I was pleading as if you could remedy it. 'Then how am I safe? It feels now as if any man is free to do to me whatever he likes.'

As I buried my head in Mam's shoulder, you reached across her to press my hand. I wept in anguish and frustration, while Mam stroked my hair, held me tight. I felt her chest rise and fall, knew she was fighting her own tears to stay strong for me. But Pap turned his back on us all, went to stand at the window, silently staring out. He said not another word.

The jury did not take an hour, William. An hour nor anything near. Just after three o'clock the bailiff knocked to inform us they had a verdict. Mam still held me as she, Pap and I walked bleakly into the courtroom. We had no doubt now what that verdict would be. From the pew, we watched the twelve men walk in to take their seats.

At the podium, the clerk stood. 'Foreman of the jury, please rise.'

A stout, greying man rose in the jury box. The clerk called to him:

'Foreman of the jury: in the case of the Crown versus Henry Allen Griffiths, have you reached a verdict on which you are all agreed?'

'We have.'

'And how do you find the defendant? Guilty or not guilty?'

'Not guilty, m'lord.'

I heard an eruption of excitement above, the judge hushing the gallery by waving down his hands, gesturing to the foreman that he may sit. The court was quietened.

'I thank the jury for their deliberations.' The judge looked to the dock. 'Mr Griffiths, you have been found not guilty by a jury of your peers and are free to go. But may I say, before you do – there is hardly a more treacherous act, one more harmful to a man than the attempt to rob him of his good name and reputation. Let me say that you go, today, from this court, with your reputation untarnished and intact. The court wishes you well. Gentlemen of the jury, I commend you for fulfilling your duty. You are released with gratitude. Court dismissed.' He brought down his hammer.

Dazed, I looked up at a pounding overhead, the Fleet Street hacks beginning a stampede from the gallery, some hanging over the balcony to note whatever the expression on my upturned face. I saw him then. Griffiths nodding with a grim smile to the judge, as he started his climb down from the dock. His eye caught mine in that moment. He sneered, his look so contemptuous, so dark, I froze under it. He turned away to stride through the courtroom doors, as Mam, Pap and I sat silent. Beside me, Pap stared straight ahead, face ashen. I felt Mam touch my arm.

'Come on, love. We'll go home.'

As if witless, I allowed Mam to lift me, guide me from the pew. Pap was still.

'Come on, Mattie,' Mam said. 'Let's go home now.'

At last he rose to follow us. We did not know then, as we passed through those courtroom doors, that we were soon to return. That the Old Bailey was not done with us.

15

The Fleet Street hacks were merciless. It seemed now I had been found so wanting, had uttered such false- hoods, lewd allegations against the gentleman who had walked at liberty from court, they had no need even feign respect. They jostled us at the court door, so close their excited spittle sprayed my face.

'Lotta, have you anything to say? What did you mean by accusing him, Lotta?'

Pap tried to elbow them back, while Mam shielded me in her arms, but there was no escaping them. They stayed on our heels down Newgate Street, all the way to Spitalfields, never once giving up their hollering. I could still hear their shouts as we slammed shut the door of Peabody House.

We spent that night in the kitchen, as if in a stupor. Mam brewed pot upon pot of tea, bringing me sooth- ing cups, putting her arm around me at the table, while Pap sat in cold anger at the hearth, his silence only broken by curses. I hardly knew my own mind. While I too felt fury, more I felt relief at the trial over, hop- ing I would never again have to hear the Man's name.

But I knew it could not truly be done, with the hacks outside our door.

They were relentless, lurking there all evening, back at first light. Although Mam was wary of them, Pap was enraged: 'We've done no wrong. I'll not hide away like it's us who should be ashamed.' Determined to present himself as normal for work, they hounded him the whole journey to Chiswell Street. Finally, at the Whitbread arch, Pap lost his head to swing for one.

'Bugger off, you slime! Is this what you call an honest living, tormenting good, law-abiding people?' He ripped the notebook from the lamped hack's hand, flinging it into the gutter. 'That's where your snake words belong – in the gutter with you.'

Mam needed groceries from Flossie Bradshaw's and two of them followed her there. Flossie came out from the counter, chased them from the shop, locking the door. She sympathised with Mam, told her the talk all morning had been of the newsboys waving their placards on every corner:

SHAMELESS! WANTON! OUTRAGE AGAINST A MORAL MAN!

Flossie spread the *Daily Express* on the counter. On page three, under bold type – *Lascivious Lotta* – was an etching of me on the stand, my face plain for all to see.

She told Mam to take the rag, she had no need of it, and Mam carried it home in her basket, intending to show only Pap, to save me from it, but I knew she was hiding something, suspected what it was.

'Show me, Mam, please,' I begged, but soon was sorry. The sight of my likeness looming large on the page, to sit in every kitchen, every parlour in England, made me feel as if I were raw flesh. Hunted, cornered like a fox.

We had no need to tell Pap when he arrived home: he knew all about it. He'd heard the newsboys calling, seen the newspapers that every Whitbread worker was reading, ferreting them away when they saw him. He hunched over the paper at the kitchen table, head in his hands.

'That's enough, Mattie,' Mam said, snatching it from him and feeding it to the stove. 'What about work? Have you seen Jack?'

Pap said there'd been no sign of Jack but he had met Tom, near the only one who would be seen speaking to him, all the other men shying away. Bertie had been downcast and shamed, saying the slagging was so great it would drive him from the brewery. I know Pap was worried too that the superintendent of Peabody House would come calling. The governors prized the respectability of their tenants above all. They would not welcome the hacks gathered outside, nor being associated with any matter of disrepute. We were always waiting for the knock to come.

Pap saw Jack, at last, on the Friday. At first, Jack had tried to scarper across the courtyard, but Pap had called out for him to stop. 'What the hell happened, Jack? What happened there in the courtroom? Why did you say what you said?'

When Pap caught up with him, Jack's eyes were like a startled hare, his voice breathy.

'I'm sorry, Mattie. I had to do it. Some lackey of Holford's came here to see me. Told me they knew things. About me and Ivy. Said I had a young family and it would be a shame if that little matter had to come out in court. Said they didn't want to attack my character, but they'd have to if I was a witness against them. I had to do it, Mattie. I can't risk losing my family, my job. You don't know what it's been like, the bashing the bosses gave me and Tom to change our evidence. It's all right for Tom, he's young, he has no family, can get another job. I had to save mine.'

When Pap told me and Mam, I remembered what you'd said about Holford being ruthless, doing whatever he could to scupper us. Still, I was shocked that he had threatened a man. That he could be so sly, so underhand.

Mam swore, called Holford every name she could think of, but Pap stayed quiet. I watched him, waiting for him to rage, but instead saw again that strange absence in his eyes. His gaze as if settled on something beyond.

The hacks were still at our door, I was captive. Even for the short times they left, I could not bear to go out before prying, probing eyes. I stayed huddled in our kitchen while Mam reluctantly went to market. Flossie Bradshaw was loyal, but Mam could hear whispering at the stalls, knew even as some smiled they were enjoying the scandal. I was the talk of Spitalfields. One day, Mam told me she'd been accosted by a woman who'd introduced herself as Annie Gordon. She'd gripped Mam's arm, told her she led the suffragettes in the East End, that it was a disgrace what had happened to me in court. She'd wanted to meet me but Mam said no. I was thankful for that.

Mam, always worried about Pap reaching work safely and unheeded, did not have to worry long. The week after the trial, he was called before the bosses. They told him Whitbread was suffering unwelcome attention due to his presence. That the whole court business had reflected badly on the brewery. They had heard of a fracas with the press near the premises. In such circumstances they felt it best for all concerned that Pap and Whitbread part company. They let Pap go. After twenty-three years he lost his job.

I was devastated when I heard it. Pap that evening had barely been able to tell us. When he finally did, he slumped down in a chair at the kitchen table, unable to look at Mam across from him, his voice a croak: 'I've failed you. Failed you both.'

Mam reached over the table for his hand. 'No, love, no.'

As he started to weep, I rushed from the hearth to hold him. I stroked back the hair at his temples.

'It will be all right, Pap, it will be all right.'

He shook his head hopelessly. 'No it won't, pet, it won't. You don't understand. I've failed you both, and you, my little girl, most of all.'

I gripped his face, turned it to me. 'How can you say it, Pap, how can you even say it? You've done everything you could for me, fought for me; you couldn't have done anything more.'

'But I didn't stop that monster putting his hands on you. I didn't stop it, Lotta. I was there, so near, acting like a fool, drinking, joking, while you . . .'

He broke down in wracking sobs like that awful night. I could not bear it.

In tears, I crouched, burying my face in his shirt.

'But you couldn't know, Pap,' I pleaded.

'I can't stop thinking of what I was doing while he was hurting you.' He was choking on every breath. 'I should have watched you more closely. Should have taken more care. And afterwards, when I saw you gone, I didn't even look for you. Just carried on with my foolishness. I don't deserve to be called your father.'

'Mattie, stop.' I could hear Mam's own voice choked.

'You're the best father in the world, Pap,' I whispered into his shirt. 'The very best.'

But my words only made him sob more.

For a week or more I watched my father crushed. I would go to him as he sat in the hearth chair, staring at the blackened wood. There, I would kneel by his feet, take his hands in mine to rub them, look up into his face suddenly so tired, so old. But he would only allow me a wan smile, then look away, his eyes as if he could no longer see me. See neither me nor Mam. It felt there lay between us a chasm, our words, however loving, unable to cross.

Those days with Pap broken I blamed no one but myself. I reproached myself for that stupid row with Bertie, for ever being so foolish as to walk with the Man. For not being courageous enough to refuse. For even revealing it to Mam and Pap, with all the hardship it had brought my family, the devastation it had wrought.

But then came a morning that gave Mam and me hope. Pap rose that morn, dressed himself in his best clothes, and told me and Mam he was off to search for work. From that day on, Pap would leave early, but return each evening with no good tidings, going to sit lifeless at the hearth, staring into it. Helpless, I could only stand and watch as my father slipped surely from our world into his own.

I often longed to talk to you during those first weeks. To feel once more your comfort, your kindness, to find in you consolation. Before we'd left the court that last day, you had seemed to care so much. I expected then that we would meet soon. But I did not see you again, William.

No, not for the longest time.

* * *

Aware once more of the rumble of the carriage, he felt the seat rattle beneath him. Those first weeks after the trial. He remembered those weeks very well. Even in defeat he had found himself the subject of much lauding, congratulations. Apparently he had done splendidly, given the circumstances.

'Excellent work, William,' Hedley had said, in chambers. 'You put up a magnificent show. I mean, the case was all but lost once they decided to charge the man with Rape rather than Assault with Intent. What were Desart's crew thinking?'

The cardinal rule in rape cases: pursue a charge of Assault with Intent to Rape rather than Rape proper, which required proof of actual penetration. Nigh impossible to prove. A pure rape charge rarely resulted in conviction.

The charge brought, of course, had not been his decision. That had been in the gift of Desart and his cronies. But so much more had been within his own.

It had been a time of invitations to dinner, the theatre and drinks parties. The trial, so notorious, had raised his profile and he found himself both professionally and socially in demand. Often, Clarence Neville, Dudley and Herbert would be at one or other of the functions, raising their glasses to him across the room.

'You see how highly they think of you, William,' Margaret had said, one such evening, in the theatre foyer. 'You did your best for that poor girl. Did what you could in the most difficult of situations.'

She'd been proud of him, he could see it in her eyes. That had been almost hardest to bear. Her complete faith in the integrity of her husband. He felt he had betrayed her. Even more than the woman, Lotta, he felt he had betrayed his wife.

The worst had come when, charade abandoned, Neville had invited him to the home of Henry Allen Griffiths in Marylebone for an intimate drinks party.

Griffiths, hosting in the drawing room, stood bumptious by the fireplace, cheeks ruddy, guffawing. He, himself, had drawn back to hover near the door, observing the man from a distance as he provided his guests with vials and powders of cocaine. He'd shaken his head, politely refusing, as one of the gathering offered him a vial for his drink.

'Perhaps a little too much of the magic powder that night, I'll admit,' Griffiths had bellowed as he lined a dusting across his hand to snort. 'Harrod's finest gave me bad taste in women. Rape maybe – but bad taste is not something I'm usually accused of!'

Everyone had laughed. But through the door ajar, he'd spied Griffiths' wife, Constance, who'd been briefly introduced to them earlier, listening. He'd watched her turn to start up the hall stairs. What kind of brute was this man?

He'd tried to avoid it, but had been surrounded by Griffiths' triumph. His own. The papers proclaimed it from every corner. Even *The Times* carried a report: Henry Allen Griffiths vindicated.

The world had declared Griffiths innocent.

He, William John Linden, sat alone in chambers, the walls of legal tomes seeming stare down to appraise him. There he passed his own judgement. Judgement on himself:

Guilty.

16

It seems we imagine there will be a harbinger of those days that come to shatter our lives. Will herald their arrival not with duplicitous blue sky, but a clutch of foreboding clouds. That we will be granted a sign. But the day it happened dawned comforting in its simplicity: sunny, fresh and bright.

Mam and I trying to cheer Pap, spoke of summer coming, of soon going boating in Victoria Park, at our breakfast of bread and tea from Flossie Bradshaw's. Mam had started working at Flossie's shop to help pay our way, and Flossie would supply us with groceries, rallying the stallholders to bag us their unsold waste. Mam said we had more fruit and vegetables now than ever we had before.

Pap left that morning, just as every other, to spend his day searching for work. Except that was not how Pap had been spending his days. No. Pap had spent his days waiting.

The day he'd awaited came, at last, on that May Monday. He walked that morning to the place he had every other. Chiswell Street.

In the mellow spring sunshine, at lunch hour, he saw him. The Man striding from the brewery arch out onto the street, two of the gaffers at his side. In their statements afterwards, the gaffers said that, humour good, they'd been in spirited conversation as they'd turned to walk towards Moorgate. Pap, watching from the far side of the arch, had hesitated barely a moment, then walked slowly behind them, waited until he was close. And then he called:

'Henry Allen Griffiths!'

Afterwards, the gaffers said that the Man turned, surprised at the calling of his name. And then Pap made a rush at him. A rush with Mam's kitchen knife he had carried from home.

It was like the most lurid of dreams, Pap said. His mind a burst of colours, fast shifting shapes and confused noise. All he could recall was his knife raising up and down, over and over, as he stabbed at the Man wherever he could, sometimes hitting, sometimes missing. He saw the Man's arm rise and fall as he tried to protect himself. The stunned roundness of his eyes. The startled faces of the gaffers, their horror, their shouts, as they grasped what was happening, their charge towards Pap to stop him. But mostly he remembered arms. Arms rising and falling. Arms reaching out to grab him. To pull him to the ground.

'For my daughter, you bastard!'

He knew he'd cried that as they'd finally contained him, dragging him to the paving, to his knees. Bystanders had sped to their aid, helping restrain Pap, locking his wrists behind his back, others hurriedly attending to the Man. Pap said his only regret, in that moment, was that the Man was still standing. One of the crowd had hailed a hansom cab, assisting the Man in, to carry him to St Bart's hospital.

Someone must have run for the police. For Pap heard the pierce of whistles, two peelers, at last, upon him to hoist him up into an arriving wagon. The police told us that Pap made no attempt to resist.

They took him to Wood Street, where they threw him in a cell. One stayed with him there, asked why he had attacked the Man, what had he been thinking. They said Pap spoke only one word: justice.

That afternoon, a constable arrived at Peabody House to tell us what Pap had done. Mam and I were stunned, bewildered, unable to make sense of it. The news shocked away my fear of prying eyes on the street. I had no care of who saw me as Mam and I pushed through the market onto Bishopsgate in our haste to reach Pap. We did not even know if they would let us see him but Mam begged the officer on duty and he took pity on her. When the iron door opened to the cell, and we saw Pap, slumped on the bench, Mam yelped and hurried to his side. 'Love, love, what have you done?'

I fell to my knees before him as she gripped his limp hand. Head bowed, he would not look at us but I could see, in an instant his face might crumple.

'Pap, no,' I whispered, stroking his knee. 'No, Pap.'

But Pap looking up, made his face stony. Although his voice was defiant, I could hear its falter. 'I did what I had to. What I should have done at the start. Except I believed in truth. In fairness, justice in this land. Well, no more. I did what I must.'

I clutched desperately at his shirt: 'But what will become of you, Pap?'

Pap shook his head. 'That doesn't matter. I've done what's right. Delivered what that bastard had coming to him. Let him know some pain now. Let him suffer it.'

'How in God's name could you think it right, Mattie?' Mam shouted, snatching away her hand. 'They'll take you away from us now. We'll be left all alone.'

At that, his eyes widened, watered. He stared up at Mam, helpless, as if he had not thought of it. He reached for her arm, but she shook him off, turned to face the wall.

'We'll get you help, Pap,' I said, taking his hand. 'I'll go to William. He'll know what to do.'

He shook his head in anger: 'I don't want him. Don't want any fancy lawyer to help me. Look how it did for us last time. I'll do my own talking. I know just what to say to any judge.'

Mam sounded a burst of frustration, Pap reaching for her skirt to pull her to him. She stayed stubbornly facing the wall, but, at last, with a sob, turned and flung herself on the seat beside him. Pap, weeping, sank his head into Mam's shoulder, rambled then of the arms, flailing arms, the knife as if a dream. They clung to each other tightly as I climbed onto the bench, cradling them both in my arms.

We were still like that when we were told we must leave. At walking away from my father, leaving him alone, so frail, so sorrowful in that cold, stark place, my heart pulsated with unbearable grief. As the officer led Mam and I from the cells, I beseeched him tell me what would happen. The officer said that the Man was being tended to at St Bart's and although, no thanks to Pap, it seemed only his arm was injured, Pap had been quite clear in his statement. He had meant to kill him. When he told us Pap would be charged with Attempted Murder, I had to save Mam from falling.

I paid Pap's protests no mind, and that very afternoon walked to your chambers to beg you come to aid us, guide us. I rattled frantically at the knocker. The clerk who answered went inside, returning to say you were still in court. Again, next day, I called, but the clerk said you had travelled on business to Somerset, and were not soon expected back. I could not reach you, William.

* * *

He shifted uncomfortably in the seat. He'd been in chambers that day she'd come. Unaware of the reason, but unnerved, dismayed at her arrival, he'd told the clerk to say he was not there, instructing that if she called again to send her away. He turned to stare out the window.

* * *

Pap was in court for sentencing within days. For Pap there would be no trial. For Pap was pleading guilty.

Mam and I were appalled by the spectre of the Old Bailey. That Friday, the hacks, hungry for any glimpse of us, jostled and harangued us on the street, all the worse this time for there were just two of us to bear it. I shielded Mam with my arms, shot out a boot at any too near, hissing: 'Get away from my mam, get away!'

The hacks perched like preying eagles in the gallery as Mam and I took our seats in the pew, waiting for a first sight of Pap. At last, he was brought up to the dock, heavily searching the court, I knew, for us. Mam buckled at his face so grey, so drawn, but I waved up at him, sending with my eyes every love I could.

I don't know whether by happenchance or design, but the judge presiding was Sir Charles Grantham, the same judge that had tried our case, stern as he studied Pap.

'Mr Rae, I am sorry to see you in this courtroom again, under the gravest of circumstances. I would have hoped that the justice we pursued and delivered you in this very court would have satisfied you. It seems it has not. Instead, you have seen fit to take the law, as you see it, into your own hands. An abomination in a civilised society. At least you have had the good sense to save the court's time with your plea of guilty.' The judge consulted his notes before again eyeing Pap. 'You stand charged with Assault; Wounding; and Attempted Murder. I note that you have, unwisely in my opinion, refused counsel. In such circumstances, and taking into account your Guilty plea, I am left to consider that although you expressed intent to kill, in fact the injuries inflicted upon your victim were not life-threatening. I am therefore minded to sentence you only on the lesser charges of Assault and Wounding. However, before I pass sentence, have you anything to say?'

Mam and I gripped each other's hands. Relief swelled in my chest. The judge was providing Pap a chance. I bit on my lip, waiting anxiously for Pap to speak. But any shoots of hope withered as I watched Pap draw himself tall and proud in the dock.

'Yes, m'lord, I have something to say. By the law of this land, have no doubt I am guilty – guilty for sure, for I meant to kill him. But I go by an older law – more ancient than yours: an eye for an eye. A tooth for a tooth. I have tried to deliver justice for my daughter, where you and your court did not. I only rue that I did not slay that devil. Then we would have seen justice. True justice.'

No, no, no, Pap. I groaned it silently, biting my lip so hard it drew blood. At his every word, with pleading looks, Mam and I begged Pap to stop but he was unfaltering, staring boldly at the judge.

The judge flushed. He leaned forward on the podium. 'Mr Rae, the court has graciously afforded you the opportunity to retract your earlier statements, to express remorse for your crime. However, you have chosen not to avail of the court's clemency. I therefore sentence you to ten years' penal servitude. Take him down.'

Mam made a low moan, head collapsed in her hands. As the bailiff gripped Pap's arm to lead him away, I leaped to my feet. 'Pap!'

His eyes chased mine, his stare wild. In that awful, bewildering moment, I could see clearly. See beyond the fire to the fear.

He was taken to Pentonville prison. We were not allowed to visit Pap or write to him, nor he to us, for six months. Through those aching, relentless days, with no word of him, I watched Mam languish. She was beset by melancholy, taking to her bed, refusing often to eat.

There was no question of her being strong enough for work at Flossie Bradshaw's. It was thanks to Flossie we had a roof over our heads. Pap a convict now, spelled the end of our time at Peabody House. The superintendent informed us that we were no longer suitable tenants. It made little difference. With only the chance of shop wages, we were not anyway able to afford the rent and it looked, for a time, that we were bound for the spike. Flossie would hear no such talk of the workhouse. She lived over the shop and opened up a room there for us. It was to that small room that Mam and I took our bags two weeks after they took Pap from us. Mam watched blindly as I packed, sorted what few spare belongings we had for the market traders to sell.

With Mam ailing, and Pap jailed, I felt my resolve grow. The worst, I thought, had been visited upon us and my spine straightened to meet it, my skin grew an armour. Hardship, it seemed, had made me a warrior. Worrying nothing now for wagging tongues, I took Mam's place in the shop. When word spread I was working there, I know full well that many came in to gawk, but I hardly cared. I'd cut a pound of butter, wrap it in brown paper and slap it on the counter, daring comment from any curious customer. Flossie would laugh: 'Keep it up, Lotta! It's good for business, bringing them in from all over London.'

Through the long summer we carried on in this way, both Flossie and I tending to a failing Mam. I would try tempt Mam with treats, coaxing open her mouth like a fledgling bird, as she sat swaddled, even in the heat, in her shawl. I whispered to her that soon we would see Pap. We wished away the days.

17

It had been the evening of that day she'd called to his chambers that he'd learned of Matthew Rae's arrest. Clarence Neville had telephoned him at home. Griffiths had been discharged just an hour before from St Bartholomew's Hospital. The doctors feared a dulling of the arm's nerves, some lasting damage. But although there was every chance he would make a good recovery, Rae was being charged with Attempted Murder.

That was when he had first suffered it. The sickly black wave that rose from his stomach, threatening to unbalance his mind. Any guilt before had been niggling, fleeting in nature, not the gripping flood he would come to know. Any rudimentary sense of shame was exacerbated by this latest turn of events. Chambers, next morning, had been full of it, society enthralled, its interest reignited by Griffiths' woes at the hands of Rae. At every event, he found himself hunted down, prey to breathy inquisitiveness, fielding eager questions as if he were under fire. The waning press reportage was rapidly restored. Matthew Rae's name marked in accusing black ink, a stigma that felt like a stain on his own hands.

Wishing for some respite at home, he'd made a futile attempt to keep the news from Margaret, but the day after Rae's sentencing she'd heard of it over a Saturday lunch with her friends.

'Why didn't you tell me?' she'd said, as they sat in the drawing room after she returned. 'The poor man. How wretched he must have felt to have been driven to something so drastic.'

He'd lowered his book. 'It doesn't matter how wretched he felt, Margaret. A man cannot take justice into his own hands. If he does we have the law of the jungle.'

Margaret had not missed the opportunity to espouse a pet cause. 'And yet, William, you believe in the death penalty. Surely that is also appealing to those very same instincts: the primal. Inflicting savagery on a fellow human being. To my mind, that is no more than what the unfortunate man said in the dock: an eye for an eye, tooth for a tooth. You have often said the law is meant to rise us above such base instincts, elevate us to reason. It is on those very grounds that I cannot agree with you on the death penalty. It is the most uncivilised, most barbaric of acts.'

It was those days following Rae's imprisonment he found himself overwhelmed by his own shameful deeds. Plagued by the part he had played first in the woman's, now her father's, downfall, no longer did he shun it, rather count the ways in which he was culpable. He would brood over that night in Cheapside. Remember

Clarence Neville's voice, mellow, as he'd leaned amicably across the table.

'Let's not make this too formal, too official, William. After all, what's said between men after a few whiskies can hardly be taken too seriously. So let us talk in confidence, as it were. If anything untoward might be said, it must be blamed on the demon alcohol. Men can talk such balderdash in drink, don't you find?'

Still far from clear, uncertainly he'd returned Neville's smile as Cecil Dudley had spoken beside him.

'You see, William, we need someone who understands, what we'll call, the special circumstances of the case. To tell the truth, no senior prosecutor wants it. As we say, Desart is loath to bring it to trial at all. So, we were wondering if you might be the right man. You've had a run of bad luck recently, unfortunately accustomed to loss, but this case could be to your advantage to lose. And no need to worry. We could manage it in a way that would not reflect badly on you.'

His confusion at being summoned was replaced by a terrible clarity. He'd realised he had been chosen not to win but to lose. *Why had he not walked away, then?* He rebuked himself in the carriage. He admitted it. There'd been a certain intoxication at being in their company, their courting of him. So long he had yearned the respect, the attention of powerful men such as these. They'd plied him with assurances, oily words like balm on the wounds of his failures.

'The case, of course, would greatly raise your profile,' Neville had said. 'And rightly so. Because we've been thinking, William, it is high time you took Silk. Your father was highly thought of, and a QC under dear old Victoria. It's only fitting that you should join the ranks. Become a KC as a reward for service.'

Take Silk. Become King's Counsel if he were to help them. Pledges like nectar to his dwindling pride. But greater, much greater than this: freedom. To be freed from fear. An end to the wakeful nights, the crippling anxiety, the despondency as he entered chambers each morning. A guarantee of status, income. Every decent bone within him rebelled, was repelled by their proposal, but the hope it brought – the means to provide, and provide well, for his wife, his son, their standing and well-being assured – that was a thing not easily dismissed. What good were principles to a pauper? Would those principles console him when Raff was removed from school, if Margaret were forced from their family home?

And so, telling himself he would merely hear them out, he'd listened. Over rounds of whisky, they'd set out their plan. Firstly, Neville said, they would bring a Rape charge, not Assault with Intent. With the nigh impossibility of proving penetration, the case was liable to fall on that alone. But failing to prove Griffiths guilty was not their sole intent. They aimed to exonerate him.

'If you could get close to the girl,' Thomas Herbert said. 'Coax from her anything you can, anything unsavoury about her. And her witnesses. We have to turn them. Find out about them. Conduct, let's say, a vigorous testing of their credibility.' He'd smiled slyly. 'After all, you have to be sure of who you're putting on the stand.'

So, that he had done. And more, so much more. Far from simply listening, he had cowed before them, a slave to their bidding. Revisited by waves of that long-ago humiliation, he rested his head on the window, revisiting too the trial, the many ways he had transgressed.

The small ways. Like introducing the fact that Tom Hawkins had heard no distressed sounds from the alleyway during the attack. Inevitably, the defence would raise it but, nonetheless, the point had been prejudicial to Lotta, and bad practice on his part. Although, he'd made sure to employ mainly good practice so the case would stand to him as a competent barrister. Such as challenging Jack Cooper when he'd turned. Naturally, he'd known his protests would make little difference, the case on course to fail. But he would have been seen do his best.

But the greater ways. He gazed out at the rain. He had not raised the issue of Griffiths' leching over Lotta, of their first encounter in the passageway, his improper chatter that could be perceived as overtures towards her, just as Tom Hawkins had testified. And their apparent chance meeting that fateful night: he had never mooted the possibility that Griffiths had, in fact, followed her, after watching her row with Albert in the hall. An inference easily drawn as Griffiths had been aware, or at least guessed easily, almost certainly due to his untoward interest, that they had argued. A vital point as it showed intent. He had not broached it with Lotta on the stand, nor confronted Griffiths with it.

He had advised Lotta, in bad faith, on the matter of resistance. Although clear to him when she told him she had not hit out at Griffiths that she had one free arm with which to do so, he had counselled her to say he had her too hard in his grip. Knowing full well that Holford would leap on the fallacy. He'd known what fate awaited her at Holford's hands. His cross-examination would be damning. She would be seen as a liar.

But the greatest. The greatest treachery. Lotta and Albert. When Holford had ambushed Lotta with their relations, he had called Albert immediately, under the guise of an attempt to refute; in truth, allowing no opportunity for Lotta, or any other, to warn Albert, leaving him vulnerable to the surprise attack. He'd had the choice not to call Albert at all. Just as he would in any other case, to delay Albert's testimony, gaining time to caution him, or simply not put him on the stand, for fear of what damage he might do. He had known that with Albert caught unawares, Holford would destroy him.

He had known that Holford would destroy Albert, because he had known what Albert would say.

She had told him.

* * *

Your mind only whispers it. Almost as if you, yourself, do not want to hear. Do not want me to hear. But I know, William, of course I know. Know that I confided in you, just as I did about Jack, what I feared I had done with Bertie. It took me much time to tell you, to trust to you my shame, but one afternoon in chambers as you urged me again be truthful, for you must know all – yes, I told you then.

And that day the court heard it, when I clung to you, swearing I had told no one, I never counted for one moment that I had told you. Why would I? My loyal counsel, my faithful confidant, my friend.

So turn now and look upon me. Look upon me as you never do. And whisper again but to me. Whisper what you did with the secret I laid in your palm, with the faith of a child. Relieve your soul of it. For I know how it festers, what stain it has left there. I who am witness to your every pondering, every reasoning, every working of your mind. In your deepest silence I hear you, William. Hear you just as surely as you are damned to hear me.

So, come. Turn now. And unburden your soul. *Confess.* Confess to me now, as you never did in life.

Look upon me this dead girl.
And tell me what you did.

* * *

He thrust his head against the window. Pressed it until the glass bit like ice upon his forehead, trying to push out the torment of her. *Her voice, always her voice. No.* He closed his eyes. *No.* He would not, would never look upon her. He *would* not.

* * *

Then only speak it softly. Softly and I will hear. Come, William. What harm in whispering your sins to a ghost? I who can reveal your trespasses to no one.

* * *

He gripped the seat as if his grip might drive her out. *Yes*, then. Yes he would confess now if only that would quiet her. If only for blessed moments she would let him be. He thought back to the days preparing for trial. Back to that day in chambers. How from his briefcase he had taken the carefully chosen cheap paper. Had lifted the lid of the inkwell on his desk. Filled his pen, made his mark. Spread the black liquid like venom on the page. Malicious words. Spiteful. Anonymous.

Sir,

I have noticed much in the press of the upcoming case of Miss Charlotte Rae and Mr Henry Allen Griffiths. I would like to bring to your attention some facts that might not be known to you and may be of interest. I know a little of one of the lady's witnesses, a Jack Cooper. It is well known in these parts that Jack Cooper, despite being a family man, and his wife just recently with child, has long been carrying on with one known to me, an Ivy Bullock of White-cross Street market. It strikes me that Jack Cooper is a man much wanting in morality.

And of the lady, Charlotte Rae, herself. You may wish to turn your attention to herself and her gentleman friend, Albert Townsend. It is known that the lady is a frequent visitor to Albert Townsend's lodgings in Moor Lane. And known to me, as a fact, that the carryings-on between them are not right or proper. I have it on good account that Albert Townsend has had his way with Miss Charlotte Rae.

It gives me no pleasure to write these things. I bring these matters to your attention only as a dutiful citizen and wishing to see justice served.

I wish you good day, sir.

He'd laboured over his language, made it fitting to perhaps a shopkeeper or such in the locality. He had not worried greatly. He knew Holford would care little from whence the information came, only that it had come. His opposing counsel would pursue it mercilessly. Flimsy envelope in pocket, he'd travelled in a cab to just beyond Whitecross Street, posting it there so the postmark would tally. Needing the air, he'd walked back to chambers.

Yes, he confessed it now. But he remembered too the well of self-loathing in his stomach, the shake of his hand as he slipped the letter in the pillar box, how it shook still with every step back to chambers. In the carriage, he felt a growing desperation.

Will you relent now that I confess it? Will you grant me even a little peace, some rest? Wretched, he leaned back his head. *Begone from me, for pity's sake. Begone.*

* * *

Ah, William, a wish so desperate yet so hollow. If only it were so simple to find rest. Peace. If only your pleas alone could set my spirit free, let me fly, go where I imagine other souls drift easy on a stream of silver light. I yearn to join them, but there is a rot within me that keeps me bound to you. For all the days that came after, every suffering in my life, rose from that solitary act, the soft strokes, the violence of your pen. It is as if my soul is severed by that cruelty. That it cries, drives me to dig my cold dead fingers into your own soul and bury in my ghostly nails.

For even as you have confessed yourself of one sin, we both know there was another. Its shadow is like a shroud suffocating your heart. Your deepest secret. And it is we alone that know it.

You are not done, William. Not done.

18

At last, in November, Mam and I walked under a thunderous, grey sky towards the great, foreboding fortress that was Pentonville. I had known a little of what to expect. Flossie had introduced me to a street cleaner in the market, Percy Capp, who had served six months in Pentonville for theft. I did not like the man: he had a shifty air, but when he sat with me in the shop's small backroom I clung to his every word, for I was desperate to know of how Pap might be faring.

I was soothed when he told me the bigwigs were mighty proud of Pentonville. They held it to be a vision, counted it most modern in its quest to rehabilitate and reform after the gruelling punishment, the hell that had been Newgate. But my heart grew sore when he told me of the stifling cells, only the length of two men, barely over the width of one man lying. He said the ceiling hovered overhead like a coffin lid.

He told me that once the cells had water closets but the pipes always blocked, so the prisoners would crouch in a foul-smelling pit, or use a slop bucket. He told of the hard plank beds, only slits of light through the iron bars of the pitiful cell windows.

He tried to cheer me by saying the prison was far from dirty, that it gleamed, the prisoners every morning scrubbing before their work, but they'd work long, fifteen hours a day. But they had it good, he said. Hard labour had only just been done away with, and, one day, when a warder heard him moaning at his hands raw from washing the coarse blankets, the turnkey shouted: 'Count yourself lucky. I'd have you ten thousand rounds on the crank if I had my way. If those whining liberals hadn't kept bleating about it.'

With Mam eager, but frail, that long-awaited day, I linked her arm tightly on our climb to the forbidding gate, waiting for the drawing back of the hatch, to show our papers. A warder led us over the cobblestoned yard, where the buildings looked near courtly, the prisoners' quarters hidden from view. As we were led into a vast hall, with towering stone arches and iron-barred windows, I caught sight beyond of five giant curved wings, row upon row of cell doors, stretching as if to the sky. My bones chilled to think of Pap behind one.

We were quickly turned to a cold, echoing whitewashed room, reeking of harsh carbolic. We searched frantically for Pap amongst the lines of uniformed men at the tables. At last, when he turned looking for us, with a bolt of shock I realised the man with the hair hacked to the scalp was Pap. He sprang up when he saw us, but was shouted at by the warder to sit.

'Love, oh, love,' Mam cried, weeping the minute she saw him, rushing towards him with outstretched arms, but Pap, weeping too, warned her.

'You can't touch me, Moll.'

As we sat there, opposite Pap, I hid my dismay at his clanging, chained hands as he spread them on the table, Mam and I doing the same so our fingers were all but touching. We did our caressing with our eyes. I tried to keep mine only tender, so not to reveal my horror at Pap's appearance. His shorn hair only made more gaunt his sore-pocked face, the grey uniform clinging to his withered frame. Even through his yearning, there was a deadness in his eyes.

'How have you been?' Pap urged us, voice earnest but weak.

'We've been fine,' Mam lied. 'Flossie Bradshaw has been a saint, taking us in. You don't need to worry. She is looking after us. We want for nothing.'

'And I'm working in the shop, Pap,' I said, anxious he know I was rallying. 'Earning good money.'

Pap shook his head. 'I let you down. I did nothing but bring more trouble upon you. I was a bloody fool. All that's happened is that bastard is still strutting around like a peacock while I'm rotting in here, instead of taking care of you.'

'He isn't strutting, Pap. You've clipped his feathers nicely,' I said, trying to hearten him, but I could see in his dull eyes, hear in his voice, where once would have been anger, a terrible defeat. He had lost all defiance.

Although Mam was eating little herself she wanted to know that Pap was nourished. He told us the food did him all right, mainly bread, porridge, potatoes and water. He didn't tell us any of what Percy had said, just that he was working, mostly washing and sewing uniforms.

'Well, that's good,' Mam joked. 'You can start doing our washing, Mattie Rae, when you come home.'

His look when she said that did not pass me by. I caught the flinch, a sad resignation in his eyes. I knew then that Pap did not believe that day would come. I tried to make him believe it.

'There's work in the market for you, Pap. All of them on the stalls are saying it, they all want to help. You're so missed. They say your big old guffaw would charm the pennies from the ladies, so they're eager to have you. Everyone wants you home.'

But it seemed the more I talked of home, the more his spirit faded. I stopped, let Mam fuss over him a while, until, too soon, the warder rang a bell.

At the bell came a change in Pap's eyes: I saw them startled. His fingers gripped the table as the warder ordered all to leave. Mam and I stuck to our bench, desperate for a cherished last moment, the panic in Pap's eyes making me wretched. I knew he was terrified of being left alone.

'We'll be back soon, Pap, don't fret, please.' In my distress, I leaned to cup his haggard face, drawing the wrath of the warder. 'No touching!' he shouted.

The warder marched over: 'Out now. Time to leave.' He grabbed Mam's arm, pulling her up, Pap leaping up too at the warder's rough handling. 'Down, Rae!' the warder yelled, shoving Pap back onto the bench, Pap unable to keep his balance with his shackled arms, nearly toppling.

Mam yelped, starting to cry at the warder's brutality. I wanted to strike the bastard but knew I would only worsen things for Pap. 'Mattie!' Mam screeched as the warder hauled her away, Pap's eyes anguished.

'It's all right, Moll. It's all right, love,' he cried after her. As the warder came back for me, Pap looked up, implored me. 'Look after her, pet. Look after your mam.'

I nodded fervently, calling as I was pulled away. 'We'll see you soon again, Pap, I promise.'

From the door I turned to take a last look at Pap. I wish I had not. For in his eyes was a terrible pleading. A pleading, I knew, for us not to leave him. Even though I had no choice, I felt as I walked away I had abandoned him. It was a look I would not forget.

Back at Flossie's, Mam was inconsolable. We knew it would be another six months before we could see or hear from Pap again. Although haunted by Pap's look, I kept myself strong and tried comfort her. She felt small, feeble, an old woman, in my arms. My mother was withering like a September flower, my father's body and spirit enchained. And so I vowed to make my innards of steel. I must fight for all of us.

* * *

The wind rattled the cab window. While the woman had battled he'd been living the life sprung from the devil's pact. Attending parties, dinners, professional functions, receiving briefs galore. In those early days, any joy at the rewards of his deviance did not penetrate his skin, reach to gladden his heart, but dripped from him like water from oilcloth. He could not drink in the golden pleasure, for the blackness of his guilt.

But as time passed, the darkness waned. He had employed reason, become master of his wits. The deed done, there was no changing it. His acts had been abominable but his aim true, intent selfless. He told himself he had offered himself up a sacrifice. Had relinquished all morality and dignity for the good of his wife, his son. If he had not chosen that course, where would they be now? He reckoned that, now done, he must make good of it. He would toil to make atonement.

So resolved, he'd worked feverishly, relentless in his bid to right wrongs, to prove himself again to worthy bearer of the Golden Lady's sword, deliverer of the justice in which he had once believed, in which he wanted still to believe.

Whether through luck, skill or fervour, he did not know, but he won now more than he lost, and his reputation grew. He became known as a fierce champion, yet just, a man of ethics, integrity. Ignoring his mind's shadow, he told himself it was a reputation rightly earned. For never had a thing been more true. No man was more scrupulous, no better servant to the law than he. He had sinned, but never again would he stray from the righteous path. Stumbling upon that perverse byway had almost cost him his sanity, made clear he had no stomach for it. He was not that man.

In the autumn of 1908, from his seat in Westminster Hall, he'd watched the mace-bearer lead the procession. As he awaited the lord chancellor, regal in wig and embroidered gown, to beckon him, he persuaded himself this honour resulted purely from his own endeavours. He did not glance to where Clarence Neville, Dudley and Herbert sat. Standing before the lord chancellor, bowing to receive the scarlet pouch, the parchments bearing the Royal Seal, he declared readiness to serve His Majesty, to wear the silken gown. He'd walked from the hall the man he had wanted to be:

William J. Linden, KC.

19

Through that dark winter, Mam called upon the intercession of her god. I would be wakened by mutterings in the wee hours, to the shadow of her on her knees by our bed, whispering prayers, pleas, making bargains with her mute companion. To bring her comfort I'd walk with her through the market to Christ Church, sit there in the pew while she knelt. Sit there in the silence. It struck me then, as I watched her pray, that God was so good at that: silence. Mam called him our loving father, yet he surely watched a thousand wrongs done his children on this earth and not a murmur. I thought of my own father, what, rightly or wrongly, he had done for me, leaving me in no doubt of his love. I knew Pap to love me more than any heavenly father.

Faced with such a lax god, I determined I would be the one to carry Mam, to guide my family over the abyss, see us safely home. I prepared for battle but theirs was not mine to win. For, no matter how I crouched by Mam, begged her take a morsel, however I sent my father the force of my love like a shield to protect him – for all my iron will, I could not make it so. In April 1908, one year after the trial and one month before we were to visit, came word from the prison, summoning us. Pap had been refusing to eat. He was failing.

Mam became hysterical when she heard it. Flossie had to calm her, help me ready her for the journey to Caledonian Road, Flossie paying for a cab. When we reached the prison we were led by an indifferent warder to the infirmary. In the cool, tiled room a trusted prisoner, acting as nurse, showed us to the furthest bed, curtained off at the wall. I nearly fell; Mam wailed, when he pulled back the curtain. Pap was lying deadly still, eyes closed, near bones on the bed, face grey and sunken.

I hurried to his side, the prisoner nodding we could touch him, he was no danger to anyone. Sitting each side of him, we both took a hand. I clasped his fingers, stroking over the scabs, the flaking skin. He did not seem to know we were there.

'Mattie, Mattie,' Mam tried to rouse him.

His eyes twitched under their lids, flickered open, then closed. His lips parted, but his mouth was too parched to speak.

'Will you get him some water?' I begged the prisoner, but he shook his head.

'He won't take it. You can try to wet his lips.'

He fetched us a glass and I stood, trembling as I dripped the water onto Pap's cracked lips, but he started to thrash his head, shake the water away.

'Pap, please.' My words came with a burst of tears. 'Take some water.'

He groaned, head still thrashing. For just a second, his eyes opened and I saw with horror a wildness there. My pap had lost his senses. Mam was moaning, face pressed to Pap's hand, as I called again to the prisoner. 'Can you not make him take it? How long has he not been taking food or water?'

The prisoner told us he had been refusing food for over a month, water for the last week. They had waited until the last to summon us. I cried out in anguish. 'Could you not have sent for us sooner? We could have talked to him, persuaded him. He cannot hear us, he can hear nothing. He is too weak.'

At last the prison doctor came. An older man, wisps of white hair at his temples, gravely he took Mam and me aside.

'Your husband is near the end, Mrs Rae. His organs are closing down, all his faculties are failing. I fear you must prepare to say your goodbyes.'

Howling, Mam dug her nails into my arm, while I desperately searched the doctor's face as if I could not fathom his meaning. 'What are you saying? Can you not feed him, please, give him water? Make him take it. Please.'

'It's too late,' the doctor said.

With a cry, Mam fell to her knees. I dropped to mine to hold her. 'I can't say goodbye to him. I can't,' Mam was moaning over and over. 'He is my life. My very life.'

'Mam,' I said, gripping her arms. 'Come with me. Come to Pap. We will pray. Come, Mam, I will pray with you.'

As we sat by his bedside I fixed on Pap's face, the festering sores, collapsed cheeks, his eye sockets like deep-purple valleys. His hand, so frail, felt as if it had the bones of a sparrow, as if it might break in mine.

Mam began to pray over him and for her sake I mouthed with her the words. As my lips moved, I whispered too in adoration, not to any god, but to my pap: *You are the love of our hearts. The great love of our hearts.* Adoring every inch of that ravaged body; each of his laboured breaths I took with him. I could not bear his chest's rattle, the suffering of it, yet could not bear what it would mean for that suffering to end. I hoarded each second of life as if it were gold, treasure forever mine to keep.

As evening fell, Mam and I talked to him of times gone by. Each memory felt like torture, yet sacred, as we gathered for him those moments, the great riches of our lives. I whispered to him of Saturday walks to Liverpool Street Station for humbugs, my screams at frothy troughs in the brewery. Mam spoke of my days skipping through the market, of slapping Pap's cap on his head, sending him out to chase me home.

At this his lips moved. He tried to speak, but I could not hear him.

'What, Pap?' I said, a thudding at my ribs.

'Ludgate, doff your hat . . .'

My heart tore open at his voice so tiny, so feeble. He was speaking of my song, the City gates he had taught me.

163

'That's it, pet, sing,' he said.

'He thinks you're a child, Lotta,' Mam said, agonised. 'He thinks you're a child again.' Her voice broke. 'Sing for him, love.'

Through searing pain I mustered every strength I could. Slipping my palm under his, caressing his fingers, I faltered as I started to sing: '*Run Aldersgate to Smithfield, mind, no fat!*'

Every word crucifying, I forced myself on, making my voice chirpy as a child's. I looked at Mam as she raised a hand to muffle her sobs, but then saw her drop it. I followed her eyes, suddenly brightening.

Lighting at Pap's mouth curving in the softest of smiles.

That evening we left the prison; I knew it would be Pap's last on earth. He would not see his last sunset, nor look upon his last moon. As the wind on Caledonian Road touched my face, I knew it would never again touch Pap's. That long night Mam and I held one another, sleepless in the bed, Mam keening against me as I gazed through the window upon that moon Pap could not see, made hopeless wishes upon it.

Early next morning the sun had hardly risen when I heard Flossie's steps beyond the door. She came like a shadow to the doorway, looked down upon us. I did not want her to speak. I knew what she had to tell. I stared at her, in terror.

'Is it over?
She nodded silently.

I moved like a sloth those days after. For days clocks would chime a time that had no meaning. Every minute felt an hour. An hour could have been a week. It did not matter to me. I passed through that endless tunnel of time in a trance, a murky fog from which I could not, did not want to emerge. For Pap had gone.

On the morning we laid him to rest, our friends and neighbours gathered around us. Those same friends and neighbours had saved Pap from a prison grave, raising enough for a single plot in Bow Cemetery. In the church the priest talked of each of us as God's children, cherished souls. I thought God had so many children, perhaps I should forgive him for forgetting one, pardon his oversight as I held Mam. A soul claimed cherished, yet so badly broken in my arms.

After church I gathered Mam close as we led the procession, followed the Spitalfields men bearing Pap's coffin down Mile End Road, near the rest of Spitalfields behind us. Pap's workmates from Whitbread were there too, Bertie also. I looked at them, took their hands as they came to comfort me at the cemetery, but they seemed as if from a different life.

Mam and I stood linking arms, holding hands tightly, beneath the arching oaks that rose over Pap's grave. There in the damp, my face chill with misty rain, I could smell the wet earth as they lowered him down, Mam swaying against me as the men took up their spades. I turned her from the brutal thudding of the sod, walked her away, blind now to all those gathered. As we walked I heard a rustle in the thrashing branches of a great oak, looked up at the screeches and flapping wings of a flock of birds. I watched them fly. Fly free, far, far from this place of sorrow.

I longed to fly with them. And I wondered if Pap's soul flew now.

That night, with all in bed, I sat numb, ghostly still in the silence of Flossie's parlour when from the bedchamber, I heard Mam's cry: *Am I to believe myself your beloved soul?*

Flossie said it was a blessed release when she found Mam cold on the kitchen floor the first day of summer. When Flossie called out to me in the shop and I chased up the stairs to see Mam lying there, so ghastly white and twisted, it was as if she had been struck by lightning.

166

Struck down, Flossie reckoned, by the merciful hand of God. The doctor said it was apoplexy. Her heart, her brain. From the Greek, Apoplexia he said. Struck down by violence. To my mind that made more sense than Flossie's talk of mercy. For it seemed to me that if there was a God, then every suffering in Mam's life had been writ by his Almighty hand. While Flossie cast him Mam's saviour, I cursed him as her tormentor.

No matter what he ordained a heathen like me, the god Mam had been faithful to all her life had been faithless. And I would hear no more on mercy. I'd been swathed in the mercy of Flossie, our friends, neighbours as they'd gathered around us after Pap, as they gathered to me when I lost Mam. I had witnessed both goodness and mercy in humankind but not in any god.

Those days after Mam's death, the bitterness crazed me. I had seen madness in Pap's eyes before he died, now I suffered a madness of my own. I lived with horror, anguish, love and hate in equal measure, my mind a carnival of confusion. My wits stripped by grief, the flood of love for my parents only spurred a rage, a hate so pure. All I blamed for their deaths, I damned. The Man. God. That hate became my abiding passion. And I was to come hate another.

20

Those days after Mam's death, Flossie did her best to comfort me. She urged me to be courageous, the strong girl my parents raised. But even evoking what Mam and Pap would have wished could not rally me, or drag me from my pit of grief. In the shop, caring little for myself, less still for others, I found it impossible to grant my customers a smile, their chatter lost to the maze that was my mind, my heart an organ scarred, toughened against the world, yet weakened. There seemed scant reason for my work. Mam and Pap had gone. I had no one to strive for. No purpose.

Dreading the suffocating hush of Flossie's parlour, I would wander, but those once-loved Spitalfields streets seemed only now to smother me, besieging me at every turn with visions of bygone days. I felt a growing desperation to escape.

Once, my feet aching, I slumped down in a doorway. The summer evenings were light, but I did not worry who saw me. Some lads passed and one of them stopped.

'Hey, here, here.' He called back his friends. 'Look who we have here. It's the girl from the papers. Boys,

I do believe we are looking upon the face of Miss Lotta Rae!'

His companions gathering around to gawk. I looked up through dazed eyes. I cared nothing for their jibes.

'You're famous, you know,' the boy said. 'Here.' He thrust his hips towards me. 'Will you make your mark on my crotch?'

The others laughing, an anger flashed through me. 'Sod off, you little bastards, or you'll see what kind of mark I'll make!' I scrambled up, swinging my foot to boot the boy in the groin, sending him flying, creasing with pain. Startled, one of his cronies tried to save face with a jeer.

'Oh, a real lady *you* are. Look at you in the gutter, nothing but a tart. Come on, boys, we might catch something if we stay too close.' They called back as they scarpered. 'Slag!'

But their words held no sting, for the world's judgement was no longer my concern; it had lost all power. I was beyond any hurt it could inflict, for I had suffered the deepest hurt. I could hurt no more.

During those wanderings, my well of hate I turned upon myself. It was I who had caused this horror. I with my stupid, girlish foolishness. Not wishing to offend had made me go against all natural feeling and walk with the monster that night. If only I had refused my arm. Had turned back to the party. I would torment myself by imagining it. I would see Bertie smile, relieved at my return; Pap lift his mask, raise his hand in salute.

I would wonder what my life might have been. I could not fathom that from that one sorry moment I had lost everything. My life, Mam's, Pap's.

Flossie would be waiting in the parlour to reprimand me when I returned.

'What are you thinking, wandering the streets alone at night? What will people think? Pull yourself together, girl, pay mind to what your mam, your pap would say.'

But Flossie's words could not reach me. There grew a silence between us. To her I was a stranger, not the girl I had been. To me she was a reminder of all that had been lost. I would look away for I could see mirrored in her eyes the girl that once was. That girl I could no longer be.

And then came the letter.

The letter, William. You never knew of it, did you? That late June day I was listlessly stacking the shelves behind the shop counter when I glanced around to see a woman there, grey hair tucked up under her hat, carrying no basket for messages. She was slapping down an envelope on the counter, casting me such a strange look as she scurried away, it made me curious. Instantly I reached for the envelope and, seeing my name, opened it, expecting perhaps a letter of condolence about Mam, but not understanding why it should come from a stranger or the need for such secrecy.

I looked immediately for a signature. There was none. The letter was written in a strange hand, large and small letters set apart as if someone were trying to disguise their writing. Quickly I searched the lines. I saw condolences not for Mam, but for Pap. And then I saw words that made no sense to me. Words that at first stupefied me, then made me chase through the door, after the woman. In strong ink, I saw your name.

The market was busy but I was lucky: the woman's age made her slow. I spied her up ahead amongst the stalls and pushed through the heave to catch her. When I touched her shoulder from behind, her face, as she turned to see me, was terror-struck.

'Why have you written me this letter?' I said, breathless from the run. 'Who are you? What do you mean by it?'

She shook her head, stepping away as if to make off. 'It wasn't I wrote it,' she said. 'Just read it. And heed it.'

She turned to go but I grabbed her arm.

'Who wrote it, then? Tell me. I have a right to know.'

Again, she shook her head, trying to pull away from me, but I had her gripped tight. At last, seeing I would not loosen my grip, she said, 'My mistress. It was my mistress wrote it.'

'And who is she?' I demanded.

She kept tight-lipped but at my dogged tugging of her arm, finally relented.

'Mrs Allen Griffiths,' she said. 'Constance Allen Griffiths.'

We talked much that day, Nellie and I. After she had made me swear never would I confront her mistress or reveal where I had received the information, she sat with me outside the nearby tea room. I cared little anyway, but, knowing Flossie was in the back room, she could mind the shop.

Nellie told me how she had been with her mistress over twenty years. How during those long years she had seen and soothed her bruises, had hovered anxiously when her master returned late from his night jaunts, crazed with cocaine, and turned from his own room to his wife's. How she had stood helpless on the landing as she listened to her mistress's whimpering, her muted protest at her husband's attentions, his bellows. How all she could do was go to her own room, wait to tend to her mistress next morning.

Her mistress had not cared those nights she suspected her husband entertained by the prostitutes in King's Cross or Soho, only been glad for it meant for one night at least she would be left be. She told me something then that shocked me. That this was not the first time Nellie had laid eyes on me. It seemed her mistress was greatly interested in me. That many times she had sent Nellie down to Spitalfields, to look upon me, see how

I fared. For her mistress felt with me a kinship, a bond. One, like she, who had been subject to her husband's brutality. For she had no doubt as to her husband's guilt. But something had happened now. Something that had made her write. When I asked what it was, Nellie seemed loath to tell me.

'It's in the letter,' she said. 'All you need to know.'

But I entreated her: 'Tell me, please, what happened.'

As she spoke, I realised why she had been reluctant to tell me. For she spoke of Pap. And she knew how it would hurt me.

'There was a man called Clarence Neville came to see the master,' she said. 'I was in the hallway with the mistress arranging the flowers and they were in the drawing room, drinking, joking. We could hear them through the door ajar laughing about your father. The master was saying it was good he was gone now, for he'd always worried he might resurface to cause more trouble, that he seemed that sort. The mistress looked at me. It was the first time either of us had heard he'd died. She was shocked and saddened.'

'So she has written me this letter of condolence,' I said. 'But what of these other words I can make no sense of? What of them?'

Nellie reddened. 'They went on to talk of other things then. Of the trial. They were talking about your lawyer; Linden, is it? Of how he'd worked on you like a snake charmer. Got you to spill all your dirty little secrets. How Holford, the master's lawyer, was singing a Hallelujah chorus when he'd got the information. How he'd never known where it had come from, and hadn't cared. Only said it was gold and would win the case for them.' She hesitated, looked down at her cup. 'That you would be done for.'

At first I could not believe what she was saying. I was assaulted by her words, found myself denying them. But as Nellie talked on, I thought of your unflagging interest, how you had coaxed from me every particular of my courtship with Bertie. How you had urged me to tell you all. I thought too of how you had wooed me and Mam. At the time Pap thought it strange you could devote so much time to our family. By the time Nellie left me, I felt the greatest simpleton ever to have walked this earth.

For now, with savage clarity, came the reason.

21

The news of Matthew and Moll Rae's deaths had shaken him. He had been staggered by the vastly contrasting fortunes of they and Allen Griffiths. Word was the man loomed large around town again, his arm all but healed. He could hardly fathom the inequity. Mercifully, however, the demands of his new position allowed him little time to brood. With work and whisky he had succeeded, for the most part, in driving the Raes from his mind; become proficient in the art of denial. And he had another problem to contend with, one that occupied his thoughts. Raff.

The boy was becoming a trouble to him. Raff had turned eighteen the very autumn he'd taken Silk, but there was absolutely no question of his going to Oxford or Cambridge. He'd shown little interest in his studies in recent years and they'd only just managed to scrape him into King's College on the Strand, fiddling in the Arts. Even as he'd tried to guide him towards law, the boy had no intention of it. He'd grown tall, taller than himself, exuding an almost frenetic energy.

He'd inherited his mother's sensibilities, her liberal leanings, but more so. Where Margaret was calm, measured in her beliefs, he was unpredictable in temperament, volatile. The boy's fervour, his passion, alarmed him.

It felt the world was going mad, his son along with it. The turning of the century had seemed to turn also people's minds, ignite and scatter their senses. These days the city had a near-frenzied feel, as if stood on a rumbling earth threatening to quake. It was all the fault of the lunatic Liberals. The Tories had imploded, the country left at the mercy of those radicals in cahoots with the raving trade unions, pandering to the poor, undermining all stability with their dangerous ideas of empowering the working classes, doling out free schools, free meals, free everything. It was insanity.

They were no better than that godawful new Labour party which wanted to bring the country to its knees, granting every right to everyone, rousing the mob with their tirades. And his son had fallen under their spell. One evening when Raff had gone to some rally he'd found particularly odious, as they'd sat in the drawing room, he'd found himself blaming Margaret.

Margaret had laid down her sketch. 'For goodness sake, William, you can't blame me for this. You know I have little time for the Pankhursts. They are far too violent, they only bring the cause of women's suffrage into disrepute. I am a follower of Millicent Fawcett and her far more peaceful organisation and Raff knows that. If he has fallen under the thrall of Emmeline Pankhurst, that has nothing to do with me.'

The insufferable suffragettes. Margaret was right; she had only aligned herself with the far more civilised Fawcett organisation. In the months before the trial, under flags and banners, she'd marched with them and an impressive number of women, from Hyde Park Corner to the Strand, calling for the vote. He hadn't been too keen. After all, she'd be exposed to every class of woman on that march. But they'd laughed on her return, for the heavens had opened that day, her skirt soaking, splattered in mud, and they'd come to call it the Mud March. It had been peaceful, good-natured, and garnered much sympathy in the press. Unlike the march that same week organised by the Pankhursts.

He remembered reading the descriptions in *The Times*, the headlines of a shocked press. Women organised like an army, striding like men, the Pankhurst woman rallying her angry swarm, 'Rise up, women! Now!' Police had tried to halt them at Parliament Green, but the women had hurled themselves at them like drunken navvies, refusing retreat, struggling on until nightfall. Many had been carted off to the courts and jailed. It had been the talk of chambers. It was a disgrace.

And now his son was associating with the likes of these women. Such an unmanly pursuit. It filled him with shame. He shuddered at its becoming known in their circles, in chambers, at court. He and Raff had argued about it. Just as they did so often.

'For God's sake, Father, you are living in the last century!' Raff had railed. 'The world is changing and we're changing it. You'd better get used to it, Papa. It's a new century. A new world. And we're going to make it a better one.'

In the carriage, he pinched his throbbing eyes.

We're going to make it a better one.

* * *

Him. You think of him. He haunts you, William, just as surely as I. Just as you haunted me. So long, you plagued me, a ghost in my mind until I made you flesh again. For you cannot rid yourself of a ghost. Cannot slay it. Only flesh can be destroyed. Only flesh can bleed.

22

I did not betray Nellie's confidence. The letter begged the
same as she, that I heed it but never reveal how I had
come by the information. I suppose Constance feared
that if I showed any the letter, her writing, no matter how
she tried to disguise it, would be recognised. I tell you
now and only now. When it can make little difference.

After Nellie left, I was crushed. Pushing past Flossie in
the shop, hunkered in my bedroom, I clenched the letter
in my fist, railing at it. Nellie had told me that Constance
had written not only through genuine sorrow over my
loss of Pap, but rage over what wrong you had done
me. Not knowing Mam had died, she wondered if Pap's
death would cause us to have further dealings with you.
If we might seek your advice and counsel. She wanted to
warn us that you were not our friend.

Although the letter spoke only of your cunning as to
Bertie, I thought of Jack. And wondered if that treachery too had been your work. The anger, the hurt, burnt
me like scalding water, washed through me with its rise
and fall. It was then. There, in that moment, that I lost
all faith. Every faith in the world, any shred I still clung
to, was ripped from me. Now that world held only

charlatans and foes. I welled with a hatred so pure, my blood turned to venom.

That day I wandered far from the shop, far from the market cries and alleyways of Spitalfields. I cannot say where I walked, I was unseeing. I thought of going to your chambers, to do what, I do not know. To confront you. To pound you with my fists, spit in your face. Perhaps to kill you. Many days after, I would envision it. How I might kill you. I would picture myself taking a knife, like Pap, driving it deep into your deceitful heart. Watch your life seep away, by my hand. Your life for Pap's. For Mam's. Those imaginings brought me solace. Soothed me like a balm.

From then I spoke to Flossie in a hiss and I know she was eager to be rid of me. I was unable be still, only finding release in pounding unfamiliar streets, a stranger amongst faceless crowds. When I could walk no more, I would catch an omnibus, a mindless passenger, travelling wherever it was bound.

One day I found myself West. On the broad Charing Cross Road, dazed by the hordes in their finery, I slipped into the side-streets, to a maze of laneways I did not know. I found a small green and sat there a while, rising at dusk to hear life all around me; the clatter of horses, omnibuses, shouts from taverns and eating houses. I saw vagabonds, dirty men and women crouching in doorways. And I felt at home amongst them. There amongst the soiled and sullied. The unwanted and unclean, slithering in the underbelly.

At a boarded-up shop, I huddled, just as they, in the doorway. And did not go back to Flossie's. Never again. Mimicking my new companions, I cupped my hands to beg. For days I cared nothing for food, but, my throat parched from sunlight and street dust, I drank thirstily from the nearby pump. I carried on in this way until one afternoon a woman passed, dropping a farthing in my palms. As I looked up to thank her, she caught my eye.

A robust woman with a wide girth, ringlets of red hair beneath her hat, dress bright and gaudy, she looked quizzically at me, holding my eye.

'You look familiar, girl,' she said, her way of speaking like my own. 'Where do I know you from?'

I shook my head, shunning her, but she continued to stare. Her eyes widened. 'Here, you're not that girl, Lotta Rae, are you? Bloody hell, I do believe you are!' She bent to lift my chin. 'Is it you, girl, under all that filth? You have the look of her.'

'I don't know any Lotta Rae,' I said. 'You have the wrong girl.'

'No I haven't.' Her voice was excited. 'I was there that first morning at the court and I saw you with my own eyes. My very own eyes. It's you, girl, I'd swear to it. What are you doing here in this doorway? Get up, get up, let me look at you.'

She bent to lift me with her sturdy arms, and, too weak to resist, I rose, standing limply before her. She looked me up and down.

'Lotta Rae.' Her face was gleaming. 'Well, I never. What's happened to you, girl? You're going to come with Mamma May now, and tell her all about it.'

She took my arm and linked it as, legs cramped, I hobbled beside her. We reached a tall brick house with a red door, climbed the steps, out of the grimy heat into a cool hall.

'There we are, love,' she said, unpinning her hat, tossing it on the coat stand. 'You're all right now.'

Mamma May. May Cotter of Soho was my saviour. Her round, jolly face and canny eyes she only painted at night, but all day she wore a smile and filled the house with her raucous laugh. There were other girls there. 'My brood,' she called them. And I became one of them. But to Mamma May I was special.

'You're my star, Lotta,' she'd say. 'You're going to pull them in.'

She ran her business from home, there in Old Compton Street. A lounge she called it. For soirées. Classy, not like those others, she said. Not like the brothels, the whorehouses. She provided, purely, a little harmless entertainment. A drop of wine, music, some female company for the gentlemen.

I was never sure if that was true. Mamma May insisted her house was respectable and if the other girls were providing something extra for the gentlemen, they were not permitted to talk of it. Certainly, Mamma May never said different. If that was the case she kept it from me, protected me. I wondered often those early days why Mamma May had taken so to me, why she showed me such care. But soon I came to know. As we sat in her comfortable parlour, with its chintz chairs and curtains, lace nettings blowing in the breeze, shading us from the sun, dust kicked up by the traffic of horses I'd catch her watching me.

One day she held my eye and said: 'You have the air of her. Her way.'

I looked at her, curious, and she told me then. Of her sister, her little sister Polly, who had died a young woman from tuberculosis. Even though long ago, I could see her pain raw, although she would shake off the memory, try to smile. And I knew I was touching that part deep within that yearned still for Polly.

That, with my notoriety, was why I was deemed special, set apart from the others. And Mamma May believed that holding me distant would only make the men more eager.

'You don't have to do anything, Lotta,' she said. 'Anything but talk to them, flatter them. There's many a man would pay plenty for the chance of being in the company of the famous Lotta Rae. All you have to do is charm them.'

At first, I was dismayed, baulked at it. Mamma May knew something of my life, now I told her all. All about you. Told her I wanted nothing to do with any gentleman, any man, ever again, but Mamma May said, 'Lotta, it's the highest form of revenge. These men are gullible; you're slipping money from their pockets for nothing. Laughing at them even as you smile. See it as getting your own back. Play them for the fools they are.'

And so it began, my life at Mamma May's. I found some joy there, was happy in her house, the finest I'd ever known. It climbed three floors, each covered in rose wallpaper, polished corner tables with delicate ornaments on every landing. I thought it refined, clean and homely. Mamma May gave me my own room, bought for me clothes and anything I wished.

There, in that house, I came to know the ways of a lady. Mamma May had been a beauty in her time, had travelled all of Europe on the arm of her 'special' gentleman, one who had taught her of books, art and music. Now with me she did the same. She tutored me in a fine way of speaking.

'Don't talk so fast, Lotta,' she said, as we sat in the parlour. 'Slow your speech down, consider before you speak. Think of what you're going to say and say it slowly.'

Rounding and stretching her mouth to show me how to pronounce my vowels, I'd howl laughing. 'If I make a face like that, they'll toss me pennies to leave them alone!' She'd cackle alongside me. She also put an end to my East End stride: 'No more booting men in the privates, Lotta. You're going to learn how to glide.'

Practising my walk along the hall, head held high, spine straight, at her face so serious, I'd poke out my wiggling bottom, turn a proud head, teeth bared wider than any chimpanzee's.

'I believe I have perfected my smile,' I'd say as she hooted.

Always I'd loved reading, now she gave me many books, poetry to learn. The novels I loved best were those of Charles Dickens, for he wrote of many characters I recognised: the poor and needy of the slums Mam and Pap had told me of. It surprised me for I had assumed him a gentleman and wondered why he would bother with such lives. When Mamma May explained that although he had become wealthy, Dickens had been poor as a boy, his father in a debtors' prison, I liked him even more.

As we leafed our way through Mamma May's book of art, I'd marvel that some of the paintings were displayed there in colour. When I began to recognise the artists' names she said I had blossomed. From Mamma May I learned so much, and more again from the gentlemen themselves.

The working room, the lounge, had rich-red walls, low-lit paraffin lamps, couches and chaise longues, an elaborate Turkish rug running the wooden floor, and at the wall a deep mahogany sideboard from where Mamma May, as hostess, would serve wine.

Every evening, in my beaded gown, hair dressed with feathers and pearls, I would make my entrance.

The other girls reddened their hair, but Mamma May wanted me keep mine dark to distinguish me, render me aloof, mysterious. But, just like the others, I rouged my cheeks, painted my face.

'Hide those freckles,' Mamma May said.

The men would look up from their tables as I entered the room. Every one of them wanted me to be their companion. Each night came the same ritual. I would sit alone, watching them take Mamma May aside, whisper to her, make generous offers for the privilege of my company. Allotted to the highest bidder, I'd sit with the victor at his table, or on the chaise longue, laughing, smiling, listening, seeming to find him the most witty, engaging, most captivating man in the world.

I had my own special gentleman, an older man, a regular who was named George Connard, but we called him George Conned. One evening as we sat on the chaise longue, wine in our hands, he grew silent for a moment, fixed me with his eyes, 'Tell me truly now, Lotta. I have often wondered. Do you like it here?'

I smiled, held his eyes. 'I like being in the company of gentlemen such as you. Who would not like it?'

He laughed. 'You flatter me. But you are a bright, young thing. You cannot be serious about the attentions of an old codger like me.'

'On the contrary,' I said, voice earnest. 'I find younger men dull. From you I learn so much. I find your experience in the world, your travels fascinating. It makes me feel I've been to those places. That I've seen the art on the walls, the chapels and the piazzas. I looked up in my book the painting by Raphael you talked of. Tell me again of the colours, of seeing it in Italy.'

So it went on in this way. All the girls would take their turn at the corner, by the tall fern, to sing. My favourite to perform was by songstress Amy Woodforde-Finden, 'Till I Wake', a ballad that would lull the gentlemen, cause them to sway under my voice, dig deeper in their pockets.

At the end of the evening, Mamma May would press money into my hand.

'There you are, Lotta,' she'd say with a smile. 'They're paying their dues.'

But for every reward, the fondness I felt, the happiness and comfort I'd found in Mamma May, often my own wiles would sicken me. Although in bewitching the gentlemen, lightening their purses, I took my revenge, sometimes, as much as I despised the men, I would despise myself.

In the hours before dawn I'd leave the gaiety of the lounge for the crushing silence of my room, the horrors that gripped me in the still of night. Many nights I could not sleep for yearning for Mam and Pap. For thoughts of the Man. Of you.

The nights I did dream, oftentimes brought dark visions and Mamma May would hear me shouting in my sleep. One night she came to my room. She coaxed me to sit up, and I saw in her hand a small vial.

'Here, love,' she said. 'A little something to help you rest.'

I flinched as she trickled the reddish-brown liquid, a tonic she called it, bitter, on my tongue but, as she slipped from the room, and I settled back down, I felt the warmest of waves. A feeling so mellow, one I had not felt since I nestled in Mam's lap as a child. It washed over me, embraced me as if I were in her arms. I drifted that night into a sleep of the strangest, most vivid of dreams, but they held no spectres, did not terrorise me as my nightmares.

From that night on, I took Mamma May's tonic, soon coming to crave it by day, but Mamma May said I must keep my wits about me, after work I would get my reward. I found myself longing for my room, my bed, my potion. To slip again into Mam's arms, let her lull me to another world, that kaleidoscope land of spinning light and colour, my hand in hers. Roaming that curious carnival, we would spy Pap, smiling, happy, burst from a ripple of pale-crimson mist to greet us. Together, we three wandered that oddest of worlds; that world I clung to. For to me it was a heaven, a blessed release from the one I must now bear.

This world without them.

23

I had been at Mamma May's two years when first I saw him. I often thought afterwards how fragile a thing is fate, William. How what seemed to be our destinies could so easily slip from us; if we were to enter just a moment too soon; leave a moment too late; turn to look too quickly; not quickly enough. For, if I had not stepped from the witness room that April day of the trial, simply for air, I would not have seen him. There in the corridor with you. I tried to stay hidden, for you were embracing him, your face buried in his hair, and I did not want to disturb such tenderness. But for a moment you looked up and met my eyes. And so it was. That simple choice to step out caused me to see him. If I had not, I would not have known him.

But that night, from the chaise longue in the lounge, I recognised him straight away. Although at first his height confused me, I could not mistake those black curls, those strong, dark features. He was being bullied into the lounge by a group of young men I had never seen before, teasing, cajoling him with good-natured banter. It was clear he had no wish to be there. He was raising his palms in protest, stepping backwards as if to flee. But they bundled him in, up to Mamma May's sideboard of drinks.

I was startled. Wits scattered, I knew only I needed to escape, have time to calm my mind. Hurriedly, I made my excuses to my gentleman, retreating to Mamma May's small accounting room aside the lounge, leaning against her desk to steady my breathing.

I stood there, now and then peering around the door to watch him. Still he was protesting that he wanted no drink, making gestures he was leaving, and, at last, throwing up their hands in defeat, his friends let him go. I watched him leave, his companions shaking their heads, laughing, as Mamma May served them wine.

Nerves steadied, I returned to my gentleman, begging a moment's indulgence, looking to where the young men stood. I guessed them a harmless bunch, buffoons, not well versed in the ways of Soho, who had stumbled across one of her parlours. Three leaned on the sideboard, busy with their chatter and wine, while I went to speak to the one who stood apart. Sturdy and broad-shouldered, his reddish hair was tousled, cheeks ruddy from drink.

'Excuse me,' I said. 'May I ask? Who is the young man who has just left?'

'Hah!' His eyes, bleary, glinted. 'Young Raff! Why? Have you taken a fancy to him?'

His tone jovial, I took no offence. Just as I'd suspected, it was clear he was not privy to the secrets of Soho. He had no idea who I was. 'No, no,' I said. It's just that I think I know him. Or at least know his father . . .'

'What, old Linden?' he interrupted, seeming amused. 'Don't tell me the old boy's a regular here?' He laughed, swigging his drink.

'No. I met him in different circumstances. William Linden. The barrister. Is that correct?'

'Yes, indeed. Raff's his boy, all right. But nothing like the old man. Raff has no stomach for this kind of thing, he'd much rather be sounding off somewhere or other. He's going to some bore of a meeting, a rant at Caxton Hall tomorrow and wants to have the head for it. He said he had no desire to see painted women, and left. Whereas I,' he leaned forward, 'have no objection to such delights.'

At his leer, I knew it time to take my leave, so thanked him, returning to my gentleman on the chaise longue. I must have seemed attentive, taking care to laugh at every quip as if greatly entertained. But all the while my mind worked.

And on it worked. Long into the wee hours, William, as I lay in my bed, casting aside my medicine. I had no desire for it, for I had plans to make.

By next morning, as I asked for directions on the Strand, walked from Whitehall to Caxton Hall, as I studied the notice of the public meeting at three o'clock, I had made up my mind.

For, you see, I had watched you in the corridor that day. You there with your boy; I had seen how you loved him. And it came to me now, that I did not have to kill you to take your life. I could take it another way.

I could take him.

* * *

He turned bleakly to the carriage window. He knew. He'd always known. She had set out to snare him. Had laid his son a trap. Looking out upon the rain, he cursed her. Cursed himself.

* * *

I was restless as a tightly tethered horse that morning, anxious for the afternoon to come. I'd dressed plainly in preparation; a charcoal skirt, white blouse, a simple hat, for I had paid mind to what I'd been told. Your son did not care for painted women.

A July Saturday, hot and bright, I bided by the cooling Thames, strolled in the shadow of Westminster Palace, sat upon the green to watch Big Ben tick down the time. Knowing the meeting to be one of suffragettes, I wondered what a man would want at a thing such as that. But I was glad, for I was hopeful that, amongst many women, I would go unnoticed.

When the clock boomed the hour, I made my way the short distance to the sprawling red-brick building. I was jittery as I climbed the outer steps into a maze of corridors, searching out the hall, at last the echo of a woman's voice drawing me to a door. Edging it open to a swell of women, I saw beyond them, speaking from the podium, another woman, dressed, to my relief, much the same as I.

Slipping into the hall, hovering at the back, the force of her surprised me. Her frame was small but she held it firm, eyes defiant. Her voice was Northern, clear and bold.

'And now is the time for we women to cast off our shackles! No more will we be mere chattels of our men, marked like cattle, our ears clipped, herded out to graze, like witless beasts in the fields as we sit pretty and silent in the parlour. It is time now to claim our voice. No longer will we tolerate the patronising tripe of chivalry, bow to male guardianship of our chastity, but use that voice to demand justice!'

As the crowd sounded their approval, I searched him out. I spied him easily as a man amongst the women, but there were other men, perhaps ten or more. He stood out with his tallness, his mop of black curls. I stayed back, keeping him in sight. He had his arm raised in answer to the woman's call.

'The Government has made us a promise and we must keep them to it. These are crucial days as they consider a bill that sees women granted equal voting rights to men. For the first time in our history we have a Government stripping the rich to serve the needy. They are doing right by the poor, the elderly and infirm. Now is the time for them to do right by women!'

Again the crowd called their approval. The woman spoke on but I hardly heard, so absorbed was I with him. At last, by the shuffling and murmuring around me, I realised she had finished. A woman brushed by me, handing me a leaflet but I was blind to it. I was solely fixed on him.

I watched him join some women and two men up ahead. Pushing my way through the crush until I was near, I waited for a lull in the conversation, before drawing close.

'Excuse me.' He turned to look at me, with deep brown eyes. 'Pardon me, but I do believe I know you. Am I right that you are Raff Linden, son of William Linden?'

I had taken him by surprise. 'Why, yes. Yes, I am.' His manner was friendly, curiosity in his eyes. 'You'll have to forgive me, I can't think where we've met. Please jog my shoddy memory.'

'We have not met, not exactly.' I was greatly nervous, trying to disguise my tongue's tremor. 'But I knew your father well. He represented me in court some years ago. My name is Charlotte Rae. Lotta Rae.'

I was hoping he might know of me, the infamy of my case cause my name to stand out in his mind. Hoping also it would not prompt him to shun me.

'Charlotte Rae.' His tone lowered, registering recognition. 'Why, of course, I know of you. Know of your case.' His jaw tightened. 'What a travesty of justice that was. The rich and powerful victors again. Their antiquated views on chastity.' I was taken aback as he reached to touch my fingertips. I had not expected him to be so forward. 'It is a pleasure to meet you. A real pleasure.'

He offered his hand, shaking mine firmly as if I were a man; the woman who'd spoken on the podium then appearing from the crowd to greet him.

'What-ho, Raff!' Her mock-grand tone masked her Northern lilt. 'How are you this fine day?'

'Annie.' His voice was excited. 'Do you know Miss Rae?' Seeing us mute, he went on. 'Let me introduce you. Annie, this is Miss Charlotte Rae. Miss Rae, this is Annie Gordon, one of the London leaders of the WSPU.'

'Women's Social and Political Union.' She smiled. 'Or better known as Pankhurst's Pesky Suffragettes. Charlotte Rae?' She paused. 'I think I . . .'

'Lotta, please,' I said.

'Lotta. Lotta Rae. Of course.' Her eyes softened. 'It is you, isn't it? Charlotte Rae, who was so greatly wronged in that trial. Well, I'm mightily pleased to see you here. I looked for you soon after the case. Wanted to offer our support.'

'Thank you,' I said, remembering now her name, how Mam had told me of her seeking me out in the market.

I could not have wished for better that afternoon. Bait bitten, Raff and Annie insisted on taking me to a tea-house in Convent Garden, and at the table I felt a glut of pleasure at the haul from my hunt, content to sit quietly considering my prey, watching the two in avid conversation. Annie had piercing-blue, birdlike eyes, wearing her fair hair high, tendrils coming loose, so engaged she was with her topic. Raff startled me by banging the table in ire or enthusiasm.

'These are such exciting times, Lotta,' he said. 'The mayhem at the Government daring to tax the rich to fund the poor! The House of Lords came down like an avalanche to stop it, but the Libs and Labour fought them like tigers, and won. But the old fogies in the Lords haven't given up, so now the Government is out to strip them of their power. The whole thing's causing chaos amongst the upper classes. They're outraged!'

'Practically civil war,' Annie said.

'Then, poor old Edward. The King dying just as the Act to fleece the old boys of their riches was passed.' He laughed, biting his scone with gusto. 'They must think it an omen of the end of world.'

I had little interest in what he said, but found myself captivated by the way he said it. His eyes were on fire, words tumbling rapid as a waterfall. It was hard to believe him your boy. To imagine one so forthright, so unguarded, sprung from one so devious. The spawn of a liar.

'But I'm afraid,' Annie said, slicing a tea-cake, 'very much afraid, they won't pursue this Bill on equal voting rights. I think they'll try to wheedle out of it, say they want to give the vote to more men first, or want Universal Suffrage. Emmeline is sure of it.'

I must have seemed unsure, for Raff said to me, 'You know, at the moment, only wealthy, landed men can vote? Well, many Libs want to give the vote to more men, working men, whereas Labour wants Universal Suffrage so all men and women, no matter what class, may vote. So there's quite a struggle going on. I'm with Labour on it, but the group I belong to, the Men's League for Women's Suffrage, would settle for equal rights, women voting on the same basis as men.'

'So would we,' Annie said. 'It might only be wealthier women at first, but it's a start. But I think with all these conflicting views, plus the hordes entirely against us, we won't get it.'

It seemed outlandish to me. That men such as Pap, all the men I had known at Whitbread, in the market, would ever be allowed to vote. That was the business of toffs, not for the likes of them. Even as I nodded I thought them foolish, dreamers, all this talk of women voting nothing more than fanciful.

'We've got to keep them to their promise,' Annie said. 'Got to keep the pressure on somehow, though Asquith is urging us to tone down the violence. We'll comply for a while, see how the Bill goes.'

'That's a good girl, Annie,' Raff said, laughing, patting her hand across the table. 'No more chucking fireballs into those pillar boxes!'

They started to talk of things then that shocked me. Of Annie's setting fire to pillar boxes, women striking politicians with dog-whips, hurling rocks, smashing windows, police battering them at marches, onlookers manhandling them as they were dragged off to jail, starving themselves there in protest. I was astounded by it. My closeted life at Mamma May's had shielded me from it all.

'The police brutality is disgusting, a total injustice,' Raff said, before looking quietly at me for a moment. 'But you have suffered your own terrible injustice, Lotta.'

'Yes,' Annie said. 'Society would cast every woman as virgin or whore, Madonna or Magdalene. Say yes to one man, say yes to every other. It never occurs to them that we might be selective in our bedfellows.'

But I was concentrated not on Annie's words but Raff's. On his expression. His look was tender but inwardly I stiffened, knowing it time now to play my part.

'Yes.' I met Raff's eyes. 'It was an injustice. But your father tried so hard to help me. I would dearly love to see him again. Do you think it possible? I would so like to thank him.'

Now I was so close I could not wait. I was overtaken by the urge to see your face. Witness you cornered. Forced, once more, to look upon mine.

24

He grimaced in the carriage. That August day. Never would he forget it. The day Raff had brought her home. The afternoon sun had been merciless, a glare through the balcony window as he'd sat in the drawing room, quietly reading, with Margaret. He'd been about to suggest abandoning their reading and drawing the shutters when Raff had burst through the door.

'I have a surprise for you, Father,' he'd announced, holding back the door as if concealing something. 'A guest. Someone you have not seen for a long time. Someone who is eager to see you again.'

With a curious glance at Margaret, he'd looked to the door as Raff pulled it open. At the sudden sight of her coyly raised eyes, her demure smile, a white blaze of shock roared through him, obliterated all thought. For some seconds he could make no sense of what he was seeing. He'd risen abruptly, in his haste knocking against the table at his side, his newspaper flapping from his lap to the floor.

Raff had laughed. 'I thought you'd be surprised, Papa. Well, here he is, Lotta. And this is my mother,

Margaret. Mother, this is Miss Charlotte Rae. I'm sure you remember Papa working on her case some years ago.'

In his alarm, he still had not managed to speak. Thankfully, Margaret had stood, held out her hands.

'My dear,' she said. 'Of course I remember. And what a surprise indeed. Sadly, we never met during the case, but I am so happy to meet you now.'

At last, he'd found himself mustering some words. 'How did this come about?' His faint smile an attempt to feign pleasure.

'We ran into each other at one of your favourites, Papa,' Raff quipped. 'A suffragette meeting.'

The woman's hands were clasped in Margaret's, as she'd turned to him.

'Yes. Such a chance encounter.' She'd walked from Margaret, to stand before him. 'It's so good to see you again, William. I was only remarking to Raff that if I had not seen him at the Old Bailey that day, I would not have known him. Such good luck.'

He'd stared at her as if through a turbulent sea. Was there a sting in her tone? A taunting? He appraised her quickly. She was different. Very different to the girl he'd known. Only three years had passed but that girl had become a woman: self-assured, so much more confident. She held herself differently. Head high, she was poised, backbone straight, proud. Her way of speaking was strange to him: grander, measured, almost eloquent, but her words seemed clipped, pointed. Spiked. But she could not know. She could not possibly know. He must calm himself.

'Well, it is a delight to have you in our home,' Margaret said. 'Please sit, Miss Rae. I'll ring for tea.'

'Call me Lotta, please.' She'd gone to settle beside Raff on the couch, Margaret rising from her chair to press the bell on the wall. He'd taken his own seat, struggling to still his mind.

'I was so sorry to hear of the death of your father,' Margaret said. 'Is your mother still living?'

'My mother has passed away also.' She'd glanced at him. A deliberate glance, he was sure. His neck felt moist.

'I am so sorry,' Margaret said. 'But, my dear, where are you living?'

'I lodge with an old family friend near Charing Cross Road. A lady who is now infirm and I am her companion. Her house is very homely. I am very comfortable there.'

'I'm so glad,' Margaret said, gesturing to the maid for tea.

Stupefied, he'd realised the woman was speaking to him.

'I thought afterwards, William, that I never had the chance to thank you properly after the trial. For your devotion, your untiring work on my behalf. I wish to thank you now. I shall never forget your kindness to me.'

He'd shifted in his chair. 'No, not at all. Please.' He'd felt some relief. Allowed her words to soothe him.

She was thanking him. Grateful. No, she did not know. Her goading of him, any meaning in her glance, was mere imagining. Of course she did not know. It was impossible.

'But you were so good to me, my family. Such a friend. Mam and Pap could never praise you enough for the time you spared us. And I the same.'

'William was greatly dedicated to your case,' Margaret said. 'He worked so hard on it, I know. He was very distressed with the way things turned out.'

He'd never known Margaret had noticed his distress, albeit for reasons very different to those she'd supposed. But naturally she had noticed. She knew him so well. *Not so well. Not well enough.* The guilt he had not felt for so long swelled in his gut.

'Just a bloody shame that the bugger got off,' Raff said.

'Raff! Show some respect for the ladies.' His tone was overly terse, he knew, but he seized the chance to release the crippling tension.

'It's quite all right,' the woman said, smiling.

'They're grown women, Papa,' Raff said. 'Quite capable of telling me off themselves if needs be.' His son and the woman had exchanged a look he didn't like. Too familiar.

He longed for a reason to excuse himself, to find a way to put an end to the ordeal, but could not. It was the weekend. There was nowhere he must be. He knew he should be making conversation, show an interest in the woman's present circumstances, but he had no wish to know, was loath to ask any questions. He was aware, though, how odd it must look.

Luckily, Margaret was so good at chatter. The three of them began to speak of the unbearable London heat, and Raff and the woman's happening upon one another. He'd tried not to think the unthinkable. To quell the torturous suspicion that this had been no random meeting, but one somehow calculated by the woman. He'd told himself such doubts were mere torments of a guilty mind, for he could not fathom how she could know where to seek out his son or, more crucially, oblivious to any wrongdoing against her, why she would wish to do so.

Buried in thought, for once he was thankful for his son's unfettered tongue, his and Margaret's shared passions, for soon the three were busy bleating about the plight of the poor, the needy, so engrossed in a torrent of hopeless causes, he hoped they hardly noticed his silence.

At last, afternoon growing late, the woman rose to leave. He and Raff stood as she bid goodbye to Margaret, coming then to shake his hand.

'I hope we will not be strangers now, William.' Her hand lingered in his. 'That we will see one another again, now we have had the good fortune to meet once more.'

Stomach seizing at her words, he'd nodded, uttered some pleasantry. Raff had escorted her from the room, offering to hail her a cab, she adamant she would take the omnibus.

Following, standing at the top of the stairs, he'd listened to them below in the hall, Raff insisting that he walk with her. Then, finally, the door closing behind them.

And there, he'd gripped the banister, with a desperate prayer.

Please, let that be the last of her. Please.

25

But your prayers, like Mam's, were to go unanswered, William. Perhaps your god could not hear, perhaps I had rendered him powerless, for I had cast myself like a storm cloud across your skies, there to reign in his place. To deal you your fate. Deal you yours, as you did mine.

I saw the shock, the bewilderment on your face that day. Saw as you struggled to greet me, not surprise in your eyes, but horror. I'd had little doubt as to your guilt, but any I might have harboured was swept away. Your obvious dread delighted me. Made me all the more determined to work my wiles on your son.

As summer turned to autumn, I saw much of he and Annie. Those days we spent in Hampstead, in a high, rambling house near the Heath where Annie lodged with three others. The house belonged to a spinster named Patience Wakeman, a woman like no other I had ever met. In the airy drawing room, with arched sash windows, couches strewn with Afghan throws, floor scattered with rugs and cushions, like a silver-haired grand old dame, she'd recline on her rattan chair, feet roughshod upon the table, telling bawdy jokes, boasting of her past intimate encounters with men as I tried to hide my shock at her candour.

'Bring me a gin-cup!' she'd call. 'And for God's sake, where are my cigarettes?'

Annie and the other women who lived there would laugh, happily doing her bidding, brewing Russian tea in a silver urn on the sideboard, entertaining the other suffragettes, wild with plots and schemes, and men, like Raff, who would plot and scheme with them. Many of the women were ladies, others from working families like me, while the men were mostly young, like Raff. The afternoons I'd arrive to meet Annie and Raff, I would find a melee sprawled about the couches.

'For goodness' sake, will one of you oafs get up and give the poor girl a seat?' Patience would bark. 'Or is that too chivalrous for you?'

Raff would always leap up, offer me his place, while some of the men teased him.

'Easy to see you're a true gentleman, Linden. Breeding is showing,' one of them, Eddie Long, often ribbed him.

Always he would take it as an insult. 'I most certainly am not,' he'd retort, ears reddening. I would make sure to give him a consoling smile before landing myself amongst the crush on the couch.

Eddie would sometimes ask after the mythical lady to whom I pretended be companion. I'd named her Nancy Connard, after my gentleman, George.

'How is your old lady?' he'd say. 'Is she as cantankerous as Patience?' Annie, beside him, hooting while Patience would scowl.

'She has not yet mastered that fine art,' I'd reply, having learned over those months to tease back.

As I joked with Annie and the others I'd glance over at Raff, catch him staring, only to swiftly look away. I was glad to see him no longer so forward, so sure, his growing nervousness, his shyness around me, boded well. I planned to play my hand slowly, to reel in my catch. And I had now a different ploy.

At first with Raff, I had set out to charm him, to laugh and listen, just as I did with my sorry gentlemen. But I quickly learned that Raff and his comrades were not like those men. These were men who did not make a show of chivalry but were earnest in their respect. Though more refined, they reminded me a little of those I had known at Whitbread, the fun in them, the comradery we might have known if I had lowered my guard. But I did not.

I realised that Raff did not want me to pander to him, to make him feel special. Raff wanted my opinion. Wanted me to believe in his causes, to feel as strongly as he. So, as if eager to learn, wanting to appear as rebellious as they, I abandoned my carefully acquired ways of a lady, hitching up my skirt to sit beside Raff cross-legged on the floor cushions, as his passion caused him to forget his nerves.

'Do you feel it, Lotta?' he said one afternoon as the others chatted excitedly about a recent exploit, the ruination of a fashionable putting green by some of the women. 'The charge there is in the air? I truly believe it's our generation that will change this world. To us the new world belongs.'

With eyes sincere, I reached to cover his hand with mine, watching for his own eyes shyly averting. 'I do believe it. I feel it too.'

He could never suspect, no matter my words, my apparent accord, I did not, could not believe anymore in anything either in this world or beyond. Faithless in any god or man, I was deaf and blind to him. It was as if I wore armour held before me, a shield his ardour was unable to lance. I could see him only as your son. A pawn in a game. A game between you and me.

Mamma May, needing me only at night, did not care how I spent my days, but, knowing of my dalliance with Raff, warned me to be careful. Often, as I left Hampstead for my work, and my night-time medicine, Raff would want to ride the omnibus with me, see me to my door, but every time I refused. I told him my companion too fragile, too sickly for visitors, but I must be there every evening to tend to her.

Always I would ask him pass on to you my kind regards. So you would know of the time I spent with your son.

It was a dull November afternoon, Patience puffing smoke from her rattan chair, Raff and I idling on the couch, when Annie rushed through the door, greatly agitated.

'Well, that's it!' Her pale cheeks were burning. 'Asquith has betrayed us. He's shelving the Bill.'

'What?' Raff bolted upright. 'Why? Has he said why?'

Restless at the window, she stared at us. 'The suspicion is he's intending to call a General Election. One to give him a mandate for the only thing he cares about; to reduce the power of the House of Lords. That'll give him no time for the Bill.'

'No time or no wish?' Patience said, tartly. 'Probably frightened that pushing through the Bill would hamper his chances in the election. Us bloody women getting the vote.'

'The Judas, he's never been on our side.' Raff was furiously wringing his hands. 'Well, he's very wrong if he thinks we're going to take this quietly.'

It was there in Hampstead the preparations began. Annie was constantly on the telephone to Emmeline Pankhurst, Raff beside her avidly taking notes, while I was on my knees, helping the other women paint banners for the planned march. It was the talk of the house. If Asquith dissolved Parliament without mention of the Bill, we must be ready, Annie said. Ready now for a fight like no other. Prepared to go to any ends. Prepared to go to jail.

My sincerity, my resolve, for the first time was being tested. I was anxious to pass that test in Raff's eyes but, in truth, I was alarmed at their zeal, terrified at what might be expected of me.

Two days before the march, Raff and I sat by ourselves in the Hampstead drawing room. A fire burned
in the grate but the room was cold as we sat either side
of the couch. I could hear Patience in the hall, loudly
issuing orders to others who had arrived, Raff fiddling
with the golden throw's fringes. I could sense his tension at being alone with me and he seemed to be thinking intently. Suddenly his hand grasped mine.

'Will you march beside me, Lotta?' he said. 'Stay at
my side?'

Startled, I looked at him. He had caught me off guard.
It was always I who made any advances; offering and
withdrawing my hand at will, I who had so far devised
and dictated the steps of this dance. I could see it had
taken him much courage to make this display, could
feel his urgent need for my answer.

'Yes, of course.' I squeezed his fingers, but, disturbed,
lowered my eyes.

For where before I would have taken my chance, held
his gaze to beguile him, in that moment I could not.

For I realised he had touched my heart.

26

We met at Caxton Hall on a November Friday at noon, that winter of 1910 at what they called the Women's Parliament, one to match the men's own at Westminster Palace. Raff beside me, we looked up to the podium where the woman I'd heard so much of, Emmeline Pankhurst, stood, her daughters and Annie by her side. Behind them sat a panel of women, four rows strong, beneath the giant banner I had helped paint: *Not Words but the Bill, the whole Bill, and Nothing but the Bill.*

Emmeline was the most striking woman. Dressed entirely in black, she held herself proudly, dark hair piled high, face made noble by chiselled cheekbones and soulful, almost sad eyes. She looked to me imperial, like a Russian empress I had once seen in a storybook. We were deathly quiet as her clear voice echoed through the hall:

'So, now we await word. Word from Westminster. That word will determine whatever our actions this afternoon. We have complied with the Government's request to cease all militancy this long year. Today, if Asquith dissolves Parliament with no mention of the

Bill, our time of peaceful resistance will have passed. We will once again show them what force they are dealing with. The women of this country united. As one!'

She had me spellbound, when a woman pushed through the crowd, climbing the podium steps to whisper into Emmeline's ear. Emmeline nodded, leaning to talk to her daughters and Annie. She turned back to us, holding us a moment with her eyes: 'Women. Comrades. The time has come! Asquith has dissolved Parliament with no mention of the Bill. So now we march. We leave this place and on to Parliament. We do not stop until we have forced our way into the House of Commons. That place of sham democracy, a voice denied us there so long. Now we make them hear! We show them ours is not a voice that can be ignored. Rise up, women! Prepare for the fight of your lives!'

The hall sprang alive with nervous excitement, shrill chatter, calls to form groups, my anxiety rising as Raff took my arm to lead me outside, into the cold air. The clouds brooding, we gathered there beneath the red-brick building, shuffling into line. Up ahead, I saw Emmeline in black fur coat, scarf over her hat, flapping in the breeze, Annie beside her. Patience, slower, had joined others behind us. I shivered in the blustery wind. Raff gently touched my hand. 'Are you all right? Ready?'

I nodded, but felt far from it at the bristling tension. The women before us raised their banner: *Where there's a Bill there's a Way*. I set my jaw, wanting to seem as fervent, as bold as they.

Slowly at first, then gaining pace, we marched, Raff chanting with the others by my side. The women broke into song: '*A Promised Land of liberty, the Dawn of Freedom's morn we see*', as at last Westminster Palace came into sight. Spying burgeoning crowds on the street, leering, jeering, I felt the urge to take Raff's hand, but neither wished to show weakness, nor recognise in myself that need. Ahead, Emmeline and Annie were already upon the iron line of police. Urgent calls rippled to all behind. Asquith had refused to see the delegation of women sent ahead.

At this there was a surge, thrusting me forward, nearly toppling me. The women beyond were trying to push nearer the House, police swarming around them like buzzards. Suddenly a fan of black swept the sky. Horrified, I watched the batons speeding down, rupturing the front lines as women, like matchsticks, began to fall. The crowds were growing larger, louder with heckling and goading whistles.

'Come on!' Raff shouted to me. 'Push, Lotta. They won't stop us.'

He gripped my hand, pulling me onwards, but from the crowd sprang a capped man, mouth twisted spitefully at Raff: 'What kind of a man are you? Are you wearing skirts under that coat?'

In an instant, more men had leaped upon Raff, dragging him from the line, landing him vicious punches as

I stood trapped within the swathes of women. Desperately, I tried to elbow through to reach Raff, but the force behind me was too great. I turned to see a mob of men.

'Want to scrap like a man, love?' The jeerer and his cronies jostled me from side to side, as I tried to wrench myself free.

At that moment the heavens opened in a torrential downpour. Rain pelting me, the men's spittle in my face, with a rush I felt myself released, snatched away by the marching women, hurtled ever closer to the House. Blinded by the rain, I turned to look for Raff, but had lost all sight of him.

Finding myself upon the wide-open road beside the green I gaped at the terrible chaos. Mounted police drove their way through the downpour, drenched women clawing, screeching at them as they were hauled away by their outstretched arms, trampling over others toppled on the ground, abandoned hats and scarves drifting in the puddles.

Without warning, a peeler was upon me. Face in a frenzy he raised his baton, swiping it down hard on my shoulder. I cried out, lifting my arms in defence, but he swiped at me again, landing a blow on my ribs. As I creased in pain, his boot flew into my stomach, flattening me. Lying winded, dazed, as if I might vomit, I saw an elderly man in a topper, staring stunned down at me. He held up his hands to the peeler.

'Stop! For goodness' sake, man, stop!'

He reached down to help me, but shock and anger rose in me like a storm.

'Get away from me! All of you! Get away from me!'

Amidst the cries, roars and screams, I was on my feet, running, when I lost my footing, tripping over a fallen woman. Her face gashed, I grappled with her to lift her, when ahead I saw one I knew from the Hampstead house: Rosa May, in her wheelchair. Two peelers had heaved her from it, leaving her lying limp on the road. They started to drag her away.

Scrambling up with the fallen woman, intending to follow Rosa May, I felt a mighty wallop on the back of my neck, knocking me to my knees. As I clutched my neck, two hands were suddenly at my breasts, squeezing, tugging at them to haul me up. I screeched at the searing pain, flailing my arms to thrash my laughing, unknown assailant, only to be tossed once more to the ground.

Crawling with grazed hands through the puddles, I felt the shove of another boot, rolling me over, the kicks coming fast. Over and over my ribs were kicked as I cried out, curling myself into a ball. At last they stopped and as I lay there fighting to breathe, I felt more hands upon me. Screaming, I pushed them away, but recognised then Annie's voice.

'It's all right, Lotta, it's me! Come on now, come on.'

She and another woman hoisted me up, Annie leaving me in the care of her companion as she disappeared into the fray to rescue others. Limping, sobbing, clutching my throbbing ribs, I let myself be led back to Caxton Hall.

The hall was crammed with the injured; battered, blood-ied women groaning but defiant, sat stemming the bleeding from their noses, cradling arms in knotted scarves, the able tending to others, prepared with bandages. I sat rocking in a corner, nursing my ribs. No longer was I sobbing, but silent, my mind numb.

Hearing Annie's voice at the doorway, I looked up to see her with some Hampstead men, carrying Rosa May, Annie shouting to take care. Behind them I saw Raff with Eddie lifting in Rosa May's wheelchair. Too dazed to mind my swell of relief, it was quickly tempered by the jolt it gave my ribs. Annie settling Rosa May beside me, Raff hastily lowered the wheelchair to crouch down at my knee.

'God, Lotta, are you all right? Where are you hurt? I'm so sorry; I let myself be pulled away.'

His eyes were tender, but their sockets were moons of crimson and purple, his face a sight, nose nicely red-dened and swelling.

'Please pardon my appearance.' He smiled. 'I found myself waylaid by some gentlemen.'

The spurt of laughter hurting, I moaned. 'I got a right kicking too. My ribs.'

'The police?' His look was fierce. 'They were bloody brutal out there. I've never seen anything like it. In all my time marching.' As he reached to softly touch my side, I flinched. Bothered both by his closeness and the sting.

Annie called him away to see if there was any hope of fixing Rosa May's chair. As he worked with Eddie, Annie told us they'd detained many women. Emmeline. Patience too. I was stunned to hear of Patience being arrested.

Beside me, Rosa May was shaken but unbowed. 'I hope they keep their hands off Patience. They took me down a side-street, swiped the valves from my wheels so I couldn't move, and left me there. They had other women down there too. They were pulling down their bloomers, then running away like schoolboys, laughing.'

'What the hell were they thinking?' Raff raged from where he knelt. 'How can they justify such savagery?'

'They wanted to humiliate us,' Annie said. 'To teach us a lesson we wouldn't forget. And we won't.'

27

Black Friday. That's what they'd called it. In the carriage, he thought of the outcry there'd been. The grotesque images in the press, women wrestling like dockers as they were hauled away, the accusations of police brutality, calls for a public inquiry. He remembered his own outrage that day after, when he'd learned of his son's involvement. The evidence had been all too clear. He'd been skulking about the house, eyes blackened, swollen. Calling his son to his study, Raff had stood sullen at the desk, refusing sit.

'For God's sake, look at you!' he'd thundered from the desk. 'You're a mess, an utter disgrace. You look like a thug, some drunken lout. You could have been arrested. Do you not realise the shame that would have brought upon me, your mother? Did you not think of her when you were out brawling with those women?'

'Being assaulted, you mean, Father!' Raff flushed with fury. 'Battered, beaten, bludgeoned by those so-called bastions of the law, those heroic guardians of the peace; your friends, the police. Assault and battery, pure and simple. They should be charged, tried and strung up!'

'Don't be so bloody ridiculous.' He'd shifted, exasperated, in his chair, despairing of the boy. 'The police were in an impossible position. What were they meant to do: abandon the rule of law for the whims of hysterical women, allow them to overtake the streets, seize the House? For heaven's sake, Raff, sometimes I think you are losing your mind.'

'My mind, maybe.' Raff's jaw was set tight. 'But not my sensibilities. Not my heart.'

'Oh, for pity's sake, listen to you. Your very words are like a woman's. Bleating about your heart. In the name of God, Raff, shape up. Be a man.'

'A man?' Raff's face was puce. 'A man like you, you mean? One who thinks nothing of others, only of himself and what gains he can make?'

'How *dare* you!' He'd sprung up, rage coursing through him. These days his nerves were taut. The reappearance of the woman had made ghastly raw that lapse of his morality. He wanted to shout what he'd endured then, what he had sacrificed for the boy, his mother, how he'd committed those awful acts to protect his son; how he longed to protect him now. 'How *dare* you accuse me of not thinking of others. I think only of my family! I have thought of nothing else but you and your mother. Have worked every day to provide for you, cater for your every need, and look where it's got me. Look what you've become.'

'What? What have I become? A shame to you, Father? Is that it?'

'Oh, for goodness sake, stop with this whining. You sound like a sulky maid servant or shop girl. Just like . . .' He'd hesitated.

'Just like what?'

Her dreaded name was on his tongue, but he refused to speak it. To do so would render her too solid. Too real. Too undeniable a presence in his son's life. He could not bear to countenance such a thing, bristled whenever Raff mentioned her, passed on to him her wretched regards. He'd suffered tortured nights, a plague of questions since the woman's visit. Constantly he would wonder: did she know of his misdeeds, relay her good wishes solely as taunts? If so, what was her intention? To expose him, undo him? But what in hell did she want with his son? He would overhear Raff talking of her too often to Margaret. He wondered if his son was even aware of how much he spoke of her.

'Those damn women!' he'd finished.

'You are a Neanderthal, Father.' Raff's voice was ice. 'I don't know how Mamma bears you.'

'Raff, stop it.' Margaret was upon them in the doorway. 'Stop it, both of you. Whatever your differences, this is not the way to solve them. Raff. Leave your father and I alone, please.'

Raff had shaken his head in frustration, brushing past his mother in the doorway. He'd sunk exhausted into his chair as Margaret had spoken softly:

'Don't you see, the more you confront him, the more he will fight you? I don't like this militancy, these Pankhurst women, any more than you, but try to let him be, William. He is young, with his whole life to learn. We have nothing to fear, for his heart is good.'

* * *

Ah, Margaret. With her kind, candid face, eyes honest and warm. She had a beauty. True beauty. One of the mind, the spirit. A grace. And strength. When first I saw her, I thought her tall, upstanding, as if she had strong, solid bones. Like a stallion. Noble. Yes, Margaret would believe a good heart a blessing, a protection from the perils of this world. But I had learned through Mam and Pap the way of good hearts. And the Man had taught me only too well a willing, a trusting heart to be no blessing but a curse.

But such a heart can also be a fire. A beacon. A light that draws others to you. And Raff's heart was that. A heart like a flame you could warm yourself by. And I was to bask in that warmth. In the days after the march as I lay in a bed in Hampstead, nursed by Annie and the women. By Raff. Annie sent for the doctor, a spindly, grave-looking man with a Roman nose, who said no ribs were broken but they were badly bruised. Rest would heal them.

Raff wanted to carry a message to the imaginary Nancy Connard to explain my absence, assure my lady I was safe. But I implored him not to trouble. I concocted a tale, told him, as luck would have it, the lady's niece was visiting for a week, I'd been given leave, so I would not be missed. I knew Mamma May would be concerned, probably riled, at my disappearance but also knew she would not come searching for me in Hampstead. She'd no notion of the house's whereabouts and, besides, would be canny enough not to seek me out there.

I was entertained at my sickbed by Patience, regaling me with tales of her night in the cell, how she had shouted and sworn, banging on the iron door, permitting the warders no peace, singing sour as a crow at the top of her voice to torment them. I smiled at the idea of a furious Patience, allowing even a little sympathy for those jailers become the jailed, lashed by her tongue. They had only to suffer her one night, as all women arrested had been released without charge. Annie told us the authorities wanted the whole sorry incident forgotten. They most certainly did not want to make of the women martyrs.

I was badly shaken by the march. The others were hardened to it, but I had never witnessed such brutality. To have been savaged, beaten, kicked like I was street dung had touched within me that same feeling I had suffered at the hands of the Man, of being not a living, breathing soul, but merely a thing dumb and numb, less than a creature, solely a receptacle for his desires, whatever degradation he wished to wreak upon me. This time, though, I had fought back against that assailant who had mauled me, dragged me by my breasts from the ground. For that I felt some pride. Even so, Annie and Raff by my bedside saw my distress:

'They use violence because their cosy little world is being threatened,' Annie said, holding my hand. 'Like wolves they attack us to protect their pack. Their pack of privileged boys that rule the forest, all of society, the laws, the courts, the Government. Beating us into submission. Determined to keep us down and in our place.'

'Just as with you, Lotta,' Raff said, gently. 'That court case was always set to fail. They weren't going to let a little upstart from a working family, a woman to boot, ruin one of their gentlemen. It was doomed from the start.'

As he spoke I could only stare, my mind whispering: *By your father. It was doomed by your father.* But it was becoming clear to me now, it had been more than you, William. It had not been just you, one man, who had betrayed me, betrayed Mam and Pap, but many men; those of your ilk who'd colluded against us, ruthless in their mission to keep men like Pap, and any woman, down.

From that day, Black Friday, those powers that conspired, they too became my enemy. I'd find myself captivated by the women's talk, a fire in my breast, glancing at Raff, that boy with the same fire in his eyes, wondering what horror he'd feel if he knew the acts of his own father. The very boy who sat by me constantly, helped me sit up to sup tea, showed such endearing devotion to bringing me my broth at five o'clock. Who, those first evenings, had held back my hair, rubbed my shoulders when I'd been stricken by a mysterious sickness, my every bone aching, stomach cramping as I sweated, vomited into a bucket.

'I must say, Raff, I think you make a fine nurse,' Annie joked one afternoon, as he carried a tray into my room when the sickness had passed. 'I think I will fetch you Patience's pinny, give it an outing. It's never been worn. You must give it a twirl.'

Next evening, as I sat propped against the pillows in the dwindling winter sun, Raff appeared in the doorway with my broth, sporting a blue, red-spotted pinny. Annie hooted as I clutched both her arm and my aching ribs in laughter.

'Take it off, Raff, take it off!' I begged him, the pain of the mirth too much.

'Why?' he said as if offended. 'You don't find it fetching? Perhaps blue is not my colour. Or is it the spots?'

'No,' I managed, in fits. 'The spots are delightful. But I think it too short. You are disgracefully flaunting your ankles.'

'My ankles are in fine shape.' He twirled his foot. 'In fact, they are ankles made to be flaunted. You are both jealous because your own are not in such good repair.'

As he read to me late into the evening, not stirring until time to sleep, in turbulent thought I would watch him, disturbed by my feelings. It had once been the simplicity, the trustfulness of my heart that had led me unwitting into a deceiver's lair; now I led Raff's trusting heart into a lair of my making. One to which I knew him all too willing to walk, should I beckon him. It was that very sweetness, that openness of his heart that caused my own to contort. I battled with myself. I could not surrender to this tenderness. I thought those nights of running from the house, far from Hampstead, back to Mamma May's to escape him. To save him. But I could not.

For his heart had become to me a sanctuary.

I found myself those dark November evenings talking to him of Mam and Pap. Of Mam's warmth, her shrewd wit, her strength before she lost Pap. Of Pap's pride in his family, his work, his passion for truth. Of how I missed them.

'I feel I have betrayed them.' My words, at last true, felt a blessed release. 'When I lost them it seems I lost myself. I am no longer the girl they raised.' Even though his warm eyes felt to me like feathery down where my deepest secrets could nestle, I did not reveal I felt I had betrayed them most through my wiles, my sordid life, playing the coquette at Mamma May's.

Although he couldn't understand all I meant, he took my hand. 'Then be that girl again, Lotta,' he urged me. 'Be the girl they raised. Live your life and live it well. That is the greatest thing you can do for them.'

My ribs were all but healed, and I knew it was time to return to Mamma May's. My heart was sore as I climbed into the hansom cab that Raff insisted on hailing for me. As I waved, watched his tall figure fade, I missed instantly the camaraderie of the house, the women. I missed him.

In Soho, with trepidation, I turned the door key, my voice timid as I called for Mamma May. As she appeared in the hallway, she could not mask the relief in her eyes, but, instantly, lips tight, she delivered her barb. 'Oh, you've decided to grace us once more with your presence; well we are very grateful, I'm sure. Where the hell do you think you've been, little lady?'

I could tell it an anger born of worry, and although my ribs complained, my nerves eased as she squeezed my shoulders, taking my arm to lead me in to the parlour. As we sat and I told her what had happened, she gave me a curious look. 'But did you not get sick without your medicine?'

I looked at her, surprised. 'Is that what it was? I didn't know why I was so sick. The doctor told Annie it was the shock.'

She shook her head. 'No, love, it's the opium. I've noticed myself when I don't take it I get sick. But you are past the sickness now?'

As I nodded, she said, 'Perhaps, then, if you're over the sickness, you shouldn't take it anymore. If needs be, a small amount of laudanum from the pharmacy.'

But I had no desire for any potion, then. For as I sat with Mamma May, in that house that before had felt a haven, I knew I had changed. Once I'd yearned for the magic of my medicine, to be cradled once more in Mam's arms, to walk again by Pap's side. But somehow, now, I felt them with me. Within me. Their simple ways, their truth, seemed to rise easy, surely as the sun to light my heart. As if I no longer needed to chase that strangest of worlds but stand firm in this one, my steps guided by all they had taught me, all they had been.

It felt as if the tender care of Raff, the women, had stirred inside me the lifetime of Mam's love, rooting me, feeding me strength, allowing me to draw from that deep well. That our bond forged from struggle, honest endeavour, had awakened in me Pap's spirit, enabling me to hold my head high, no longer with false pride but honour. I believed again: believed in the righteousness of our cause. I would walk beside my comrades as I had once walked beside him.

Live your life and live it well. I would be Mam and Pap's girl. The girl they had raised.

I knew then, no matter my fondness for Mamma May, I could bear no longer the insincerity, the hollowness of my life there. That my time in Soho was over.

For, in Hampstead, I had found something lost: a faith. Faith in others, and so some faith in this world. And now with my fortified heart, something more. Faith in myself.

28

From the carriage, he stared upon a passing row of dim, decrepit houses, thinking of that awful Yuletide evening when Raff had insisted on inviting her to dinner at their home. He'd feared then the worst had come to pass. That his son was smitten.

'Try to be pleasant, William,' Margaret had said in the drawing room, as he'd poured himself a sherry, awaiting Raff's arrival with her. 'I know you are not best pleased, but try to be welcoming. She is Raff's guest.'

'No, I am not best pleased,' he'd said fiercely, turning to her. 'Are you? Will you still be pleased if we learn that they're courting? Is this the kind of woman you wanted for your son? One who hails from the rookeries, the slums? One who is . . .'

Tainted, he'd wanted to say. One who had been defiled. It was not simply poverty that rendered her unworthy, but notoriety. Her lack of virtue, even before the event of Henry Allen Griffiths. The stain on her now, afterwards.

'William, please, you know that's not true. She's far from a slum girl. From a working family, maybe, but there's no shame in that. And you advocated for her so passionately, were so disheartened by your loss. Yet now you turn so ardently against her. I don't understand what's wrong with you.'

Margaret was being deliberately obtuse. Her principles were making her mealy-mouthed. She knew very well a woman of such lowly class, with her sordid history, was a far from palatable consort for their son. She couldn't possibly think otherwise. Whatever her protestations, at least their mutual misgivings offered Margaret a reason for his ire. Thankfully, she would think that all that played on his mind.

Raff had burst through the door, a torrent of glee and cold night air, face glowing with frosty nip and pleasure.

'Evening, Mamma, Papa. Here she is. A little like an icicle,' he'd said, smiling at his companion. 'So needs some warming alcohol, immediately if not sooner.'

'Lotta, please,' Margaret had said, standing. 'Come warm yourself by the fire.'

He'd forced himself to look at her as she'd smiled at Margaret then cast a greeting glance, a nod at him, going to stand by the fire. He'd done the perfunctory thing of offering her a drink.

'A sherry, Lotta? Or something else?'

'A sherry would be lovely, thank you.'

Immediately, he'd been aware of a difference in her. Something in her manner. She seemed not as spiky, not as aloof. Did not hold herself so proudly, stiffly. Although she refused to meet his eyes as he'd handed her the drink. He'd noticed that.

'Sit down now, my dear,' Margaret said. 'And tell us all you've done since we last met.'

She'd sat beside Margaret at the fire, began to tell her of her new lodgings in Hampstead. That dreadful house. Raff never stopped talking of it, seemed never to be anywhere else. He imagined him there amongst that clucking coven.

'But did your lady not need you any longer as her companion?' Margaret asked.

'No,' she answered. 'Her niece has come from the countryside, Sussex I believe, and now lives with her. I was no longer needed. And so Patience took me in. I love it there. I have so much company.'

'Well, I am very happy to hear it,' Margaret said. He'd wondered if that were true. Or if she thought, just as he, of how it afforded the woman and Raff many hours unhindered, alone. Of what they might be doing.

'Lotta acts as Patience's companion now.' Raff laughed. 'When she heard, she said, "Oh, come here and be my blasted companion. This lot are no good. Too slow with my gin and cigarettes. I'll look after you, girlie."'

'Yes.' She'd smiled. 'She is so kind to me.'

Aggravated by their good humour, he'd drained his glass. Still, as he'd observed her, he'd been somewhat pacified by her tone, her demeanour. She was much more amicable. Not as sharp. She directed her conversation only to Margaret and Raff, but he allowed himself the thought that perhaps he'd been mistaken in his suspicions. Perhaps she and Raff honestly had simply happened upon one another. He was encouraged in that he could spot no intimacies between them. No hand placed upon her shoulder, or brush of her arm. Perhaps she was merely one amongst many of his awful cohorts. Perhaps it had all been a matter of chance. Perhaps.

* * *

I was only too conscious as I chatted with Margaret, that you watched me. That you were desperate to know my mind. Once, that would have been part of the game. To torture you with doubt. Leave you never sure-footed, uncertain if you faced an opponent or what measure of opponent that might be. Yet, since our last meeting, the game had changed. Yes, I despised you still. Not even for my own sake, anymore, but for Mam and Pap. But I had come to care deeply for your son. However I denied it, I could not quell the feeling. Even so, I held him at bay. I could not cleave to him with the truth I hid from him. The truth of you. The depth of my bitterness. Such falsehood between us would sully him, sully me. And I felt guilt. Guilt in how I had snared him, the devious way in which I had lured him to me.

Now, with the honest, pure feeling I had for him, that act seemed dirty, vile. I had set out to trap him, but it seemed I had set a trap for myself. Unable to pledge myself to him, yet unable to forgo what joy and comfort I had found in him.

So, as I sat under your scrutiny, my thoughts were confused. It was as if I now too held a secret. It was not only hatred that caused me to avert my eyes that night, but fear. Fear you knew all too well my deceit with your son. Fear my eyes would reveal to you their shame.

* * *

He'd been placed directly opposite her at dinner. The worst possible arrangement as he battled to avoid her eyes, sensing she did the same. Luckily, Raff was brimming with conversation, he and the woman laughing together too often, Margaret her usual graceful self, whatever her qualms, displaying the pleasure of a mother at seeing her son so happy.

'You know they're thinking of making Papa a judge?' Raff had said, mouth full, Margaret slapping his arm, chiding him for it. 'What do you think of that, Lotta?'

There. It was then. Then he had known. In that moment all doubt was banished. She'd met his eyes properly for the first time. Held them. The spark of malice was unmistakable. The intensity of her look, the blackness of her stare. She knew.

'I think it a great responsibility.' Her every word was measured, eyes refusing to leave his. 'To sit in judgement of others. To be chosen to determine another's wrongdoings.'

He'd withered under the weight of her words. Throat seizing, he diverted his eyes to his glass. Taking some wine for a mouth run dry, he'd answered, gruffly.

'It is the jury which decides any wrongdoing. They who make that judgement.'

'But the judge that decides their punishment,' she said. He could feel the fix of her eyes.

'No.' He'd kept his own eyes on his plate, feigning interest in the food. 'The sentence is often specified. The judge does not have free rein on punishment.'

'Oh, come off it, Papa,' Raff said. 'He may not have free rein, but he has great sway. You know, weighing up the circumstances, considering what led to the crime, whether there's remorse and so on.'

'Yes, to be remorseful is so important.' She swooped on it like a bird of prey. He could feel himself jabbed, clawed at by her words. 'Pap was not. Not remorseful at all for what was seen as his crime. And so he received the harshest of sentences.'

This was unbearable. It seemed his skin was penetrated by her eyes. Without raising his, he watched his son's hand reach across the table for the woman's.

'If justice had been done in the first place, your father would never have been driven to commit his so-called crime,' Raff said. 'That is the tragedy.'

He'd felt he might suffocate.

'And that justice is something your father strived for, but was so sadly denied,' Margaret said. 'And why he'll make such an excellent judge. He'll do everything in his power to prevent such travesties. He will be an invaluable addition to the Bench.'

Overtaken by the urge to escape, he'd scraped back his chair, going to the sideboard, under the guise of fetching more wine. 'Nothing is decided yet,' he said. 'So let us not speak of it anymore.'

* * *

It was in those moments our minds met, didn't they, William? No longer two boxers warily eyeing one another from our corners, but alert and ready, mounted like jousters, lances raised. You must have wondered then if I sat before you, your own judge. What nature of punishment I was minded to inflict. Once, I'd have had no doubt. At the beginning, my course was clear. To beguile your son, as you had beguiled me. To entice, entrap him. Spark in him desire, to grow in time to what he might think of as love. Only then to spurn him, shatter his heart, deliver my final, lethal blow: that I had played him for a fool. Reveal to him your wrongdoings, strip him, like I, of all faith in his own judgement, any faith in you as a father, as a man. Finally, to reveal the truth of you to Margaret. To destroy your family as you had destroyed mine.

But now all had changed. To declare your wrongdoing would be to declare my own. For, no matter how I might protest myself true, Raff would know I had been lying from the start. Would know my proclamation of admiration for you a deceit, perhaps arouse in him suspicion that our meeting had not been fortuitous, lead him to guess at my scheming. He would not forgive me for it. To Raff, like Pap, honesty was all. To reveal myself a liar would destroy me too in his eyes. And to devastate your family would be to devastate Raff. I could not countenance inflicting on him such pain.

I had agreed to accompany Raff that evening for a sole purpose: that you be forced to look upon me, see me just once more. And in that seeing, see again Mam and Pap. See yourself. The truth of yourself. I had determined it would be the last time.

For I was decided. I would have no more to do with you. I would take my revenge on you, on those of your ilk, another way. Would strive to undo your dominion alongside my fellow suffragettes, help forge a world you did not want. With them I would endeavour to put an end to you: the supremacy of men like you. And do so in a way that honoured Pap's memory, would make Mam proud.

Even if I could foresee no happy union with Raff with this spectre of you between us, he would not hear of your treachery from my lips.

It was my intent to stay silent.

29

From that night his mind had known no rest. Certain now she knew, he spent his days always on guard, terrified by what she might say, what she might do. When she might do it. Any guilt, or culpability for the situation he found himself in, was overridden by fear. With a word she could sweep away what he held most dear. His family. He did not worry for his career, for he realised, with some small shame, she would not be believed; Neville and the others would see to it. But, at a whim, she could reveal his wrongs to Raff. The boy already held for him little respect: this would finish him. And he would run with it to Margaret. There would be no hiding from it then. He could not hide from the eyes of his family, nor their damnation. He could not bear that they might come to think him a man so low. He could not bear to think himself that man.

Whether or when she would act he could not know, but of one thing he was sure: she was intent on hurting his son. Raff's infatuation with her was palpable. He could feel her goading him with his son's devotion. At the idea of his son being played for a fool, his terror turned to fury. He began desperately to search Raff's face for signs, for any fresh animosity towards him or disenchantment with his new companion. But none had come. Rather, his son's mood was elevated, affable, almost chirpy. It was clear whatever the nature of this dalliance, it was suiting him.

Margaret was pleased by their son's good spirits. Even as he'd tried to draw her, she would not fully admit her reservations; only counselled him to let the thing run its course, allow Raff to employ his own good sense.

He did not have such confidence in his son's judgement. He knew him to be headstrong, dogged when his sights were fixed. Still, he tried to heed Margaret's advice. With difficulty, he stood back, suspecting her right, that the more he challenged Raff, the more it might encourage him to persist. If the woman's name was raised, Raff talking of her to his mother, he would find a reason to withdraw from the room.

Often Raff would accompany his mother to a West End tea-shop. He knew the woman was sometimes there. Margaret would return home, mentioning something amusing the woman had said, titbits of their conversation, but seeing his expression, she would grow quiet. It became an unspoken understanding between them. Do not talk to me of her.

Yet the silence only made her louder, denser in his mind. He thought of attempting to put an end to the torture by going to her, confronting her, imploring her: *Do what you will with me, but leave the boy be.* But he was certain what would come of it. Gratified by his torment,

she would only persevere. He could finish it by unmask-
ing her, confessing all to his family, but their contempt
was not a thing he could countenance. He felt himself
hunted. Taunted. Trapped.

* * *

I knew you would be feeling so, for I felt it too: that you
were the greatest obstacle to my happiness. A shadow
that stalked Raff and me, a dark stain on the bright trio
that we sometimes formed, those days, with Margaret. I
would find myself taking tea with mother and son, pretending Raff and I were one, just he and I, just we three.
I would imagine this a world free of the curse of you.

I was often able to cast you far from my mind for there
was much to occupy us at Hampstead. Asquith promising us a second Bill on Suffrage, there was constant
bustle, planning of marches, rallying of support, a great
camaraderie and fun in the house amongst we women
and the Hampstead Harries. It was I who put that name
on the Hampstead men, and we would laugh as together
we conjured up ever-riskier slogans for our publications.

'I pray to God this Bill will pass,' one of the women,
Lilian, said, one afternoon as we were crouched on the
drawing room floor, rolling out banner cloth.

'Don't bother about your praying,' I said. 'Your only
business on your knees is to paint these banners.'

'Pagan!' Eddie shouted from where he hunkered on
the floor beside Raff, fixing finished cloth to poles.

Raff smiled. 'Yes, comrades, I'm afraid Lotta shares my heathen heart. We can't quite fathom how God's apparently wholly sacred, one true word comes so often amended by his rivalling prophets and disciples.'

'Exactly,' I said. 'If the Almighty truly wanted peace in the world, if he would give his word to one man – *God* forbid, a woman – why not all? Then there would be little room for misunderstanding.'

Raff laughed with the others, but then grew serious. 'But all those different religions and their symbols, it's ironic. Because they're not, in the end, any symbol of the divine, but a symbol of something only too human. An all-too-human struggle to give form, a face to the mystery of creation.'

'How about the mystery of how to attach this bloody material to the pole?' Eddie said, looking defeated. We all howled, but Raff was earnest:

'Human, like Jesus,' he said. 'It was no divinity that made him shine. Not Godliness, but his humanity. His heart. That great human heart. It's not about worship. It's about love.' He glanced at me as he lingered on the last word. Taking his meaning, I looked away.

I had been put to work at the suffragette shop on Charing Cross Road, selling our knick-knacks and publications, attempting to recruit curious women browsers. I was nervous at being so near Soho, worried Mamma

May's girls might spy me, but none ever appeared. At times, I had a hankering to visit Mamma May, but somehow I did not dare stir that sleeping dog. We had said our sad and fond goodbyes and I knew Mamma May was pleased for me. That life, I was certain, lay behind me now.

It was a time of such immense hope. It seemed a constant spring, a time of budding; fragile flowers of a new world emerging from deadened branches, like green shoots of awoken life. Warring against the gentry, the Libs and Labour had crushed the Lords, bringing higher wages, pensions for the elderly, aid for the sick and unemployed, and better working conditions. Lloyd George's aspirations truly seemed within grasp, his oration sounding like a great, beckoning bell in Parliament. One evening Raff leaped from the couch where Annie, Eddie, the women and Harries sat, to pounce upon an unsuspecting Patience, spinning her around in her rattan chair, as she spluttered on her gin. Arm raised in salute before her, he sounded Lloyd George's words: 'I cannot help hoping and believing,' he bellowed, 'that before this generation has passed away, poverty and the wretchedness of human degradation will be as remote to the people of this country as the wolves which once infested its forests!' He snatched Patience's cup from her. 'And may we all drink from the gin-cup of life!'

We all stamped our feet and cheered, I clapping my hands in laughter and delight.

Some evenings, Raff would follow me to my room. It was then I was most troubled, for I knew what was in his heart. What was in my own. We would sit on the bed, I struggling at his closeness as we lay, talking long into the night.

At last, one such night, I confided in him my years at Mamma May's. Guilt at what I concealed about his father so often overwhelmed me. I yearned many times to confess it, unburden my heart. Knowing it impossible, I gave him whatever gift of truth I could.

'I made something cheap of myself,' I said. 'Something Mam and Pap would be ashamed of.' I could not meet his eyes, afraid I'd become something lower in them. I felt too the sting of being unable to admit it was the very lounge he'd frequented, for fear he might guess I had first seen him there.

He gripped my hand, but still I would not look at him. 'Not cheap, Lotta, strong. You have such strong will. You were simply trying to survive after all you'd endured. I have nothing but admiration for you. For all you have overcome.'

'I'd lost all faith,' I said, reassured by his words. 'I never had faith in any god. But I envy those who've had good fortune enough to believe their fate guided by a benevolent hand.'

He reached for my face, turning it to his, gently: 'And yet that fate has brought you here. Not merely surviving now, but thriving. Become a woman your mother and father would surely be proud of. *I* am proud of you.'

He stroked my face so tenderly. But even as I was soothed, I was shamed. Shamed by his pride with all I hid from him. And fate. It had been my own steps that had dictated my fate, had led me here, of that I'd made sure. I had hunted him out, stalked him. I longed to return his touch. Longed that night, as I had so many others, to embrace him, caress him, pull him to me. To reveal my heart fully, let it fly, settle where it ached to abide: at one with his. But I turned away. The secrets I held, held me in turn. Held me from him.

Such were the nights; the heat of those summer days in Hampstead matched our own as our Bill was debated. However, by winter, it was clear Asquith determined to frustrate it, proposing the vote be granted to more men first, in some distant future. We knew this simply a way to cast the Bill aside.

With outrage and vigour, we lost no time. We marched, as they expected, but also did something they did not. Under cover of night, making ready at the Charing Cross shop, with rocks and hammers, we set out to do our work.

Swiftly we moved through the streets, striking, hurling our weapons at the grand Government houses' windows in Whitehall, at the newspapers in Fleet Street, at the vast panes of the West End shops. Raff and I ran together, the cold biting our faces, filling us with verve, the shattering glass speeding us as we fled, panting in thrill and fear.

That night we heard whistles blow all over London. Raff and I escaped but, by morning, hundreds had been arrested; Annie amongst them. In Whitehall, she'd waited defiantly for the police, wanting her day in court. It seemed we had shocked the whole of England. Never before had we inflicted so much damage on Government buildings, never at all on the city businesses.

As we gathered in Bow Street Court, beneath the dock where Annie stood, we listened in awe, the furious magistrate imposing a sentence of two months in prison, as Annie declared she did not recognise the country's laws for they were solely man-made. Like God's law, Raff mused later. Laws deemed God's but, in truth, fashioned merely by man for the satisfaction of men.

They took Annie to Holloway where we were not allowed to visit as, refusing food, she was kept in confinement. We soon learned they were inflicting on her, not for the first time, the torture of force-feeding. Growing too sickly for prison, within four weeks, Annie came home. She arrived feeble, using a stick to walk, her once-forceful voice weak, face gaunt. For a month she lay in bed, as we nursed her back close as we could to health. But there was a fragility ever after in our proud, strong Annie.

* * *

He'd only learned later of Raff's part in that night. Unknown to him then, soon after his son had flouted the law he himself held sacrosanct, a conviction only deepened by his own transgression, he had been appointed a judge.

In the Royal Courts of Justice, he'd stood before the justices, amongst them the despised Neville, himself now a judge. Neville's cohorts Dudley and Herbert sat near Margaret and Raff, watching from the pews, in his mind sullying his wife and son with their presence. Their knowing of him a thing so vile while his wife and son remained innocent of it, seemed as if he colluded with them to mock his loved ones, felt something putrid, festering.

He hated Neville's eyes upon him. He had been a good King's Counsel. He needed to believe this honour, at least, had arisen solely from his own good works, awarded on his own merit. But he was no longer a fool. At the proposal of his selection for the High Court, much as he'd fought to deny it, he'd been only too aware it more likely reward for favour granted, 'services' to the Crown, than any recognition of legal excellence.

As he'd raised his hand to take the Judicial Oath, swore by Almighty God to serve the King, at what he must next speak, his throat had grown dry: . . . *and I will do right to all manner of people, after the laws and usages of this realm, without fear or favour, affection or ill will.*

Favour. Ill will. The familiar black swell in his gut. As he signed the Oaths book, he battled against it, told himself what had happened lay firmly in the past. That from this day on, he would stay true to his oath. He would be true.

The justices smiled as he was presented with his ceremonial gowns, inviting him to take his seat beside them on the Bench.

Taking his seat, he looked down. Avoiding Dudley's and Herbert's eyes, he dwelt purely on Margaret's, Raff's. In Margaret's, he saw what he'd anticipated: pride. But what he found in his son's eyes brought a surprise akin to shock: for where he would so often see scorn, he saw there that same pride. He felt a spring of joy.

But quickly that joy plummeted. In its place was left a gripping shame. Because he was not worthy of his son's admiration. It was now, especially now, he deserved that scorn. For, although the seat beside his son was empty, it pulsated with a presence. There, he saw another face. Another pair of eyes staring up at him. Hard. Accusing. Eyes that could see him. See his stain.

Always she was there. Always.

30

Never did I imagine your shame that day. That would have brought me, at least, some solace. Far from any shame, those days I pictured you just as I once had the Man, like a peacock strutting, puffed-up, proud. Fouling on the graves of Mam and Pap.

In Hampstead, when Raff described to me the ceremony, for all his scorn of hierarchy, he could not help the pride in his eyes. For seconds, I thought of abandoning all care. Of having done with this charade. Of screaming at him just what sort of man his father was, this man who now dared sit in judgement of others. I wanted to rip him from you, cause him to hate you, make him want only to cleave to me, but I was held captive by my lie. And although Raff would gripe about you, be furious sometimes at your staid ways, your bigotry, I knew he loved you. I could tell by his anger. He was so inflamed by you, it was clear how much he cared.

While you were bestowed with accolades, in Hampstead we waited anxiously for the outcome of another Bill on Suffrage, only to see it defeated. My rage at that, and at your elevation, spurred me on and made me reckless. One March evening, with others I set out on the rampage, our targets the Strand, the Dilly, the elite shops of the West End. Alone on Vere Street, I eyed my charge: Marshall & Snelgrove, straddling the corner of Oxford Street. In the still of the narrow road I swung my hammer, striking blows on the majestic panes, leaping back from the shattering glass, the ring of it like a tumbling crystal waterfall in the quiet. I could have made my escape then. Instead, stoked by anger, inspired by Annie, I ran onto Oxford Street, the smashing glass bringing a clutch of passers-by. In plain sight, I raised my hammer, driving it through the window, the shocked crowd gasping, jumping to avoid the flying shards.

'What in God's name do you think you're doing?' a man in a topper shouted, deserting his female companion to grab me, tussling with me as with sharp elbows and kicks, flailing my hammer, I tried to fend him off.

Before long two peelers had chased through the broad thoroughfare to contain me. Hurtling me off to Vine Street station, I was still flailing and fighting as they tossed me into a cell.

'There you go, darlin',' my jailer said, before slamming the door. 'No windows for you to smash in there.'

In the tiny cell, I huddled at the corner of the bench. I thought of Pap. Of him at Wood Street, and the thought only made me stronger. I would be as defiant as he. Through the endless night, the dark, the ice in my bones, I remained unbowed.

'Tamed yet, love?' A peeler jeered at the hatch. 'Have we taught you to behave like a lady? Improved your manners yet?'

'No more than I've improved yours,' I spat.

At last, came morning. Now I took my turn in the Bow Street dock, lighting at the sight of Raff, Annie and Patience and the others in the pews. Raff smiled up to hearten me, but his eyes told me his struggle. His wrestling with his principles. I knew his mind. Knew he would want me to stand brave, firm, while also wishing me contrite in hope of leniency. But I was determined to face that court, like Pap before: unrepentant.

The magistrate, a greying older man, studied me. 'You stand before this court, Miss Rae, charged with Malicious Damage. How do you plead? Guilty or not guilty?'

I drew myself up. 'I plead neither guilty nor not guilty. I do not recognise the charge nor the law, as no woman had a hand in making it.'

The magistrate looked outraged. 'Your brazenness appals me. You have caused enormous damage and immense cost to a long-standing and much-respected business. For that reason, and in light of your impertinence, I sentence you to six months' imprisonment. That is all.' He brought down his hammer.

I gripped the dock. In my frenzy, I had almost sought my punishment, but I was shocked by the severity of the sentence. I could see dismay amongst Annie and the others, Raff staring at me, stunned. He tried to make his eyes proud, of comfort to me, but I saw their distress. I lingered on them before I was led away.

The wagon jolted my already sickened stomach as I sat stiff, trying to calm my nerves. At the wagon halting, the back door pulled open, I stayed frozen to the bench until a stony-faced peeler tugged me down. 'Welcome to your new home. Enjoy it, girl.'

I hardly dared look at the spectre before me. The grim towers of Holloway, known to all in Hampstead as The Castle, its mammoth gateway flanked by grotesque griffins clutching keys in their claws.

From the cobbled yard, the peeler led me through a forbidding black door into a vast hallway, then to a gloomy room with ochre walls, leaving me to the charge of a stern woman warder in ebony cap and dress, belted with a brown pouch which I'd learn held her keys.

'Been a naughty girl, love?' Making notes at the desk, she beckoned another warder. They steered me through the hallway to a dank, tiled room. 'Take off your clothes, all of 'em,' the first warder said.

She took my skirt as I stepped out of it, unbuttoning my blouse to stand in my chemise and drawers. 'All of 'em!' she repeated. I fumbled with the chemise, pulled down my drawers, feeling suddenly powerless, humiliated in my nakedness, shivering in the damp.

Roughly, they began scrub me down with harsh-smelling carbolic, at last throwing me a coarse towel. They handed me a bundle, my uniform, watching as I put on the black dress with white arrows, white apron with black. I pulled on the white cap.

Marched out into the long, echoing hall, women chattered, cackled, peered down from a rise of iron balconies. One of them called: 'You going to the Skeleton Sisters' wing, love? Think you can get me the vote?'

Others laughed behind her as the warders hustled me on, finally coming to a studded metal door. They pushed me through, leaving without a word.

At the bang of the door, I stared around me: at the stark, clammy wall slabs, bleak light struggling through the bars. A brown horsehair blanket on the bed, beside it a tiny table. I sat on the bed, thinking of Pap. Of he too sitting in his cell. Somehow this did not sadden me, but brought me comfort. Made me feel him close, as if we were one. For now I must endure what he did.

Those early days I was comforted too by the company of my fellow suffragettes kept on the same wing. Those I saw were also new to the prison, our longer-serving comrades weakened, confined to their cells, having refused food. Just as I did now. A warder that first evening summoned me to the eating hall. From the bed,

I shook my head. 'I want nothing. I will not eat while imprisoned for what is only a just and righteous cause.'

She curled her lip. 'You'll go where I tell you to go.'

In the eating hall they made we suffragettes watch the other prisoners eat, putting plates of potatoes, soup and bread before us, while we sat stoic, trying to rally each other with glances and smiles. Every morning they would order us up from our untouched bowls: 'Eating or no eating, you're working!'

Our chores we did together, scrubbing floors or washing down walls, long hours at the brush making my hands sting, cracked and sore.

'I think they're trying to teach us real women's work,' one, Alice, joked.

I grinned. 'Better make a lousy job of it then.'

In the laundry, washing bedding and uniforms, I soon faltered, my stomach gripping at the steam and heat with the lack of food. I trembled under the weight of the soaked blankets, my head light, pounding with pain. The labour became torturous.

The warders forced us on, trying to weaken our resolve, break us. Some of them, I knew, were sympathetic to our cause, but most mocked us.

On the fifth day I was unable to rise from my bed. The warder tried heave me up, but I fell back limply as she cursed me. From that day I was confined to my cell.

As I lay there those endless days, stomach seized, limbs weak as air, mouth rancid and dry, I tried imbue my father's spirit. *I hunger like you, Pap. Just like you*. It was then that you would come then to torture even more my mind. How it was your treachery had brought Pap his suffering. With a half-crazed hate I would raise my head to stare bleary at the dreary light through the bars, whispering to Pap, over and over: *I suffer just like you.*

They came for me. In an empty cell, three warders hoisted me into a chair, manacled my wrists to it, pulling a white sheet up around my neck as I yelled. Two held my kicking legs, the third pouring a putrid mixture of raw eggs and milk into a jug, ignoring my screeches, slapping her hand on my head, forcing it back.

Silently readying his equipment, the doctor leaned over me. He tried to prise open my clenched mouth. Finally, with the warder's aid, he yanked it open, thrusting a stinking rubber tube into my throat. I retched, choking as I heaved it up, three times or more, screaming when it was out of my mouth.

They left me and I thought, for a moment, they had given it up. But the warder was back, squeezing all air from my nostrils, forcing her fingers into my gasping mouth, the doctor seizing my gums with a metal lock, my jaw as if it would break. Gagging, as if I would smother, I felt the tube pass my breast as if to pierce my heart. Then came the foul mix, landing leaden in my stomach, making me want to vomit.

The days became agony as, my throat shredded, they tried to drive the rubber through my nose, twisting it in vain like a dagger beneath my eyes, feeling they would be wrenched from their sockets. Beaten, they returned to the steel gag, locking it over my bleeding, blistered gums as I writhed in pain.

Afterwards, back in my cell, I would curl on the bed, sobbing, shaking with the violence of it. Being strapped, held down like a wild animal brought visions of being fixed against the wall by the Man. My throat raw flesh, gums ripped with sores, I would spit out great globs of blood into my bucket.

And whisper . . .

I am your girl, Pap. I am your girl.

31

The carriage rumbled as he looked out into the misty night. He well remembered that time. How Raff had come to him. Stood over him as he'd sat at his study desk, begged him to help the woman, use his influence to gain her early release.

'I will not help her!' The words had escaped him in a rush. So many months of stifling all sincere feeling, struggling to stay silent at his son's gullibility, had finally erupted at the boy's impassioned plea. 'What's happening to her now she has brought upon herself. What did she expect with such abominable behaviour? Running berserk through the streets. Behaving worse than any lout, like some common vandal. Let her reap now what she has sown. May it teach her a lesson.'

'How can you be so heartless?' Raff's eyes were pleading. 'They're torturing her in there. Please, Papa, I implore you. I don't know if she'll survive it.'

Agitated, he'd shifted in his chair. 'Don't be so bloody melodramatic. If she's tough enough to run riot around London, lobbing hammers at hard-working, law-abiding businesses, capable of inflicting such grievous damage, she's tough enough to do her time. And these ridiculous hunger strikes. Hysterical nonsense. If she wants to survive, all she has to do is eat. We won't give into blackmail.'

Raff had spat. '*We*. We won't give into blackmail. Well, you have made it quite clear just what side you are on, as if I didn't know it.' He drew himself up as if to score a point. 'You might like to know, Papa, that I've lobbed a few hammers and rocks into some law-abiding businesses myself. Been quite the criminal. Would you like to cart *me* off to jail now?' Raff had turned sharply to leave, but he'd risen quickly, grabbed his son's arm to stop him.

'Do you do these things just to torment me? With these women? This *woman*? What are you doing, Raff, consorting with someone like that? Is all this carry-on with her a deliberate attempt to goad me? Is that it? To hurt me? Your mother?'

'What the hell are you talking about?' Even in his anger, his son had seemed genuinely nonplussed. 'Mamma likes Lotta.'

He'd released his son's arm in exasperation. 'You bloody fool. Your mother simply tolerates her. Do you not see that? Do you really not have the sense to realise what shame this flirtation with a bit of totty brings on us all?'

'How dare you. How *dare* you.' His son was flushed, furious. 'Don't you ever call Lotta that. This is the furthest, the very furthest it could be from a flirtation. And Lotta could bring shame to no one. I know many, many fine women, I can tell you, Father, and she is one of the finest. I only respect and honour her.'

'Hah!' He baulked, looking up at his son. 'Respect and honour. A woman like that? How can you say it even in jest?'

'You hypocrite. You bloody *hypocrite*.' With a step closer, Raff stood over him bent at the desk. 'After all your fine words in court, after you advocated for her. That's what you mean, isn't it? Her past? What was done to her? That the crime committed against her has sullied her, dishonoured her? In my eyes it makes her only brave and strong. One who's had the dignity to rise above what one of *your* ilk has done to her.'

He'd straightened in fury to face his son. 'One of *my* ilk? Do not dare compare me to Griffiths! If you mean one of my class, then, yes. Yes, he was one of my class. And yours. *Yours*, Raff. Stop playing, pretending you sprang from the gutter. And it's not only what was done to her, but her own deeds. What she did with that boy long before Griffiths. That alone shows her character. Shows her not fit company for one of *your* class.'

Raff snorted in derision. 'Oh, yes, her lowly status. Let's not forget that. You are an unbearable, entitled snob, Father. But we won't have to suffer pompous prigs like you much longer. Your day is nearly done. We're ridding ourselves of the tyranny of your class. I can't wait till your world is no more, Papa.'

He'd roared into his son's face. 'You are so naive as to be bordering on stupid! If you go any further with this dalliance you'll be an outcast in all good society, any prospects you have will be ruined. You'll only be sneered at, a subject of scorn, gossip and tittle-tattle.'

'And so will *you*. Isn't that what you mean, Father?'

'Yes! Yes!' he'd shouted. 'And so will your mother. Is that what you want for her? For God's sake, Raff, believe me, it's not simply for your mother's sake, nor my own that I implore you to stop this. All of this. It's a waste of your life. You've finished college and what are you doing? Only clowning around with those women. For the sake of your good name, your future, I beg you, stop. And I warn you – if you persist I will not support you financially much longer. Nor have you living in this house.'

In frustration, Raff had stormed from the room, slammed the door. He'd slumped, defeated, into the chair. At last he'd spoken truly, he felt spent. But it was what he could not say that sat heaviest on his heart. It was in those unspoken words he failed most utterly. Failed as a father to protect his son. In keeping from him the woman's true intention. Her only aim. To hurt them both.

* * *

I was to spend four weeks in Holloway. Four torturous weeks before I became too sick to stay. When Annie and Raff came to fetch me in the cab, as Raff rushed to the prison gate to take my arm, I could tell him shocked by my appearance, even as he tried hide it. I knew well

I was all ashen face and bone. Too weak to care, my heart nearly ruptured with relief at seeing him.

In Hampstead, Patience, waiting in the hall, shrieked when she saw me:

'Oh my God, my poor dear, what have they done to you?'

Fighting my fatigue, I tried to jolly her. 'It's all right, Patience, it's all the style. Suffragette slender.'

Annie and Raff helped me to my room, where they'd placed spring flowers for my return. While Annie fussed around me, I noticed Raff was quiet. As I laid down thankfully on my soft bed, he silently took my hand. The tenderness in his gaze nearly undid me. But I was determined not to cry. I let my hand rest in his, closed my eyes to slumber.

I spent the days often sleeping, always waking to find Raff by my side. Many times in the wee hours I'd find him still there, leaning his arm on the bed, watching over me. When roused from sleep I could stomach little but Annie cooked clear broth, Raff spooning it to me or stroking my back while I supped. He'd bring sweetmeats to tempt me, sometimes sitting on the bed, brushing my hair to soothe me.

Morsel by morsel, I felt the fledgling blooms of health. It was then that Annie presented me with a medal, just as she wore, fashioned by Sylvia Pankhurst to honour the hunger strikers. The Holloway Brooch, set upon the gratings of Westminster Palace, a convict's arrow and chains. Annie pinned it on my bed-jacket.

'Good,' I said, resting my head back. 'I'm a proper jailbird now.'

My manner was deliberately hardened. I had not wanted to talk of my confinement, revisit that horror, afraid of what weakness it brought in me. The brutality of the force-feeding had awakened feelings that disturbed me: that same powerlessness I'd felt for a time after the Man, the vulnerability of the girl I'd once been. I'd long despised that girl who'd been led so haplessly to her fate, so I had cast her from me, buried her deep within my gut. Now, in my fragility, I felt her stir. I tried again to bury her.

More than a month had passed, Raff lying one night beside me on the bed, when I found myself talking of it. The grip of the manacles, agony of the metal gag, the suffocation of the tube. Without warning, a gasp escaped me.

Raff, his eyes welling, reached for me. I tried to look away but found myself watching those eyes. Watching in wonder at his tears falling so freely as I held back my own. If I could not cry he would cry for me. His eyes become huge, soft as a child's, I felt the purest wave of love. At his beauty. The beauty of his vulnerability. And I thought, if I loved it so in him, how could I despise it in myself? For I did love him. I loved him beyond measure. That was a truth, in my frailty, from which I could no longer hide. That was the only truth. The greater truth. A truth greater than any lie.

I reached for him, drew him to me. I searched those eyes so radiant, felt the fire in that soul light mine. Felt his tears touch that shunned girl, ease and lift her free, gently guide her from her hiding place. Softly, I kissed his lips, my heart soaring; soaring yet finally truly at rest. For the first time since I had lost Mam and Pap it felt I released my breath. That, at last, I had come home.

32

He rested his head on the carriage window. Gripped by a sweet anguish, he saw amongst the raindrops, a face. The guileless, earnest face of a child, dark eyes quizzical, rosebud smile revealing a shocking gap where a milk tooth had been. He pictured that child's black curls upon the pillow, in the bed where he'd left her peacefully sleeping, unsuspecting of what the morning would bring. He closed his eyes. Of that coming morning, of only one thing he was sure.

He would not be there to see her waken.

* * *

Even though tender, your eyes upon her, your very thoughts of her I cannot stand. That you hold her in your arms, your heart, your mind, repels me. Perhaps it is because of she that I dwell cursed in this limbo, bound endlessly to you. Perhaps because you watch over my child, so I must watch over you. Perhaps it is not all that went before, nor even what came after, that keeps me in bondage, but she. My girl.

At first, I thought my queasiness still due to my prison spell, although I was mystified for I'd seemed to improve so greatly. Only when I found myself each morning retching over my washbasin, when I realised I'd been too sickly to pay my monthlies mind, did I confide my fears to Annie. The doctor, she said, would be of little use. Whatever test he had offered no certainty. She said we must bide our time. Must wait and see.

It was impossible to hide it from Raff, and I had no wish to. When he came that afternoon, the others left us alone to talk in the drawing room. On the couch, I held his hand, faltering as I told him, startled as he sprang up.

'What? But this is wonderful. Don't you think so?' His face was the strangest mix of emotion. Shock. Dismay. Pleasure. Delight. Like a whirlwind he filled the room, pacing before me, sitting again to hold my hand, leaping up to pace once more, tripping over his words.

'What will the child need? Where will we live? I must find work, yes, I must do that instantly. And we must get married. Right away, Lotta.' He was on his knee, gripping my hand, looking at me imploringly.

I shook my head, begging him, 'Stop, Raff, stop. We are sure of nothing yet.'

My mind felt sodden, I could not think. I needed time to order my thoughts, make some sense of this alarming happening.

By summer's end, we knew. At my belly's bulge and swell, I could deny it no more. Raff was calm now, certain. We must marry immediately. I had no doubt

I wanted to marry Raff. I loved him so greatly. And I had few worries, for Patience wanted us to live in Hampstead. But the spectre of you: it was that which shadowed my happiness with Raff; the terrifying thought of a lifetime bound to you, our child through its very blood. But I had no choice. Already bound by love to Raff, swollen with his baby, it seemed your fate and mine were forever tied.

Annie and Raff made every arrangement, the wedding set for September 20th at Chelsea Town Hall. Patience insisted on gifting me an outfit and Annie took me to Selfridge's. We chose a dress of pale-blue cotton with a panel of lace, blue silk button shoes to match. Back in Hampstead, I modelled it for Patience.

'Count your blessings these modern dresses are so loose,' she said. 'In my day, the boning would have crucified you.'

That September morn dawned bright as my mood. I determined to put you far from my mind as excitedly I dressed with Annie and the women upstairs, knowing Raff was below, getting suited with the Harries. He left with them before we – Annie, Patience and I – followed in a cab, more travelling behind.

Into the elegant room with pale-green walls and grand white arching, extravagant flower displays at the corners, I carried a posy the women had made, Annie walking beside me. I needed no man to give me away for I was no possession. Raff turned, smiling, from where he stood at a mahogany table, as I stepped to his side.

There, with all our friends looking on, we pledged our troth. Raff slipped on my finger a narrow Russian gold band from Patience's trinket box as we made to one another our vows:

'Till death do us part,' I promised. Then held his eyes, to whisper: *And beyond.*

* * *

At September's end, they'd arrived in Gibson Square. That past week, they'd seen little of Raff, his constant absence worrying Margaret. At his son's lack of consideration for his mother, his own fear of what time he was spending with the woman, he'd been on the verge of reprimanding him, when the two had appeared, without warning, that afternoon in the drawing room.

He'd seized at the horror of seeing her, both astonished and incensed at his son's gall. Bringing this woman, on whom he'd made his feelings known, into his home. She'd stood by Raff's side, in gaberdine coat and hat, declining to remove them when Margaret, clearly taken by surprise, had suggested it. Raff's face was set; it was obvious the boy was readying himself for something.

Margaret had to persuade the woman to sit, but Raff insisted on standing. He himself had remained sitting, painstakingly averting his eyes from the woman, fixing them on his son. Abruptly, Raff had started talk, looking neither at himself nor Margaret.

'You should know, Mamma, Papa, that Lotta and I have wed. We were married over a week ago in Chelsea Town Hall. Lotta is now my wife.' His tone was brash, face defiant.

He'd gripped his chair, dumbfounded, as if he'd been struck. Margaret's eyes had widened, her voice dismayed. 'But, Raff, what do you mean? Why didn't you tell us?'

Nerves alive, in seconds he'd chased through a maze of thoughts. This was unbearable. The very news he'd dreaded, every fear now realised. His son knowing his abhorrence of the woman, the clandestine nature of the act he understood, but it seemed to have been performed in unnatural haste. Quickly, his mind fell upon a reason. He sprang up.

'You stupid, *stupid* boy!' he'd bellowed at his son across the room. 'Did you *have* to get married? Is that it?' He'd made no attempt to disguise his rage. Hadn't tried to serve up his words more palatable, more delicate in the presence of Margaret. His fury, despondency, every shattered hope to be free of the woman had overwhelmed him. His certainty that she'd inflicted upon him the ultimate revenge. That this had been her ploy all along. To not simply hurt but ruin his son.

'We *wanted* to,' Raff retorted.

'But the rush,' Margaret entreated them. 'The secrecy. Is your father right?' She looked anguished between Raff and the woman.

Raff did not answer the question.

'I knew Papa wouldn't like it. I thought he might try to stop us.'

'You bloody fool.' He'd slammed his hand on the side-table. 'Damned right I would have stopped you. Tying yourself to this – this *harlot* – for life. What the hell have you done? Don't you know you can pay women like this off?'

The woman had stood abruptly. Raff dashed towards him, making a fist as if to strike him, but it was not his son he feared. The look in the woman's eyes alarmed him. They were all at once alight, dark with menace. He felt a sudden terror he had gone too far. Provoked her to spit out their festering secret. Margaret was on her feet, holding back Raff, desperately trying to calm him.

'Stop, stop, for God's sake, both of you.' Margaret looked pleadingly into Raff's eyes. 'Please, Raff, sit down. Try to explain.'

Raff was clenching his hands, expression fierce. 'There is nothing to explain. You can see from my father's choice words just exactly what I was afraid of. He has made all too clear the need for our secrecy.'

'Your father is just shocked, as am I,' Margaret said, turning to where the woman stood. 'I am so, so sorry, my dear, it's just very sudden, you understand?' Margaret went towards her, extending her hand. The woman, flushed, seemed to mellow somewhat at Margaret's approach, giving a reluctant nod as Margaret touched her arm.

The threat seemingly passed, he sat. The rushing of his blood, panic exhausting him; he was spent. He could not risk antagonising the woman further, must go easier than he'd like on both she and his son. The deed done; it was too late for truth. It would gain him nothing. The boy was trapped. Wearily, he spoke. 'Raff, since you've grown you have brought your mother and I only disappointment. You have shown yourself foolhardy and reckless, hell-bent on bringing dishonour to this house, to the family name. It is better if you go. Leave now, please.'

'Raff, no. It's not true.' Margaret rushed to Raff, begging he and the woman to stay as they walked resolutely together to the door, but Raff shook his head.

'Don't worry, Father, we'll leave this house with pleasure. But one thing you should understand. If ever you want to see me again, it will be with Lotta. She is my wife now. Mother – I hope you understand.'

With that, they were gone, Margaret collapsing onto the couch with a wail.

Later, they'd sat together by the drawing-room fire. Margaret had been furious with him since Raff's departure, veering between that anger and lamenting her son.

'You shouldn't have said that to him,' she berated him as she had countless times that afternoon. 'About being a disappointment. And you shouldn't have told him to leave.'

He'd shaken his head in frustration. He longed to shout it out to his wife. That their son had been played for a fool. Hunted, snared like a witless rabbit. That his life now lay shattered. That it was because of him, all because of him, and that he could not bear. No more than he could bear to watch it unfold.

'Don't waste your sympathies on him, Margaret. He's not worth your time. And I only spoke the truth. He *has* brought nothing but dishonour to us. He has sired a bastard. It is coarse, but it is surely a fact. He didn't deny it.'

Margaret had implored him. 'But if she is with child – if she is, William – we must make sure that child is taken care of.'

'We will not! I will not have any bastard child in this house. We don't even know that the sorry brat is his – it could be any number of men's. The woman is a trollop, Margaret. And we must have nothing more to do with either of them. Do you hear me? You are not to go near them. I forbid it.'

33

No, you wanted nothing to do with my spawn. Nothing to do with your son. From that day, at the thought of you, Raff would work himself into a fury, spitting your name in poisonous tirades, but I could see the truth of his heart. His anguish at his estrangement from you.

Naturally, I was glad to be rid of you. I was torn between hoping the estrangement would last, and sorrow for Raff, wishing his hurt away. Now living in Hampstead, those autumn days Raff would be out constantly, hunting for work, determined we'd have our own lodgings and he a job to keep us.

Margaret did not obey you, William. She visited us many times in Hampstead as my belly grew and back stiffened. Once she learned the truth, that I was with child, although she could not hide her worry, she was only kind. I came to look forward to her visits, her gentle counsel, laughing at how she would lick her finger to wet down and tame Raff's curls as she had since he was a boy.

'Unhand me, Mother!' Raff would exclaim, retreating, then protesting, acting proud as she insisted on giving us money from her allowance, saying we could not rely on Patience's goodwill for ever, and must save now whatever we could.

I thought on that money she gave us. Money in name belonging to Margaret but, in truth, belonging to you. Money you *allowed* her. If Raff had thought of it, he probably would not have accepted it. But to me it seemed some sweet justice that it should be spent in a way you would deplore.

In November came good news. Eddie's father knowing the general manager of the railway hotel, the Midland Grand at St Pancras, Raff was granted an interview, returning that sunny winter lunchtime in high spirits. Impressed by his background, the general manager had proposed he train with them with a view to management. The best news was that Midland Railway owned houses nearby and could supply us with a furnished apartment at a rent we could afford. Raff was overcome with joy, as was I.

Margaret accompanied me to view our new lodgings, a white-stone terraced house in a quiet road, a short walk from St Pancras and King's Cross. Inside the narrow and dim hall, I nervously turned the key to the ground-floor apartment, entering to gaze around me. There were three rooms and a kitchen, but even with their tall bay windows, they felt cramped after the brightness, the airiness of Hampstead. But I tried not let my trepidation show, even as I saw in Margaret's face her doubts.

On the night of February 16th 1913, in Hampstead, our baby was born. Writhing, groaning, crawling like a crab in my sweat-soaked nightdress over the bed, Martha, the midwife, tried to contain me.

'Hold still, Lotta! That's it, good girl. Push now, push, come on.'

Annie had brought Martha to prepare me before the birth, but nothing could have readied me for the unearthly pain. I gripped the sheets she'd knotted to the bed poles, biting on them like some savage beast, only thankful she had larded me below to ease the baby's passage.

At last, near midnight, I felt the final agony, the blessed relief of the child slipping from me. Exhausted, I slumped back on the pillow, staring both in alarm and wonderment as Martha held up the tiny purple being, its fierce, wailing face coated in my blood and a shocking yellow slime.

'Here she is!' Martha laid the cord like a snake upon my belly, the child upon my breast as I looked in awe at the wriggling, crying thing. I laughed and wept at the same time, laid back spent, as Martha cut the cord with a knife, taking the child to the basin to be washed before Raff, waiting downstairs with Patience, would see.

Annie was stroking back my damp hair. 'You have a daughter, a beautiful daughter,' she whispered, as I, half-crazed, watched Martha swaddle the clean child in a towel to lay it back down upon my breast. As I gazed, I could not name or make sense of my emotions.

Astonishment, a rushing joy, the greatest fear, at this living, breathing creature with its shock of black hair, face crinkled like the oldest of souls, being mine.

In an instant, Patience smiling beside him, Raff was at my side. At his eyes so wide, mouth gaping at the child on my breast, I laughed, pulling him to me. His eyes welled as, nervously, he stroked her tiny ear, covering my head with kisses. I touched the child's head as if to anoint her.

'Moll,' I said, as I started to cry, overwhelmed by my emotions, the exhilaration at the child, the memory of and yearning for my mother. 'This is Moll.'

* * *

He'd suspected many times that Margaret was defying him. His suspicion had only deepened when she no longer mentioned Raff or the woman, or beseeched that she might see them. She seeming unnaturally sanguine about the situation, he'd confronted her, but she'd denied any meeting. He'd never known her lie to him before, and that she might be doing so now wounded him greatly. But she could no longer feign innocence or hold her tongue when the child was born. That February morning, as he finished breakfast at the dining table, she had come to sit by his side and firmly made her announcement.

'You might be interested to know you have a grand-child, now, William. *We* have a grandchild. A child born in wedlock and you must do right by her. I will no longer tolerate anything less.'

He'd never had confirmation the woman was with child, but every instinct had told him it was so. But the mere notion, now made flesh, felt as a punch to his gut. So it was done. The woman was the victor. She had stolen his son, made good her haul by saddling him with a child. It was done, but he would not be forced to bear witness to it.

So minded, he'd tried to persuade Margaret that any association with Raff and the woman would only subject them to ridicule, see their reputation in tatters. That by keeping their distance his colleagues, their mutual friends, would consider them acting correctly. Their social standing would be threatened by acknowledging the wanton woman as their daughter-in-law, her offspring their grandchild.

Margaret had scoffed. 'I don't give a fig for my social standing. If my so-called friends wish to disown me, or gossip about me, so be it. I care for my son and our granddaughter. That is all.'

Some of what he'd said was sincere. He did worry, but only slightly for his reputation. In truth, he knew his status was secure, his rank too high for this sorry circumstance to have any real consequence. Perhaps some idle talk, some tittle-tattle, but of little substance. Raff and the woman were married, after all. While the woman's background may be a source of amusement for some, by others he might be considered benevolent.

But much as he suffered agonies at his estrangement from Raff, his agony at the boy's downfall was much greater: the agony at his own part in it, what his past deeds had cost his son. The chance to protect him now lost, he could not countenance a role in the charade, watching the woman preen. He felt her volatile, feared too what his presence might at any moment ignite. But it was not simply the menace of what she might reveal but the shadow she cast: the shadow of the man he'd once been. One abhorrent to him. Worse, one that would be abhorrent to his wife. He had risen, unrelenting, from the table.

From that day, Margaret had become brazen, almost revelling in her defiance. In the morning room she would flaunt purchased gifts, furry toys and matinee jackets for the child, soothing powders for both baby and mother. Wilfully, she'd announce her visits to them, refusing to say when she might be expected home.

Deliberately, she'd raise their names. Raff. Moll. A name he hated for it pierced him, reminding him of what hell he had wrought upon that woman. And Lotta. *Lotta*. *Lotta*. The name he detested most of all. No longer Lotta Rae. But Lotta Linden.

* * *

That February night, as I bled to usher new life into this world, Emmeline Pankhurst declared war. She pronounced it now clear the Government intended never to grant women the vote. Her words sparked a fire that would rage across England, one that matched every fire in my belly.

Just nights after Moll was born, one well known to us, Emily Wilding Davison, in the unoccupied Surrey summer house of Lloyd George, secreted a bomb, blowing five rooms to the heavens.

The war cry had been answered. With the Government and country in uproar, I nestled in my bed, cradling my baby as Annie and the others gathered around, avidly plotting mayhem. Taking the first steps from my room, learning how to carry and soothe my baby, nursing her day and night at my raw bosom, I'd find the house deserted, the women gone to rampage with others all over England, torching tea-pavilions, railway carriages, smashing windows, tarnishing walls, severing telegraph and telephone lines.

Blazoning headlines proclaimed a reign of terror. Emmeline, arrested for inciting women to commit offence, answering her critics, quipped: 'We do not intend that you should be pleased.'

As I sat limp, arms aching from rocking, my comrades stood alert, braced and ready for battle. Their wits sharp, my own felt thick as London fog, their torsos taut and primed, mine like sunken sponge.

So it was, as Patience and the others gathered around the doorstep, Annie beside me in the cab as I wrapped Moll in a shawl, my heart, though unwilling, knew the time had come to part. With Raff at the hotel, I watched

Annie fuss to settle me in the apartment, spirited, working quickly, eager to return to her crusade.

At last, I kissed her, hugged her goodbye and closed the door behind her. I did not know where my future lay in the struggle. Only knew my friend was gone to prepare her weaponry while I must prepare for my new life in King's Cross.

34

Those early days were not always easy. We'd made the apartment comfortable with Patience's rugs and throws, Raff happy in his work, but it took me time to become accustomed to what changes a baby brought, the relentless call for my attention. Tired from nursing and tending to Moll, I missed the camaraderie and help of Hampstead, and seemed plagued by unending worry; worrying Moll did not take enough milk, worrying she would smother herself in her cot, then, after willing her sleep, would worry her too quiet in her slumber. Those times, though, when I watched her at rest, assured of her breathing by the rising of her tiny chest, the overwhelming worry was replaced by overpowering love. I wanted to gather her to me, absorb every inch of her into my heart.

In the perambulator Margaret had gifted us, I'd wheel Moll snug to King's Cross Station, to listen on the forecourt to the guards' whistles, the trains' great letting of steam. Passing outside I'd see vagrants, gaunt, with grimy begging hands, reminding me of my own wretchedness on the streets before Mamma May became my saviour. I saw too the painted women lingering by lampposts, touting for trade, remembering my nights as a coquette.

When it rained, the paving seemed to rise with a smoky smell of soot and, in some strange way, I came to love that blighted place. It touched in me the memory of where I had come from. My own poor flawed and filthy London. Thinking on that, I would feel an elation. At how far I had travelled, at where I now stood. Looking down upon my milky, content child, carrying her to that place I cherished. My home with her father.

Although Raff worked long hours, I was not lonely, for Margaret would often visit, lifting Moll to dote on her, eager to try her gift of a pretty matinee jacket or such. I treasured her company. Felt for her the greatest affection. I was so grateful for your absence. It allowed me to pretend, as before, that you did not exist. Let me bask solely in Margaret's motherly warmth, for the love she shed upon Moll, she shed upon me too. Annie and Patience also would visit, fresh from the struggle, bringing with them one summer day news of Emily Wilding Davison, she who'd so enthralled us with the February bombing.

On Derby day it had been intended Emily would wave suffragette colours before the King's horse, but it seemed she'd tried to pin them to the horse's bridle, been struck and now lay perilously close to death. London, the whole country, was riveted, the talk of nothing else. Raff said he'd had to fight to keep his temper, and so his job, as he overheard men in the lounge, sipping their drinks, mocking that malignant suffragette.

When word came that Emily had died, I knew I must march with her on her final journey. That June day, in dresses of pure white with black sashes, holding suffragette colours, we marched to booming brass bands, behind her flower-strewn hearse. With the other hunger strikers, I carried our emblem, Raff watching from the roadside as only women were called on to march.

The newspapers said there were six thousand of us. All I know is that London stopped. I moved along in the sea of white, looking up to see men in boaters and caps, women staring down from the open tops of halted omnibuses, more thronging the pavements, six lines deep, the police herding back the crowds as the coffin was lifted into the Bloomsbury church. As the coffin was carried out, we struck a military stance to salute it.

One woman, Elsie Howey, had ridden alongside us on a white horse, symbolising Joan of Arc, which statue they said Emily had looked upon at the suffragette fair the night before she'd fallen. The warrior stood, sword raised to the sky, plinth emblazoned with her supposed last words: *Fight On and God Will Give the Victory*. That day, we paraded banners bearing that motto. I did not believe it. If victory was to be ours I did not count on one I had always found so absent to grant it. But what those faithful, what none of us could have known, is it would be not God – not God, but Hell would deliver it in the end.

*   *   *

Hell. He rested his head back upon the leather, closed his eyes. *Yes, it was Hell in the end delivered your victory.*

*   *   *

Emily's death fanned an already flaming fire, brought a call to arms to women the length and breadth of Britain. Late at night, Raff at last home, nestling with him beneath the throw on our small couch, listening out for Moll's breathing in the cot, he would lament we could not play a greater part in the struggle. But we knew it impossible. Not only did his gruelling hours not allow it, but he could not risk any trouble and so risk his job. For me, the demands of caring for Moll afforded little chance for militancy, and the dangers posed at the marches; the chance of police or mob brutality, I could not take. I was responsible for Moll now. Even so, those days at King's Cross Station, I would try to play my part, standing with newssheets to looks of distaste from passing men and women at the sight of Moll beside me in her perambulator.

As Moll grew, she brought me the greatest happiness. I learned quickly the tricks of motherhood; how to mollify her tantrums, the art of distraction with her most treasured bear. Enchanted, I'd sit, watching her at play, my daughter bouncing a rag doll twice her size, thrashing it to within an inch of its life as with it she danced, entranced by a world hers alone.

Arriving home, eager to see her, Raff would go to watch over her in her cot.

'Come away,' I'd whisper. 'You might wake her,' but then find my head on his shoulder, as bewitched as he at the sight of our child in peaceful slumber.

If home early, Raff would lie on the rug, wave before Moll her beloved bear: 'Mister Bear wants to know if Miss Moll Linden has been a good girl today.'

'Miss Moll Linden has not been such a good girl,' I said, one such day. 'Tell Pap about feeding your porridge to Mister Bear. And how Mister Bear's mouth had to be scoured with carbolic,' laughing as Moll jumped up and down, shrieking in protest, watching with pleasure the delight in Raff's eyes, the joy her antics brought him.

The aching worry of those early days somewhat waned, my love for Moll only deepened as her feisty character showed itself. When Patience and Annie would visit, her cheeky, impish ways brought us much merriment.

'Mam is going to put on your shoe now, Moll,' I said one day, bending to put it on her foot, preparing her for an outing with us.

'Give me!' she demanded, snatching it from me, we trying to stifle our laughter at her grim determination to tug it on.

'Now there's a woman who knows her own mind,' Annie said, happily.

Making her escape as I attempted to brush her hair, I'd give chase, she screeching in glee as I tripped on her toys, eventually catching her to put her on my knee. There she would settle, sucking her finger, eyes growing dreamy as I brushed those black curls so like her father's. I would think of Margaret trying in vain to tame Raff's, knowing myself sure to do the same, destined as they were to grow unruly like his.

Blissful in this thought, there, on my lap, I would gather her close; this tiny creature that Raff and I had made. She who had become mistress of my heart.

* * *

He'd known the time of reckoning to have come the first Yuletide after the child's birth. Margaret had issued him an ultimatum. If he refused to spend Christmas with his son and granddaughter, if he would not have his own blood in his home, neither then would he have his wife. Doubting her threats, he'd found himself not feasting that Christmas Day but eating alone. Just as so many other days, Margaret had deserted him for that squalid King's Cross apartment. He knew he would have to relent.

Falling on a Sunday, the appointed afternoon was the eve of the child's first birthday. Margaret had planned a tea, gleefully decorating the drawing room with bunting and balloons. He knew for all her gaiety she was as anxious as he, obvious by her fussing over the positioning of the cake, the crockery on the table. At last, at three o'clock, they'd heard the bell, voices in the hall below. He'd stood, hands tensely clasped behind his back, awaiting their entrance.

The first sighting of his son, after more than a year, had taken him aback. To see him in the flesh again gave rise to intense sentiment. All battles, animosity, in that moment negated by a well of love, a wish to go to him, take him in his arms, hold him. But he did not. He'd not made such a show since Raff had grown, he certainly could not do so now. His son seemed even taller, holding himself with the surety of a man rather than a temperamental boy. The woman, close by his side, was bending to the child taking unsteady steps, Margaret quickly beside them, showing the child the bunting and balloons, the woman exclaiming about them. It was clear how at ease his wife and the woman were in one another's company.

'Hallo, Father.' Raff's greeting was terse, the woman looking up from the child, her own greeting guarded. 'Hallo, William.'

He was aware of Margaret's eyes upon him. He knew he must be welcoming. 'Hallo, please, please come in. And this must be . . .'

'Moll,' the woman said. 'Say hallo, Moll.'

The child unsure, Margaret bent to coax her. 'This is your grandfather, Moll. Say hallo.'

Led by Margaret, the child tottered towards him, chortling as Margaret tickled her. She stood gazing up at him.

He'd looked at the child, her scattering of black curls, and known this girl was Raff's. Never had he truly doubted it, but it was plain now through her gait, her expression. Something in them reminded him of Raff as a boy. The memory brought a surge of pain. The child's eyes, though, were her mother's. Quizzical. Appraising. Seeing.

'Hallo, Moll,' he'd said. 'I am very pleased to meet you.' He'd extended his hand, Margaret placing the child's palm in his. As they'd shaken hands, they'd all laughed, a laughter, he knew, to mask the tension.

Moll had been the greatest blessing that day, the most welcome distraction at the table, Margaret fondly tending to her with endless lemonade and sweetmeats, the child scrambling up the tablecloth in her supreme efforts to reach the cake. Her face smeared in cream, the woman had wiped it with mock scolding, Raff's adoration and amusement at his daughter obvious.

'Moll, you have the grip of a monkey,' Raff had said.

'And the mouth of a gorilla,' the woman had said, smiling, the child waving wildly her chubby arms, mimicking her mother making ape sounds.

Perplexed, it struck him that his son and the woman seemed happy. Genuinely happy. It confused him. He was not sure what he'd anticipated. Perhaps a palpable hostility, at least on the woman's part, but she seemed truly absorbed with the child above all else. Swiftly, he settled on it: it was the natural way of motherhood. That she loved her child did not mean she loved his son.

It certainly was easy to be charmed by the child. He'd found himself joining in the revelry, feeling an unexpected warmth towards his granddaughter. With some surprise, he'd realised the child seemed to bring with her not the greater threat he had foreseen, but somehow an easing of that threat. It was the strangest of feelings. As if he and the woman were now in some way bonded, bound by a being to which neither of them would wish to cause trouble or pain. Avoiding the woman's eyes, he found himself watching instead her hands. The handling of her dessert fork. Her lifting of the cup. Once or twice, their eyes had met. It seemed she shared his sentiment. For, instantly they'd lowered them to the child as if reminding themselves of what must unify them.

Raff had a certain pride about him. It was clear his new role as husband, father and provider was suiting him. He spoke animatedly of his work. 'I'm under-manager of the lounge now, Father. It's very interesting, all the people you meet, the different places they're travelling to, the types of business they're on.'

He'd nodded, trying to show enthusiasm, even though he considered what his son did lowly. It was she who had humbled him. Robbed him of the future he could have had. A real profession. A worthy wife. But the child. The child.

After tea he'd played with her, winding for her Margaret's gift of a clockwork man, enjoying her howls of delight. By the time the three left, it was with regret he bid goodbye to his granddaughter. With the sincere hope he would see her soon again. As he'd sat with his wife by the fire, he'd mused on the child, with lingering pleasure. He and Margaret agreed. It had been a happy day.

* * *

Yes, it passed as a happy day, William. Raff was overjoyed by the reunion, and it warmed me to see him so happy. I was minded then to try. To try to suffer you for his sake, for Moll's. Never would we be friends, that I knew, nor could I ever truly make my peace with you. But, perhaps, we could have abided by some uneasy truce. So much unsaid, to stay forever unsaid. But it was not to be.

For, whatever I pledged in the silence of my bed, somewhere out there in the deeper, darker silence the stars were stirring. Blinking, as if awoken by a summons, they made moan, moving not with harmony and grace but a malign groan across that ink-black sky, mutating as they came to collide, to ignite in the heavens. The stars made their own pact while we were sleeping.

And no matter our intention, they would have their way.

35

It happened in moments. Mere moments that would decree every second, every hour of every day ever after. Never could we have guessed what fate those seconds would deliver us. As I heedlessly fussed around Moll in the stifling King's Cross heat, and Raff served his customers cooling drinks, how could we know that in that very instant two shots under a Sarajevo sun would sound the knell on our serenity.

Although Raff made mention of it, the assassination of Austrian Archduke Ferdinand and his wife, Sophia, by a zealous Serb hungering for freedom from Austria, we paid it little mind. Through that hot July we heard the rumbles, yet they were as thunder in distant hills. When it came, it came quickly. At July's end, Austria-Hungary in retribution declaring war on Serbia, every country thereafter tumbled like cards. Russia vowed to protect Serbia, Germany in turn defending Austria-Hungary. When France swore allegiance with Russia, France and Germany proclaimed themselves at war. We knew then what would come. Still, it stunned us. On Tuesday, August 4th, allied to France, the Government announced us at war with Germany.

It seemed unreal. Perverse. Just the previous after-noon the country had lazed in the bank holiday heat. Now it stood ready, suddenly alert, children snatched from their play on beaches to prepare, with their fami-lies, for battle. Raff and I were horrified as instantly it seemed the country was gripped by a fever. Urgent headlines issued rallying calls, feeding a frisson on the streets, like a madness, the frenzy before Christmas. People started talk of Nation, Empire, Glory.

When Emmeline Pankhurst stated her full support, commanding that all suffragette operations cease, that every woman assist the war effort, Raff and I were dismayed. Far from all shared that sentiment. Annie, Patience, countless others in Hampstead and beyond vehemently opposed the war. On one of Raff's free afternoons, visiting Hampstead with Moll, we sat with Patience and Annie in the drawing room.

'Well, that didn't take long,' Patience said, smoking from her rattan chair.

'What didn't?' I asked.

'For all the hubris of this magnificent new century to founder. I've lived too long,' she said, voice raspy from tobacco. 'Too long to believe in marvellous new dawns. It seems for all man's spectacular advancement he hasn't wandered so far from the primal. Men and nations massing to show their might. Alpha lions prowl-ing to mark their territory, tearing the flesh, spilling the blood of other prides. Pissing on those lands to make them their own.'

And I remembered. How as a child with Mam and Pap, I'd stood flushed with midnight cold and excitement amongst the revelling crowds, lighting at the great bell song of St Paul's. How those bells had rung out over the London sky to herald a new century. The twentieth century. A time of hope. Marvel. Such great promise.

'Make a wish tonight and every dream will come true,' Pap had whispered as we gazed up upon the icy stars.

No, it had not taken long. Not long to give the lie to this enlightened new age, to trample on its buds, quench its light. Not long for evolved man to reveal the claw that scratched at his belly. His urge to be supreme. King of the Pride.

* * *

He stared out into the night. What had he felt at that call to arms? He'd been excited. Swollen with fervour, patriotic pride. Had thought the war would be good for the country so divided by Liberal lunacy, those militant women shouting the odds. This was just what was needed to unite it: a common enemy. The Germans had been a threat for years with their ever-burgeoning weaponry and warships. Now they would show those Huns who was master.

He'd been fired by belief. A belief in his countrymen, his homeland. This war was a matter of honour. One that demanded sacrifice. He'd been anxious to talk of it with his son.

Lord Kitchener was calling upon men to serve. With word it would be over by Christmas, he'd been fearful Raff might miss his chance. One, at last, to make of himself a man, show his mettle. To be the son he'd hoped for, one he could be proud of.

He'd seized the opportunity one evening when Raff was visiting alone. Out of earshot of Margaret, who did not share his passion for the war, he'd invited his son into the sitting-room beside the study. Handing him a port, he'd raised the subject. Immediately, Raff had rebuffed him.

'Don't try to involve me in your imperialist rubbish, Father, I don't believe in it. I don't believe in this war. It's simply all the old empires parading their power, trying to dominate, and grow their territory, the victors sure to plunder and colonise yet more African lands. Kings and lords keeping the mighty safe while sending the peasants off to fight. I will have nothing to do with it.'

Deep disappointment making him indignant, he'd stood facing his son. 'Do not insult the Empire in this time of need. How can you be so treacherous? This is the land of your father, your grandfather, your forefathers. The land that bore you. Show some loyalty, for God's sake.'

Raff had snorted. 'Ah, Blood and Soil, is that it, Father? King and Country? And God too? For God and Country?'

'Yes! Yes!' He'd been outraged at the boy's scorn. 'For God and Country. Is that principle so abhorrent to you? Does it mean nothing to you and that bunch of men in skirts you run around with?'

'Don't cite God to me, Father,' Raff had scoffed. 'You don't even truly believe in God. I doubt you've ever given it much thought. You *believe* because your father believed. He because *his* father believed. It's not God you're faithful to but they. Faithful to your kin, your blood. Well, it is blood that blinds, Father. Turns us into maniacal tribesmen, baying for the blood of other tribes, deprives us of our senses.'

Enraged, he'd roared. 'How dare you. How *dare* you. You stand in my home and insult me, your grandfather, your country and the faith of our fathers. Sometimes I cannot even recognise you as my son.'

Despairing, he'd sunk into a chair. Raff had watched him, put down his drink as he prepared to leave.

'Blind faith, Father. That's what you have. Thought-less, blind faith. If there is a God may he at least protect us from that. It's those blind with faith who wreak the most carnage with their zeal.'

* * *

When Raff returned home, he told me of that argument. He was greatly saddened by it. After your recent reconciliation, he'd wanted no more trouble between you. Sitting close on our couch, I stroked his hand as Moll slept peacefully in her cot.

'But I don't think it is for any God when even in his name we fight, Lotta,' he said, caressing my arm. 'But for all we've ever known. For the God of our fathers, our *father*. For our tribe, they who worship him, our own. It's not for any higher being we fight, but against any who would dare rip at our roots.'

It is blood that blinds. That I understood only too well. The blind hatred I had felt when my own blood, my mother, my father had been so greatly wronged. The girl I'd been had died and been reborn an avenging warrior. In those days, William, the thought of your pain was my pleasure, your suffering my joy. I would revel in it. Yes, I think in those days I was mad. As Raff spoke, I was certain I knew only too well the mania that drove war.

Yet even as he talked that night I felt it stir within me. My love for Mam and Pap, so untouched by death. Even as I knew that love's very purity can turn it malign, a love become loathing for any who would threaten it, if Raff wished against the force of such love I could not comply. I felt it still. I feel it still.

Even through the cool of autumn the national fever soared, soldiers marching the city streets to cheering crowds, boys and men clamouring to serve, many from the hotel. Raff said they were hailed as heroes, parties held in their honour to see them cheerily on their way. Raff felt the silent judgement of those too old for service, while others would make only too clear their opinions.

'I'd have thought a young man like you better occupied serving your country, rather than cocktails,' one older male customer said.

Still, in those early days, the jibes were fewer. For we all believed it would soon be over.

And then in September we heard talk of the trenches.

*　*　*

In the carriage, he smiled ruefully. The September Battle of the Marne. They had called it the Miracle of the Marne. A *miracle*. He shook his head. Such bitter irony. Heralded a miracle because in France the allies had driven back the Germans; bitter for now there was stalemate. Each army stalled, dug deep in French soil, entrenched in iron lines.

All along the Western Front.

*　*　*

At home we heard only of the glories, the victories, the newspapers forbidden to report anything that could lead to alarm, talk that might affect morale became a crime. The war not over by Christmas, there were rumours of conscription. Raff said he'd be jailed before he'd be forced to fight.

His job became harder as the country's mood grew more sombre, unseemly now for gentlemen and ladies be seen engaged in trivial socialising. Losing their young men to battle, the hotel was hiring older men in their place. Older men. And women. We made wry note of it. It seemed, now they were needed, women were well able to do the work of men.

At last, the general manager made it clear the hotel expected Raff to do his duty. He said it did not reflect well on them that they retained one better employed in the military. Raff found a white feather, a symbol of cowardice, left for him on a plate. He was refused service in a shop because he was not wearing a uniform.

'I can do nothing for you here, lad,' the leathersmith said. 'We don't do work for traitors, those shy of putting on the King's uniform.'

With his job all but lost, knowing it would be impossible to find another, horrified, I sensed him waver. One night, as we watched over Moll in her cot, he said, 'I don't know if I can bear to leave her.'

'Then you mustn't,' I said, gripping his arm, desperately searching his eyes for his promise he would not desert us.

My own entreating failing to quell his doubts, I asked Margaret to talk to him.

'No, Raff, no, you mustn't think of it.' She clasped his hands on our couch. 'I'll speak to your father. He'll support you and Lotta until the war is over. It will surely be over soon.'

Raff wouldn't hear of Margaret's petitioning his father. He was adamant. 'No, Mamma. If anything's to be done, I'll do it myself.'

When Patience and Annie would visit, they'd join with me in reminding Raff of the new world we'd fought for, a world fair for every woman – and man.

'Think, Raff,' Patience urged him. 'Think of all those men. Those not considered worthy enough to vote, yet good enough to serve King and Country, being sent to their slaughter. Play no part in this perversity, please.'

Those days I'd wheel Moll to King's Cross, hearing the kiosk vendors talk to customers of the wounded soldiers who'd been carried home under cover of night. The platform guards had whispered to them of the gore, the fleshy mess, the absent stare of the soldiers' eyes. Some soldiers had spoken of the slaughter out in Gallipoli, before others warned them to hold their tongues. My blood was ice at the thought of Raff amongst them.

Then came what you will say finished it. What was done to London that May night. The Zeppelin bomber that glowed like a moon in the heavens, spat its shells north and east, from Stoke Newington to Whitechapel. And Spitalfields. On my Spitalfields. They cleared the slums that night.

Margaret watched Moll, as I walked those streets, once my own, two mornings after; walked amongst the rubble, the ruins, houses and shops torn and jagged, innards rising like monsters against the sky, men, women, children wandering, dazed from what had been wrought upon them.

I saw no one I knew, only cast my eyes on what had been done. To be certain none I knew was hurt, I asked a passer-by of Flossie, of my friends amongst the stallholders and was told they were unharmed. Flossie's shop was still there, Peabody House still standing. But as I looked upon them in that wasteland, stark and ghostly, it seemed all my days there – every childhood day, sweet and dear – was consumed by that sickly pall of dust.

You will say it was that. The rattle of that metal beast, its shower of fire, the screaming, charred children, the flames that ravaged our city that did it.

But I know different, William. I know different.

36

For the longest time he had told himself it was so. The bombing of London, that had been what sealed it. But now. Now he was done with lies. Lies to others. Lies to himself. Still, he could hardly bear to think of the truth of it. He looked out upon the dim, gaslit streets, the rain relenting. They were drawing near now. Near to Chiswell Street.

He leaned back his head. Although he turned his face from the memory, it came unbidden in misty images upon the window. The afternoon Raff had come to him. He could see his son weary that day, as if straining under a heavy load. He'd sat with Raff in the drawing room, waited for him to speak. As he did so, softly, slowly, his meaning become clear, he was struck by the fact that his son was unburdening himself, confiding in him. He had hardly done so since he was a child.

He had listened. To his son confess he had been dismissed from his job. That with war fever high after the bombing, it would be impossible to find another, and he was no longer able to support his family. He had come seeking his father's aid.

He remembered now what words he had spoken in reply. Words he could still taste like dirt, something putrid on his tongue.

'I cannot do that.' He recalled how Raff had looked hopelessly at him. 'I cannot do that, Raff. I think you know now what you must do. What is the right thing to do.'

His son had implored him. 'I can't, Father. Can't do what you ask. It would go against everything I believe, to join the bloody murder in those fields. I cannot betray my conscience.'

'And neither can I betray mine.'

Eyes locked, they'd sat in silence before he had spoken again.

'Raff, if you do your duty, if you serve your country, I promise you I'll take care of your family. I'll support Lotta and Moll and you won't have to worry for them. They will have everything they need. If you do now what you must, all will be well.'

He'd watched his son thinking. Raff had said nothing for some while, then, with the slightest of movements, silently nodded. He'd felt a jubilation.

'Good boy. Good boy.'

Eagerly, he'd told Raff he would make the necessary calls. That with his background he was sure of training at a higher rank, that of an officer. He would use his influence to secure it. But Raff refused. If he was to enlist, he would do so like any other man. On this he was firm.

At last, Raff standing as they finished speaking, he too had risen, opening his arms. As Raff stepped towards him, he'd gripped his son's shoulders.

'I'm proud of you. So proud.'

He'd seen Raff's surprise at the welling of his eyes, the welling of his son's own. They had embraced. He'd held his son close. Just as he had when he was a boy.

*　*　*

Raff told me that evening of what had passed between you. He was greatly affected by it, so greatly moved by how much his serving meant to you. The pride in him, at last, you had shown. I wanted to scream.

'But you went there for his help and he denied you,' I said in desperation.

But he seemed to think nothing of that now, his only concern your happiness. That having brought you only disappointment he had finally a chance to earn your respect. He talked lovingly of you while inwardly I wept and cursed you. You had forsaken him. You were willing to support me and Moll, but only if your son joined the slaughter.

He was lost to me, lost to my pleas. Margaret came, distraught at the news. You had told her it was the bombing that had decided him. Raff did not enlighten her, but, while he tended to Moll, I told her the truth of it. She was outraged.

'Please, Raff, ignore your father,' she begged. 'I will speak to him, make him see reason.'

But Raff was resolute. He had made peace with his father, and intended to make good on his word. No pleading would turn him.

He began to make arrangements for me and Moll. He wanted us to make our home in Gibson Square, as did Margaret, but I insisted on our independence. Not only was I trying to hinder Raff's leaving, but, of course, I could not live with you. Nor you with me. I can well imagine your terror at it, your relief at my refusal. Finally, there was no need. Now Raff was to serve, the hotel allowed us to remain in the apartment. Raff's earnings would be a pittance but, no doubt, desperate I stay from your door, you were only too happy to pay for our keep as agreed. I was to be beholden to you.

As the military judged his fitness, I willed that he be found wanting. All in vain. Too soon my gentle soul was gone to Aldershot to learn the ways of war. Margaret and I comforted each other in King's Cross through that lonely summer, ardently seeking signs of war's end, that he need not go. But it was not to be. In September Raff was enrolled in the infantry of Kitchener's New Army. He was to be dispatched to France.

That autumn day we travelled to Charing Cross station, to bid him goodbye. Opposite you in the carriage, I could not bear look at you. Margaret too blamed you utterly for Raff's leaving. She sat anguished beside you, curled like a frightened bird while Moll played clap-hands on my lap.

We found Raff on the forecourt, under the clock, our arranged meeting place. Moll was leaping excitedly at the fuss and noise, the swarming masses of troops, while Margaret rushed to embrace him, kissing his cheeks over and over. Inhaling every inch of him I despaired at the sight of him in uniform, felt the spring of tears at his brutally shorn head. Margaret started to cry as she stroked it.

'Well, you've got your way. At last my curls are tamed, Mamma. In fact they are annihilated.'

His cheeriness did not placate me. I could see him battling his own tears. It destroyed me. I glanced over to the platform, stared with hatred at the waiting Dover train, turning back to see you before him, so stoic, so calm. If there was any heart within you I did not see it. You clasped his shoulder, shook his hand, said, 'Well done. Good man,' while I wished on you damnation.

You left just Moll and I to walk with him to the train, to stand on the platform as he leaned out the window. I lifted Moll and he clapped her raised palms as she screeched with delight. Then he pulled my face to him, gripped my neck tightly as our lips lingered. I did not want to let him go. Never wanted to let him go. As the whistle blew, I caught his hand, desperately kissing it, clinging to his fingers until he was lost to the thrust of the train and he called through the roar: 'I love you, Lotta Linden.'

* * *

If there was any heart within you. Of course he'd had heart, that day. He'd felt it seize at his son in uniform, a swell of pride but also pain. But he could not display weakness. He'd had to remain strong for Raff, for Margaret. Yes, he'd felt his stomach grip as he watched him walk away. But he'd had no doubt. No doubt that what his son did now was worthy. Right and righteous. And he'd had hope. A deep hope.

That journey to Charing Cross, he'd watched her looking out the window, her expression so poisonous. He'd despised her. Been quite sure what made her so venomous. She was vexed. Afraid. Angry that having gone to such ends to entrap his son, he had now broken free. Afraid that his leaving would see her hold on him loosen. Perhaps absence would cause a rift, reveal to him her flaws, the gulf that naturally lay between them through her lack of standing. She had made a good catch in Raff while making of him something low. War might change him. Toughen him up. Make him the man he could be, should be. Her false heart, the insincerity of her troth might see her revert to her flighty character, lead her to seek the company of other men. Even to commit adultery. He would then arrange a simple divorce. He and Margaret would take the child, raise her with Raff.

Her fears had been his ambitions. With his son at war, he had hoped it would spell her end.

* * *

With Raff gone, Margaret yearned for the consolation of Moll in Gibson Square, but even as I craved her comfort I could not stand to be in your presence. Instead, she came to us, often excitedly carrying letters from Raff.

I lived for my letters from Raff. Although I knew him at the Western Front, he was not permitted to tell me precisely where, but he said in October, once the battle was over, that he had seen fighting in Loos. I could not imagine it. In Aldershot he'd said how his stomach turned at the sinister sheen, the lethal metal of the weaponry. My own stomach turned at the thought of it now.

He told me too of No Man's land, overhead the trenches. Of its vastness, its mire, a wasteland of barbed wire, smothering smoke and gas, the relentless echo and shudder of guns. He told me of the misery of the trenches, the stench of stagnant water up to his knees, the fear there was amongst the men of trench foot. He had seen it for himself. Feet swollen the size of an elephant's, so numb they could be stuck unknowing with a bayonet. He had heard the sobs of men carried to have their feet cut from them. The screams of the lucky, whose swelling had abated, the agony as feeling returned. The stink of the pus, the sores. He spoke of the drowning mud, the fat rats that clawed over them to steal their rations, the crawling lice, saying it was just as good his curls were gone, for they would surely nest there, gnaw through them into his skull.

I know, to spare her, he did not confide in Margaret the same. At times he must have said too much, for lines were struck out by a purging pen. But mostly he talked of his love and longing for me and Moll. I would take up my pen to write: *My love, my love, my love* . . .

Christmas brought its own torture. With Moll nearly three I knew I must make some attempt at revelry, understood what solace she brought Margaret, so had to endure an afternoon with you at Gibson Square.

Margaret had valiantly decorated the house for Moll, but the sparkle only made the empty chair at the table more stark. I could see in the very way Margaret spooned bread sauce onto your plate that she begrudged you even that small kindness. The coldness in her eyes, her brisk nod when you thanked her. Her resentment at your forcing Raff to go, she could not disguise. Nor I.

Moll, her usual spirited self, masked the silence.

'Grandpa, look what I got in my stocking,' she said, clambering upon the table, sitting the tiny clown upon a serving dish.

'It is the most delightful thing,' you said. 'We should give it a name. What shall we call it?'

'I've called it Milly.'

'But surely the clown is a man?' you said.

'Yes, the clown is always a man,' I said. 'Clowns who wage war.'

I held your eye as you bristled, knowing how you longed to retaliate. I almost goaded you with it, for you had no grown allies in that room.

Margaret caught my eye, as you turned your attention once more to Moll. I had no need to veil my animosity now. Margaret assumed it came only from our mutual blame of you.

You had, though, an ally in Moll. It was clear she adored her grandfather. I sat stiffly as later she played happily on your lap, wretched to see how she doted on you, you on her. I took my leave as soon as I could.

I decided I could no longer be held ransom, rely solely on your charity. Knowing you had lost maids to war work, that Annie and Patience worked alongside many women at the post office, I determined I would earn some money of my own. Conscription come: when I enquired at King's Cross Station, I was quickly employed as a ticket collector. Margaret was overjoyed at the prospect of caring for Moll, all that rankled with me was that my girl would spend so much time at Gibson Square with you.

I saw women everywhere now. In each and every place there had once been only men. Released from our bondage, at King's Cross I saw maids turned guards, conductors on the omnibuses, female peelers on the streets, heard more worked on farms, in factories, as bank tellers and office clerks. There was an outcry amongst some at we women being occupied in a deadly craft, building guns in the munitions factories. Uproar that women, the hallowed bearers of life, should forsake that sacred duty to create instead the very weapons that would destroy it. But such outrage was of little matter. No amount of outcry could turn the tide. For we were needed, our labour vital. It seemed the powers no longer doubted our capability. Were only too certain now of our worth.

Some days, free of work, I would travel alone on the train from St Pancras to Dover. Wandering far from the town, from any soul, onto the furthermost corner of the sandy shore, I'd stand there, raise my face to the wildly blowing wind. Closing my eyes, I'd listen. Listen to the distant boom, the fire. For that wind carried with it the sounds of France. In those moments I could imagine myself with him. I would listen just as he must to the thunder of the guns. Stood just as he beneath that boundless sky, that steadfast sun so untroubled by the rumbles, the madness and tussles of men below. Together, under that same sky we stood. Together we listened. My love and I.

37

We did not know then what that Flanders wind tried to whisper to us. Raff could not, would not confess it. But we know now, William.

Know of the stink, the rotting corpses that lay for days beside him in the trenches. Of the tortured cries he must endure from those blasted into the suffocating mud pools of No Man's Land, clutching the entrails of their stomachs in that rancid water. Their crying for their mothers as they held their innards in their hands, pleading for a merciful shot from a passing soldier. Or those crawling to the stares of dead men, stumbling upon random hands, arms, the scattered legs of the maimed. Only to realise, at the drag of their bodies, that one of them was theirs. Below, in the trenches, the silent pleas of those haunted by those cries: that if death must come, let it be clean, quick. Please not slow. Please, God, not slow. Hours, days, nights of dying, death become a prayer. How was it for Raff, William? How was it for your boy?

* * *

He closed his eyes, but there was no hiding place. It had been a Sunday. July 1st, 1916. The Battle of Albert. The first day of the Somme. He had often thought of it: what had he been doing those moments it began? Turning in peaceful sleep? Dressing, perhaps, for breakfast. A thing so mundane. It were as if he had lumbered foolishly about his business; as if he had missed the ringing of some divine gong. Time up. Run out. Time had come to an end and he had paid it no mind.

There had been many Londoners said they had heard it. That eruption beyond the sea, so loud it had stopped early risers in the streets. The Lochnagar mine blown beneath German trenches, the loudest sound yet known to man, the roar of the earth ripping into the sky, hanging deathly still in a malign plume, then tumbling in dust and debris over the scarred earth. An explosion so mighty it would allow the Allies to advance on the German trenches; so ferocious it would fatally confuse the Huns, disable their defences.

It did not.

The telegram had come to him. A communication normally reserved for officers, more usually the soldier's wife receiving a letter. He had supposed, later, they'd afforded him this courtesy due to his position as a judge.

It had been Wednesday, early morning, Margaret readying herself to collect Moll, he at breakfast. The maid carrying the envelope on a silver tray to the table, he'd stared at it for a long time before opening it. Instantly, he'd suspected what it was. He'd tried gather himself, banish fear. Told himself, if this brought news of Raff, he could simply be wounded, at worst, the very worst, missing. At last, slowly, he'd cut it open. It was from the War Office. He'd searched the type:

Regret to inform you . . .

They'd handwritten *Deeply* before *Regret*: *Killed . . . action July 1st . . . Lord Kitchener expresses his sympathy.*

His mind had refused to recognise the words. Desperately, he'd read them again in case he had not properly understood. Then sat rigid, blind to the paper in his hand.

Margaret had appeared at the dining room door, presumably to announce her leaving. Her eyes had fallen upon the telegram. 'What is it, William?'

He'd been unable to speak. His mouth had opened, but made no sound.

'For God's sake, what is it?' Her voice rose, shrill.

He couldn't say the words. Words so blunt, brutal. Grotesque. Killed. Dead. He could hardly fathom them; could not form, nor bear them on his tongue. She had come to the table, snatched the telegram from him.

He'd seen her there before him, fallen to her knees. But he'd seized. He'd had no ability, no resources to comfort her. Just gazed stupidly at his wife on the floor, rocking with an unearthly keening, clutching the telegram to her stomach. It seemed they stayed like that for the longest time. He remembered, finally, he'd made some attempt to collect himself. Summoned the maid. Asked her to telephone his chambers to explain his absence. With her he had gathered Margaret from the floor, placed her in a chair. But through the fog of that day, one thing remained terrible in its clarity, would never leave him. The sound of Margaret's cry. Primal, like the deepest howl of a wounded animal.

He heard it still in his waking moments. In his sleepless nights.

* * *

I had been waiting on Margaret, growing worried at her delay. When I saw both of you at the door, Margaret sickly pale and shaking, eyes lowered as if she were afraid look at me, I could make no sense of it. If she was ill, as she must be, why not send a maid in her place? Why had you accompanied her?

She teetered like a trembling fawn under your arm into the sitting-room, shrunken, withered. I had seen her robust only yesterday. I could not understand it.

'Margaret, what's wrong?' I helped her onto the couch.

You remained standing, face stern. It was then I had a glimpse of the unthinkable. Of what tidings you might bear.

'No.' I said it defiantly into your face. '*No!*' I shouted it.

'Lotta.' Margaret feebly reached out her hand, eyes pleading, starting to moan, a horrible noise. I slid down before her onto my knees. 'No,' I said again. '*No, no, no.*'

You made some attempt to touch my shoulder, but I pushed you away. You glanced over at Moll, standing staring at us from the arm of the couch.

'Granny, what's wrong?' She placed her little hand on Margaret's, Margaret slumping weeping, Moll's face crumpling as she herself started to cry. 'Mamma.' She ran to me, eyes wide with confusion.

'Take her, William, please,' Margaret implored. As you led Moll away, I could hear you coaxing her to show you Mister Bear in her room.

Margaret looked at me, anguished. I beseeched her. 'What's happened to him? He's wounded, badly wounded? Where is he?'

'Gone,' she whispered. 'Gone.'

Let me tell you of after. Of the darkness that stole my soul, that became my consort, my constant companion. Of the endless dull hours, each the same as the one before, only broken by a searing pain from a black hole under my heart, a well so deep I was terrified I would fall into it and drown.

Listlessly I'd feed Moll, but eating was a chore too great for me. I no longer worked. Instead, my days I spent with

Moll, gathering her to me on the couch, or blindly watching her at play, at night lying wakeful with her, the sound of her breathing my only solace. Even as I cleaved to her, I tried not to frighten her with my need, my mournful presence, my tears. Mercifully, she was too young to understand what had befallen us, the stark truth of death. She knew Papa was away. She thought that still.

Many days, Margaret and I passed together in King's Cross. She had no wish for anything but to see Moll. We were informed by letter of Raff's burial place, the French earth that held him but it was we who longed to hold him, ached to bring him home. To see, if only once more, his beloved face, to stroke his hand, whisper to him words of love.

With no ritual of a funeral, left with only our emptiness, it was Margaret who wanted the memorial service, while I wanted nothing but to hide away with Moll. But for her sake I agreed. That day in St James' churchyard, Moll being sheltered in Gibson Square, I wandered alone, the sun unnaturally shining as if not aware all light had left the world. I had invited no one from Hampstead, only wanted this ordeal done with. To see those with whom Raff and I had shared so much, with whom we'd been so happy, I knew would only cause me pain. There were no Harries to ask, we had lost them all to France. Along the pews I saw only strangers with solemn, respectful faces; your colleagues and Margaret's friends.

In the front pew I sat beside Margaret, assuring your distance by having her between us. I was oblivious to the dean's drone, only conscious of Margaret's hands trembling on her lap, conscious of you. Your stiff cough. The shifting of your feet on the kneeling cushion. At last, you rose to address the congregation, so pristine in your frock coat, so correct in manner. I did not want to look at you but found the loathing drawing my eyes. I detested your composure. I watched your mouth move as you delivered your oration. Heard words. *Glory. Gallantry. The sacrifice of our men.*

I stared at you. *Glory.* What glory in being fooled? They had not been gallant but witless. Deceived by the silence of the German trenches they'd been herded from their pits, flooded like cattle onto the wasteland, blindly bolting towards where those hoaxers, deemed disabled, lay in wait. But, sacrifice. Yes, sacrifice. A witless slew of cattle unleashed. Stampeding towards the slaughterhouse.

* * *

Glory. Gallantry. As he'd spoken those words, another had blighted his mind: *Carnage.* The carnage that day had been so great, a call for mercy had been granted, a truce to haul away the devastation of the dead, the wounded. Rumours were, between dawn and dusk, the nation had suffered more casualties than in the whole Boer war. It had been a bloody massacre.

* * *

In silence I travelled with you and Margaret back to Gibson Square. There was no need to pretend now. The desolation was absolute. Margaret could not even bear the brush of your arm, would shift in her seat if the carriage rocked you too close. I had no intention of lingering at the house where you had invited some from the church. I was there only to collect Moll.

While Margaret fetched her, across the drawing room I watched you shaking hands, accepting condolences from your colleagues, heard some pay tribute to Raff. I hated the sound of his name on those strangers' tongues. I heard one talk of the bravery of his last moments.

I wanted to scream: were they brave? *Was* it moments? Minutes? Hours? How long did it take for that fire, all that promise, the warm glow of life to seep from him? What did he suffer? Did he cry out for me? Plead I come to his side to soothe him, hear his last whispers? Did he yearn for the soft touch of Moll's tiny hand, hear her impish laughter as the battle roar dimmed? Did he weep for Margaret, as those death shadows fell, long for his mother, the kind comfort of home?

Did he think of you? Did he damn you? Damn you to hell as I did now?

* * *

Kneading his temples, he tried to knead away her voice. Before the memorial service, in that week after Raff's death, he had met with the Army Council, a privilege denied to most, one granted him as a judge. They had been quite clear. His son had taken many bullets. Very many. Enough to ensure that the end came swiftly. They'd assured him of that.

He'd been easily identifiable because of his tag. And his body had been whole. He'd remembered that word. Clung to it. Whole. His son had been whole.

* * *

Whole. Was that to be my consolation? Perhaps there was some in it. That my love's gentle hands, purposeful limbs, his impassioned heart lay not strewn like butchered meat across that Flanders field. That he was recognisable. But was it his face, that beloved face, made him so, or that he was tagged like a dog amongst the dead, to be hoisted with them onto the heave of bodies piled in some conquered, unconquered, corner of that cursed land.

I watched you from across the room, Moll leaping at my feet, asking me who all these people were. 'They are no one,' I said. 'Nothing to us.'

As we left, Margaret tenderly embraced me. An understanding between us, she did not bid me say my goodbyes to you, but I felt your stare. I lifted my head to meet your eyes. To send with mine their message:

You killed him. You killed your son.

* * *

He remembered that moment. That day he had watched her, found in her no sorrow, no tears. When their eyes had met he had seen there only a terrifying coldness. He had known then she did not mourn his son. That she had not loved Raff. She only hated *him*.

* * *

Those relentless days I was tormented by visions of my love lying still, stiff, staring on that slaying field. And I would wonder. Did a German man or boy lie nearby? Did they lie, unstirring together, while around them madness raged, whatever righteous quest, whatever differing creed to them so meaningless now.

I would think of what Raff had said: *It is blood that blinds.* I imagined that very blood flowing over the dried mud to join with his silent companion's to form a pool. A bright red pool. That blood, that made of them enemies in life, merging in their dying, to run as one. Their warm blood, one blood. United now in cold death.

But then would come Moll. Moll, so full of life, her wild black curls so like her father's, a balm to my wound. I would smile, lift her to hold her close. Our child, blessed child. Imbued with Raff's light and spirit.

In the year left to me I would think of that. Raff's light, his spirit. His eyes like a burst of sunlight, his heart a flame. I could not fathom it: how that light could burn so brightly, yet in an instant be gone. And I would wonder: where does it go, William? All that fire?

Siobhan MacGowan

I had thought, my soul released, I might find him. But I have wandered this limbo, seeking out his light in the dullness, searching for him, for Mam, for Pap, but nowhere can I see them. Perhaps it is my own darkness keeps me prisoner, has kept me from them. Perhaps my own darkness that dims Raff's light. Or perhaps he has risen a ghost from those Flanders fields to roam them.

Perhaps he roams them still.

38

Margaret was lost to him. She had held herself distant this past year, now her bitterness, often it seemed sheer hatred, was biting. She had moved from their bed chamber into her own, was scathing at any of his attempts to comfort her. Moll seeming her only solace, she would spend her days in King's Cross, sometimes staying there at night. The only time she would suffer conversation with him was to talk of what the woman needed, or Moll.

The silence in the house was stifling. Margaret would leave the drawing room when he entered, going to the morning room or bedroom. Finally, he'd summoned Ada, Margaret's spinster cousin from Edenbridge, one she'd always been greatly fond of, hopeful that a woman in which to confide would bring Margaret the consolation he could not. He also longed for some company in that wretched, lonely house.

It was better when she came. When Margaret was gone to King's Cross she would sit with him in the drawing room and he would probe her, desperate to know his wife's mind. Ada would not betray Margaret's confidence but say to him gently – 'Give it time, William. She is grieving.'

At times this would cause him to well with sorrow, at times it would make him angry. She was grieving. Did she think he was not? His own grief sat heavy, like a boulder in his stomach, something from which he must always distract himself. Something dark, untouchable, for which he had no words. Sometimes he resented Margaret's palpable mourning. He had no such luxury. He had to carry on, for her, for their grandchild. He must work. It redeemed him. A refuge from the unspeakable darkness within, the hostility at home. Margaret's condemnation of him only seared his own wound.

Through that agony he had tried to maintain the lie. That it had not been he alone that had forced Raff to war. It was the bombing, his dismissal from the hotel. He would have found it impossible to obtain employment, it would not have been good for him, a man with wife and child, to be reliant on his father. Even at the thought, he was aware it was ludicrous. *Not good for him,* when the worst, the very worst, had come to pass. But still he told it to himself. It was the only way he could bear it.

*　*　*

Sometimes, while Margaret minded Moll, I would wander. Just as I had after losing Mam and Pap, I hankered to leave behind the streets where Raff and I had been so happy, to lose myself in crowds, in unfamiliar sights and sounds. Although Annie and Patience tried to comfort me, their presence only hurt me, reminded me of those Hampstead days, that place that had been so dear to us. I longed for consolation but I knew not where to find it.

I found myself drawn to the West's milling broadways. One afternoon in Covent Garden, I spied a small tent, announcing the services of a spiritualist. I don't know what I sought there. Perhaps that I might somehow commune with Raff. Drawing back the drape, I saw the tent hung with the Turkish cloths Patience so liked, candles in red glasses casting a ruby glow. At a velvet-cloaked table sat a strong-boned woman, dark hair caught in a shell comb, eyes large and brown, her shawl beaded. She smiled at me, bid me sit before her.

Once seated, I did not speak. She looked at me, quietly, with her deep eyes then said, 'I can see you are suffering.'

I spared her a nod and she said, 'Perhaps you have lost someone.'

This made no impression on me. All of us, those days, had lost someone.

She asked me to spread my palms upon the table. She gazed on them, touching them lightly.

'Yes, I can see much suffering in your life. You have lost someone dear, perhaps more than one. And I see trouble there. A great trouble. Perhaps one who has hurt you badly. Wronged you greatly.'

At this she had my attention, though I wondered of which of you she spoke. Whether of you or the Man. I gave a slight nod.

'Perhaps you are finding it hard to forgive?'

I felt a wry twist in my gut. 'Yes.'

'Perhaps it is in forgiveness that your suffering will ease. That you will find your solace.'

She must have heeded my face, scornful.

'Forgiveness is not about pardoning the other person their wrongdoings.' Her look was intent. 'It is not about for*giving* but for*going*. A surrender to what has happened. An acceptance. Letting go. In that acceptance you are released. You can banish the wrongdoer from your life, for it is not *they* but your *own* feelings of hatred and resentment that keeps you bound to them. In acceptance, that forgoing, not only do we abandon the hatred and resentment but also the culprit. We are freed from them. Their presence in our minds, their power over us.'

Through my grief and turmoil I could not comprehend her fully. What I did understand, I baulked at. Acceptance. Forgoing. Even if I could ever truly accept what had befallen me at the hands of the Man, I could never reconcile what end it, and your role in it, had brought to Mam and Pap. And now I blamed you too for Raff's death. I had not the happy choice of banishing you either from my mind or my life for I was ever bound to you through Moll. I could not just take her and walk away. I could not deprive Margaret of her.

And even if I could find work enough to support us, I knew you would never leave us be. You would not be robbed of your granddaughter. I sat there, deaf to her.

'Have you ever thought our souls are on earth to learn lessons?' she went on. 'That we will come again, those lessons learned? That the one who has wronged you has their own lesson to learn, will be reborn, their soul enlightened?'

I stared at her. No, I did not think it. That the tortured on our earth lived only to serve their torturers' souls so those tormentors might return one day graced. That Pap's, Mam's, my own life had counted for nothing but submission in some way to a heavenly fate, mere sacrifices for the evolution of another's soul. The Man's. Yours.

I stood abruptly, leaving her a coin on the table as I went. She smiled up at me.

'I hope you find comfort.'

Those days my steps led me back to the streets of Soho. Feeling so like I had when I'd lain desolate upon them, there grew in me a yearning once more for Mamma May, she who had been my saviour before. At last, one late summer day, I found myself climbing the steps to knock at her door.

When she opened it, shadowing the hallway with all her flamboyant, stout fullness, I could see her shock.

'Lotta!' she exclaimed, finally. As she ushered me inside, as I saw the old sights, smelled the familiar smell, I had to keep from collapsing into her arms.

She took me into the parlour, unchanged, and as a girl I did not recognise brought tea, I told her my sorrows. She listened sympathetically, sitting beside me on the couch as I cried, pulling me to her, my head resting on her plump shoulder. With her, that day, I shed tears more freely than I had any other. She felt a mother to me.

We talked of what had passed in her life since we'd last met. I wondered if the war had changed things.

'No, love.' She smiled. 'The war hasn't affected my business, not at all. Made the need for it all the greater. Men need to know what it is to smile and laugh. Have fun again.'

I knew at Mamma May's I'd found what I'd been seeking. Through autumn, through winter, I returned. And that wintry afternoon in the parlour, as she handed me the vial, as I put it to my lips, I knew I did wrong. In that moment before the brown liquid coated my tongue I thought of Moll. But I thought also of the world it promised. A world where I had walked with Mam and Pap, a world I might yet walk with Raff.

I tipped back my head and drank.

* * *

He breathed deeply. It had been spring that Margaret had first seen it. She'd arrived home unexpectedly from King's Cross, distressed, gripping Moll's hand before he and Ada in the morning room. She had refused to speak in front of the child, sending her away with the maid for a treat. She was so fretful she'd managed talk to him without acrimony.

'What on earth is wrong, Margaret?' Ada asked, once Moll had gone.

'It's Lotta.' She'd remained in the doorway, as if unsure how to proceed. 'I think she's unwell. I found her . . .'

'Found her where?' He'd grown impatient at her hesitancy.

'She was collapsed. Slumped on the couch. Moll was out of bed, trying to rouse her. I tried myself, and woke her in the end. But she was slurring. She made no sense.'

'Is she ill? Has she a fever?' asked Ada. 'For goodness sake, Margaret, should we not fetch her a doctor?'

'No. She has recovered. I brought Moll with me, to allow her rest.' She went to sit on the chaise longue before she spoke again, quietly: 'I found something else.'

*　*　*

She'd found the vial, empty, by my side. Now I not only took my medicine at Mamma May's but bought my own from the pharmacy. My potion no longer brought me Mam or Pap nor, no matter how I willed it, Raff, but its bitterness brought me the sweetness, the blessed oblivion I craved. But returning cold to this world, I would shake, assailed by visions of torn limbs, bloody, screaming men pleading for God's mercy. So I would wait my chance to take more. Usually I was careful. With Moll in bed, I would take care to hide the vial. But that night I must have fallen into a stupor. That was my undoing.

* * *

Laudanum. As Margaret spoke that day, along with the affront, the revulsion, his outrage at the endangerment to Moll, he'd been aware of a rising elation. The woman was an opium eater. A degenerate. Shameless, as she had proven through her trickery of his son. The discovery brought with it opportunity. One for which he had long hoped.

The child.

39

Long had he wanted the child. Not only for love of her, but for the comfort, the hope she brought Margaret. Brought him. Raff's child. Through her their son lived, would in some way be returned should Moll make with them her home. Whatever rift would surely be healed as together they raised her, delivered her from a squalid life in King's Cross to the one she deserved in Gibson Square. The one she'd been born to. Her birthright.

It had required no thought. Acting straight away, he'd told Margaret that Moll could not possibly be returned to the woman, a clear danger to the child. That if the woman had fallen under the spell of opium she needed guidance, time to recover herself. Ada agreeing, Margaret, usually so ill-disposed towards him, had listened, her allegiance easily won where it concerned Moll. He'd urged Margaret to return immediately to the woman, persuade her, make her see the sense in it. They would care for Moll simply to allow her recuperate. He was aware of the need not to rile the woman. Her revenge scuppered by his son's passing, she might seek satisfaction another way. Be minded to reveal their sordid history to Margaret. Opium oiling her tongue, the threat was even greater, a danger that tongue might be loosened. He had hoped with Margaret's coaxing she could be pacified.

It would give him time.

* * *

When Margaret returned, I was frightened at seeing her, so ashamed, but beside me on the couch she was kind, stroking my hand, assuring me she understood only too well my loss, my pain. I was lulled into comfort but, quickly, as she spoke, saying they must think of Moll, as her meaning became clear, I clutched at her.

'No, please. Please don't take Moll from me. I swear I'll take it no more.'

She gripped my hands, eyes searching mine. 'Can you truly make me that promise, Lotta?'

Feeling my face wild, I knew I was lost. Knew even as I protested, I longed for more. She knew it also. She could see the lie in my eyes.

* * *

He stared out the window. Her need for that poison had been greater than the need for her child. His motives then could be seen to be pure. He'd done what he had for Moll. Solely for Moll. He looked down, rubbed the finger of his glove. That, at least, is what he'd told Margaret, what she believed.

He'd begun to put things in place. The woman had already given him a gift; he'd taken steps to see if she would offer up more. Moll safely in their care, thinking herself on holiday, the woman consenting, for a time to stay away, he'd summoned to his chamber one often employed by the Crown prosecution. A good man. A private investigator. He'd given him his brief. Instructed him to watch her. Tell him what she did.

* * *

That very first evening without Moll, I sped to Mamma May's desperate to tell her what had happened. In the parlour, she held me while I wept, berated myself.

'Hush, hush now,' she said. 'All will be well. We must work to rid you of your craving. How much medicine are you taking?' Ashamed, I told her and she soothed me. 'Then we must go easy, take our time. I will help you, love, don't fret.'

She insisted I stay with her while we purged me of its grip. With Moll away I had the chance to get well in peace, I must take it. I cried and thanked her, burrowing my head in her lap, while she stroked my hair. I knew then, it would be all right. Mamma May would make it right.

* * *

Within a week his man had brought news. Early that week he had seen the woman leaving her King's Cross residence with a carpet bag. She had travelled to another residence in Soho, a well-known house of ill-repute. She had been there since. She would venture out to stroll some afternoons, always with the madam of the house, then return not to stir again.

He'd been astounded. Never had he expected a prize such as this.

'Are you certain?'

'Absolutely certain. She has stayed there every night this past week.'

'And you can testify without doubt to that fact?'

'I can.'

Rubbing the leather of his glove, he thought of his barely stifled glee when he'd informed Margaret. So long he'd wanted to rid her of her affection, her loyalty to the woman, ever more so since Raff's passing, bitter at his wife's cleaving to her, her shunning of him. Even if she could never know of the woman's depravity in deceiving their son, with this revelation he hoped to strip Margaret of every faith in her character.

She'd sat in the drawing room as he stood over her to deliver his blow. She had stared at him, stunned.

'I don't believe you.'

'I can assure you it's true. Have you not come back from King's Cross twice this week, found her not there?'

She was ashen. 'Yes, but I assumed she was simply out. I did not wait for her.'

'Well, you have your explanation now for where she is.'

She'd started to fumble with her fingers, searching the room as if to find an answer. 'But what could she possibly be doing there, William?'

'It's a brothel and an opium den, Margaret. What do you think she is doing?'

He had what he needed now. He'd contacted a colleague, a magistrate at Clerkenwell. They'd met informally in a coffee house near the court.

'You have enough, William, more than enough to satisfy me,' he'd said, slicing his muffin. 'I'll issue an order to remove the child into your charge.'

When he'd told Margaret of it later, she'd been both relieved and pained.

'But is this permanent, William?'

'It's a first step.'

She'd fidgeted with her wedding ring. 'I just don't know what to think. If I could believe she'd simply tinkered with opium, if I could be sure she'd recovered, I would never want to keep Moll from her. But now with the . . .'

He'd heard his wife's unspoken word. *Brothel.* 'But who will tell her?' Margaret said.

'I will.'

* * *

I'd been at Mamma May's ten days when the note arrived. A messenger delivered it, waiting on the steps for a reply. Those awful days I'd longed so much for Moll, but when I saw my girl again, I wanted to be renewed. I had suffered sickly mornings, drenched nights, achings in my bones, it seemed in my very blood, but Mamma May had seen me through my fitful sleep, my tortured days. When she brought the note to the parlour I could not fathom who would be writing to me there.

My stomach gripped as I read.

'It's from him. William,' I said to Mamma May, curious. 'He wants to meet me.' As she frowned in puzzlement, fearfully I voiced her thought. 'How does he know I'm here?'

* * *

They'd met in King's Cross. Her face severe as she'd opened the apartment door, she'd left him to close it behind him. In the sitting-room, settling on an armchair facing her on the couch, he'd realised it was the first time they'd been alone since the trial. Never had he wanted to be alone with her, nor she with him. Now, she would not look at him.

'I trust you are feeling better,' he began.

She'd nodded, eyes cast downwards, then raised them.

'I'm doing very well. I feel myself almost recovered. I've hardly any need now for . . .' She did not finish.

He nodded. 'That's good. Very good.' He'd glanced at a fleck on his trousers, before looking up again. 'However, it's not at all certain that you'll be able to sustain such recovery, resist the allure. They say opium is a very potent thing.'

'It is.' Her jaw was set. 'But I'm determined. I am strong.'

Their eyes meeting for seconds, she looked away. He allowed a moment's silence before speaking slowly. 'You know, Lotta, in law, you have committed an offence. You have wilfully neglected your child, endangered her. Under such circumstances you could be charged, brought before the courts and tried.'

She'd turned quickly, fixing him with her eyes. He went on.

'And then there's the matter of where you've been abiding this past week or more. A house widely known to be one of ill-repute. Not a fact a court would look on favourably or take lightly.'

'I . . .' She flushed. 'But that's where I was getting help. It was there I was recovering. My friend . . .'

He interrupted her. 'Recovering? Recovering from a weakness for opium in an opium den? Do you really think the courts would take that seriously?'

Face bloodless, she stared at him. 'That is why,' he continued, 'all these matters combined – your wilful neglect, endangerment of Moll, your dependency on opium and your keeping, let's say, unsavoury company, I've had to take action. I have a court order that places Moll in my custody.'

She leaped up, fiercely. He raised his hands as if to assure her.

'But you needn't fear. Although you could be charged with neglect and endangerment, face imprisonment – although I could also inform the authorities of your consorting in the brothel, I will not. Not if you take this quietly. Allow the situation to be. Margaret and I will allow you visits to the child. Supervised visits. In this way both you and I win. Otherwise, if you cause trouble for me on this – or any *other* matter – I will have no choice but to pursue a charge, to begin for you a fruitless battle, one you would lose. In such circumstances I could no longer guarantee you access to the child.'

Her eyes drew wide. She made a dash towards him. 'You bastard! You bloody *bastard*!' She lunged at him as he sprang up, grabbing her flailing arms to defend himself from her clawing fingers. Crazed, she screeched into his face. 'You killed Mam and Pap! You *killed* them. We trusted you and you betrayed us, you broke them with your treachery, *crucified* them. And now you have killed Raff!'

At last. At last was unleashed what had lain silent so long between them. He felt a rush as the wound released its poison, the lance at his son's name on her hollow-hearted lips. With every loathing within, he dug into her wrists as she raved.

'And all this time you have tried to be rid of me, but I would not let you bury me as you buried Mam and Pap. You are trying to be rid of me now. But I swear on the head of my child, you will never be rid of me. Never!'

He twisted her wrists, face inches from hers, every word seething:

'I warn you. Take care what you say. Take very great care. If you utter any such slander against me again, I will be forced to act. And you will not like the consequence.'

He flung her away, swiftly leaving the apartment. In the hallway he heard the scurry of her feet behind, but did not look back.

'What have I to lose?' she screamed. 'What have I to lose?'

40

A shout roused him from his trance.

'Chiswell Street, sir.'

With his glove, he rubbed the mist from the window. Letting the carriage roll on some yards, he rapped the roof with his cane.

'Here. Stop here.'

The carriage jolted to a halt. Bending to release the door, bones stiff, he climbed onto the street. The rain had made the paving glisten, the air thick with the stench of the damp nag. He looked through the murky night at the archway before him.

'Just one moment,' he called to the driver, the man nodding, tightening the reins on the restless horse.

Crossing the slippery cobbles to the mouth of the archway, darkened, dank from rainfall, for a moment he was still, then stepped through the stone tunnel to stand at the iron-barred gate ahead.

There it was. The yard, the clock, the sheltered passageway where she and Griffiths had walked that night, lit now not with flaming torches but dimly by gaslight. He turned, trying to see the alleyway to the stables, but it was out of sight. He rested his forehead against the iron bars.

What have you come here for, William? To make reparation? To somehow undo what can never be undone?

Why had he come here? It was because of what happened here that every minute, every hour of his life ever after changed. The lives, too, of those he loved. It was because of what happened here that his life now stood on a precipice. But more. He was drawn here as one complicit in murder is drawn to the scene of the savagery. He had never truly confronted it. What brutality had been inflicted on her here. What she had suffered at the hands of Allen Griffiths. He, assigned the sword of justice, had never been concerned with the crime. He, her protector, had only been concerned with protecting himself.

He made himself think of it now. That girl, so blindly innocent as she walked. A lamb led by the wolf. For the first time, he pictured it. The thud and crack of her head against the alley wall, the force of the blow driving through to her stomach. Her stunned face as he struck it, the red welts, the tears that would have sprung at the sting. The shock, the confusion as she tried make sense of his frenzied groping, his bestial licks, his revolting groans and grunts. The violence. The degradation. The violation. And afterwards. The slow horror as she realised what had befallen her. For the first time he thought of it, really thought of it. The iron bars cut into his forehead.

'I am sorry,' he whispered.

He waited for her voice but she was silent. Silent now.

'I am *sorry*,' he whispered again.

At last, at last: I hear you. But there is more – you are not done, William.

He cast just one more glance at the sheltered passageway, then turned wearily to walk back down the archway. Once more on Chiswell Street he spied lights, heard the muffled shouts, guffaws of men from the nearby tavern. Across the road, beneath the street-lamp, a couple walked, the woman fondly chastising her companion, some men engaging in good-natured banter, one letting a raucous laugh. For a moment he watched, wondering at them: so untroubled, so carefree.

Did they not feel the ghosts around them?

* * *

Do they not feel us, William? All we who have passed here before? What are we now? Have we left our shadow on the cold, grey walls; do they harbour an echo, a sense of us? Does the paving hold an impression of our footsteps, our once-welcoming homes still hear our laughter, the ring of our young voices, or are they forever lost, unheeded by those who dwell there in our place. The same wind that touches those faces, touched mine. I looked upon that same moon. These streets knew my steps just as surely as theirs. What do we leave behind, William? What are we now?

* * *

Ghosts. Everywhere, ghosts. The ghosts of the dead. Of the living. He was haunted by her now in death, just as she had been haunted. By what had happened to her in life. In this place. At his own hands. So many ghosts. The ghosts of death. The ghosts of life. Now was time to lay his own ghost to rest.

He stepped back to the carriage.

'Old Jewry,' he said. 'Police headquarters.'

He'd been fully rehearsed as he left King's Cross that day. He'd returned home to an anxiously waiting Margaret.

'Well?' she'd said fretfully, as he entered the drawing room. 'How was she? What did she say?'

He'd sunk as if drained into the chair.

'It was not good, Margaret, not good at all. The whole thing was greatly disturbing. I am sorry to say, but I think the opium has laid waste to her mind. To be frank, she seemed almost deranged.'

Margaret, harrowed, sat rigid on the edge of the couch.

'What do you mean? What did she say?'

'If I could fathom any of it I would tell you. She spent the hour rambling. Slurring, just as with you that day. She didn't deny her time in the opium den. Rather, she seemed to revel in it. She is lost, Margaret. Lost to any reason.'

'Oh my God, poor Lotta.' Margaret was anguished. 'I must go to her, must try to make her stop this.'

He'd spoken quickly. 'Go to her where? In the brothel? She made no secret of it, that's where she is staying. No, Margaret, let her be. Let her be for now. I did not want to tell you but it's better you know – she is taking no responsibility for her actions, but laying the blame firmly with us for taking Moll. Claiming that's what has her still in the grip of opium. She is raging against us. I don't want you subjected to the same tirade I suffered today. Let's wait and see what comes. Perhaps if she calms, if we can be certain she is in her senses, perhaps then we will talk to her. But not now.'

Margaret, although distressed, had accepted it. She was more genial with him now, had relied on his counsel since the woman's downfall, her need for him greater since Moll's coming. It had brought them closer just as he had hoped. And there was no reason for her to doubt him for all he said, sadly, might only be expected.

He had set the ground.

* * *

I should have been cleverer, William. Should have kept my wits about me. I should have gone to Margaret, alone. Told her what I must calmly, as coolly as you. But you had reckoned well. That deprived of my child, I would be far from within my senses. After you left, I was hysterical. I did not even think to go to Mamma May for guidance, only feverishly paced the apartment, tormented by thoughts of Moll. Did she cry for me?

Did she believe I had abandoned her? I only knew that I must see my girl. And Margaret. I must see Margaret. She would listen. She would help me. I must see her. I must see Margaret.

* * *

That very evening she was at their door, wildly rapping the knocker, shouting from the step. Hastily, he'd instructed the maid not to admit her, urged Margaret to stay upstairs, away from the door. But Margaret had not. She had insisted on standing in the hallway, listening.

Holding Margaret back, he'd caught snatches of the woman's howls: *Betrayed . . . trial . . . worked against us, for the man, wronged us . . . Mam . . . Pap . . . killed . . . killed Mam and Pap . . .*

'What is she saying, William?' Margaret implored him.

'Raving. She is raving. I told you. Come away.' At last he'd managed to coax Margaret upstairs.

Then telephoned the police.

* * *

Two peelers came, grabbed my arms, hauled me down the steps. While one disappeared into the house, the other pushed me into the wagon. The second peeler returned, climbed into the wagon, told me sternly I must not bother you again or they would arrest me. They would take me home now, and there I must stay.

340

But his words slipped over me like water. You had my child. And nothing would keep me away. Nothing.

* * *

She'd returned before they'd arisen next morning. The maid, shaken, had disturbed him in his bed chamber, saying the woman was again at the door. Margaret, woken by the rumpus, stood in her nightgown on the landing, as in his dressing-gown he'd started downstairs. This time he'd been firm.

'Go back to the room now. I will deal with this.'

Immediately he'd telephoned the police, a wagon soon arriving. At the morning room window he'd listened to her screeches as they contained her, then gone to meet the constable in the hallway.

'Don't worry, sir,' the constable said. 'We'll arrest her now. She's had her warning. We'll take her to the station.'

'No.' He'd drawn closer, lowered his voice. 'I'm afraid the woman has been ravaged by opium and has lost all run of her senses. I don't want her arrested. I would rather she obtain the medical assistance she needs. I think it best you take her to Bethlem, place her in their charge. I will see to it from there.'

'Very good, sir. Just as you wish.'

As the constable left, he'd returned to the morning room window. To watch as the wagon rolled away.

* * *

I was battering the wagon, thrashing, yelling for them to let me out. I could not see then, but the wagon crossed the river to Southwark, along the Lambeth Road. It took me to the asylum. Bedlam. Dazed as they hauled me out, I looked about me at a sprawling building with grand pillars, a dome that reminded me of the Old Bailey. I could not fathom my surroundings but as the peelers hoisted me in, seeing white-pinafored nurses I knew I was in a hospital. The peelers herded me down a bright passage into one darkened by iron-grilled windows, these nurses rattling keys and I knew then it was no hospital, but a prison. Pushed into a room where two of these nurses, these rattlers, stood, I was so bewildered I could hardly understand the talk between them and the peelers. It was only when I heard mention of you that I started to screech again.

'No! Please, he is my tormentor. He has tortured me for years, he killed my mother and father. He has stolen my child, my husband, my life from me.' I started flail wildly, the rattlers rushing to grapple with me, one gripping me with a strong arm.

'Take it easy now, or you'll end up in the strait-waistcoat. And you won't like that.'

The peelers left, the two rattlers marching me down the dim passage to grimy stairs, climbing to a bleak gallery with iron-barred windows. Pitiful, bedraggled women roamed beneath a peculiar arced ceiling, some crouching, rocking, muttering, others standing silent, faces to the wall. The rattlers thrust me into what I'd come to know as the sleeping cell, at the bed's head gruesome black shackles and chains. Leaving, the rattlers locked the door as I sank onto the bed and howled.

After many hours, a doctor came. He was an older man, not unkind, and I beseeched him, tried make him understand I was no lunatic, that you had betrayed me, killed my mother and father, stolen my child. That you had killed your own son. I begged him listen. I wept.

With a gentle look, he said, 'But your father-in-law has done you a kindness by placing you in our care. He only wishes your recovery.'

I wailed, leaping from the bed to his feet, clinging to his legs, imploring him. He bent to release my arms, sat me back firmly on the bed. He took the cup he had carried with him from a shelf within the wall.

'Here. Take this. It will make you feel better.'

I looked down at the cloudy mixture he held. For seconds I was tempted. Drink it back. Escape to some blessed oblivion. But I thought of you. Of Moll. How it was love of my medicine that had allowed you to rob her from me. Clinging to the chance of her return, I shook my head.

'Nothing will make me feel better. I have lost all I love. And now I have lost my child. Only she will make me better. Only she.'

* * *

After three days, he had met with her physician, Doctor Adler, at the asylum. In the doctor's office, at his desk, he'd been appraised of the woman's condition.

'There is definitely hysteria there, perhaps a little melancholia, but I have yet to establish if she is suffering raving madness. However, I think I've identified something interesting. A malady much reported on. She's accusing you of many dreadful things, including the murder of her parents and, indeed, your son. This seems to me to have every attribute of paranoia. A disorder by which the patient has something fixed in their mind, an attachment to a false idea of one or more as their persecutor. She has refused sedation, so I'm afraid we are having to administer it forcibly. But, in any case, it's only a temporary remedy. It will do nothing to dislodge such fallacy.'

He'd been jubilant. He'd come in the mere hope of persuading Adler that any accusations the woman might utter against him were solely a madness induced by opium. Her being diagnosed with a sickness seemingly so severe was manna. He'd felt though a quiver of guilt. Quickly assuaged by thoughts of his son, deceived.

'Yes, I always suspected it,' he replied. 'I've long seen a wanting in her, something amiss. Although it worried me, I've done my best to help her. Tried to make her feel welcome in the family. But now the opium. I believe she's been taking it secretly a long time and it has brought to the fore her troubles. I fear she is a danger to herself, a danger to her daughter, as well as myself.'

'Indeed, I agree,' Adler said. 'But we'll do what we can for her here. How successful we'll be I don't know. Time will tell.'

The carriage rocked. They were drawing close to Moorgate. He leaned back his head. *Time will tell.* Yes. It was that of which he'd been afraid. He'd been sure that his influence as a judge could keep the woman confined for years – many years – but what of the future? What if she regained her wits, her cunning, beguiled the doctors just as surely as she had his son. What if she satisfied them she was sane?

And Margaret. She'd been the great danger. Even that first week she'd been desperate to visit the woman. Then, there'd been no question of it, they'd thought the woman far too deranged. But the day would come when that would change. When, finally, the woman repeated her accusations to his wife. Would she come, eventually, to believe her? It was unthinkable. Their union, already so fragile, would be shattered. He would lose her. He would lose Margaret.

And Moll. Moll, as she grew, would most certainly ask questions, wish to see her mother. The child had been pining for her, they pacifying her with treats and promises. Luckily, she was young enough to be distracted. But as she became older – how could he keep her from her mother, then?

No. He'd known it no good. He was trapped. Trapped within this grotesque dance. He had no hope of peace. He would have to contend with the woman for the rest of his life.

Unless—

41

The solution had not presented itself straight away, but come to him over weeks. When the idea, at first abhorrent, had flickered in his mind, he'd dismissed it as pure fancy. But the germ grew shoots. At work in his chambers, papers lying idle on the desk, he would find himself indulging the fantasy. The blissful fantasy of a world without: a world without turmoil, the unrelenting tangle in his mind. A world without fear, foreboding, the threat of being unmasked. A world without torture. A world without her.

With an intoxication akin to madness, he began to imagine, if he were to do it, how he might carry it out. When one Sunday as he sat in Gibson Gardens with Moll in the May sunshine, watching her at play, crouching to a bird to catch it, the bird wildly flapping its wings to make its escape, he was struck by an inspiration. Entranced, it seemed the path now shown, he must follow it. He would find his steps slowing past premises that would provide him with what was necessary. At first, he would deliberately pass perhaps once, twice a week, soon coming to loiter there daily. At last, he'd found himself entering covertly, eventually making a purchase. He'd left somewhat unsteady, furtive, looking about him as if every passer-by knew his thoughts. He had told himself he would buy no more.

Yet, he had returned. Not to that same premises, but others. In his chambers, his eye was constantly drawn to the locked desk drawer, where the packets lay. On the day he had finally opened the drawer to place them in his pocket, after the endless agitation he had felt a certain peace. As if he, himself, had little hand in the matter. As if he were being guided by a force over which he had no mastery. One that he must, that he would, obey.

* * *

I was beset by grief for Raff, for Moll, suffocating in the mire of my prison. They kept me locked up, stifled within my dank, dim cell.

'Allow her no stimulation,' I heard the doctor instruct a rattler. 'It will only encourage her hysteria. We must not excite her emotions but subdue them.'

I had no wish to wander, anyway, out to the corridor where I heard unnatural howls, the eerie incantations, screams of other women. What little I ate I ate in that sickly, lime-washed room, my privy a foul pot. I had no means to wash, and did not care to, but that they did for me. When I banged at the door, wailed to protest my sanity, two rattlers would arrive.

'Out!' They'd haul me out past the roaming women with vacant eyes, others cackling at my plight, to a slimy, tiled room, filling a grimy bath with cold water. Roughly they stripped me, as I yelled, wrestling to bind my ankles and wrists with leather straps, plunging me into the water, then leaving. My limbs bound I could not struggle, although I would holler, but as one hour became two, three, as the ice crept into my bones, it would numb me, my teeth chattering like door-knockers, goosepimples like boils, the agony and shock of the relentless cold striking me dumb.

'There,' they'd say, at last heaving me out stunned and mute. 'That's cooled that fever in your brain.'

I did not learn quickly enough to comply. To bend my will to theirs. When I screamed in rage and frustration as they brought food, they'd fix me on the bed, manacle my wrists and shackle me to the gruesome irons overhead, driving whatever slop into my mouth or leave me there unfed. If I continued to struggle or cried out in anguish, they'd curse me:

'Shut that bloody mouth or we'll leech you. They'll suck the hot blood out of you. Then you'll be no trouble.'

They would leave me shackled for days. Days of staring at the pallid walls, nights of raising my cuffed hands, shielding my ears from the torments of others. Chained, I had no way to use my pot. Hunkered there, my piss seeped through my drawers, soiled with my own muck.

They came for me with the leeches. Strapping me again, they attached the giant, brown, clammy creatures to my chest, my neck, taking pleasure in fixing their grotesque suckers near my lips, so I would sit stiff, afraid to open my mouth for hours, frightened even to twitch. When at last they prised them off, there were purple blotches where they had sucked every blood from me.

No longer did I resist the doctor's medicine. They had come at first with syringes but now I thirsted for their cups. I would drink them down like a dog lapping water, desperate for the escape they offered me. Afterwards, sated, I'd stare vacantly at the iron-barred window, imagining, in my haze, the world beyond. I craved the comfort of Mamma May, Annie and Patience but knew they'd have no notion where I was. On days unbound, I'd curl on the bed, wondering where Margaret was, why she had deserted me. Most of all I longed for Moll but despaired of ever again holding my girl. I lived in dread of the shackles, the baths, the leeches. Like the sucking of my blood, I felt the fight drain from me. I was losing all hope. All hope of liberty.

I would be crucified by memory. The memory of the Man, that Halloween night where the path to this torment, to you, began. I would remember happy Halloween nights of long ago, watching Mam sew Pap's mask, how Pap would catch my arm to frighten me with his tales of the Wandering Souls. Both alarmed and enthralled, I would ponder those unfortunate spirits, wonder why they should wander, what had them so restless? I thought, then, perhaps a pining: the longing to look again upon the faces of their loved ones, to feel their warmth in that cold, cold night.

I think that still. For I know in this groaning purgatory, those beloved faces are all I seek. From the shadows, I try to see Moll but she appears to me only dimly, like a wraith, like it is she who is the ghost. It is you, you alone that is manifest. You made flesh to haunt me.

* * *

At the asylum, the nurses had admitted him. He was the woman's father-in-law, more pertinently, a judge. One had accompanied him through the rancid gallery, wretched women moaning, pointing fingers at him as he passed. The smell foul, he'd covered his mouth with his handkerchief.

'Here we are, sir.' The nurse unlocked the iron-studded door. 'You've a visitor,' she shouted inside. 'Don't cause any trouble or we'll chain you.'

He'd nodded his thanks before seeing the woman there, gaping at him from the bed. He'd been shocked at her appearance. Her simple black dress was soiled with slops, hair unkempt, manner wild. He'd closed the door behind him.

'What are you doing here?' Her eyes had darted feverishly before she sprang up. 'Have you come to let me out?' Her face was alight with a joyful mania. 'Have you come to release me?'

He'd nodded slowly. She'd rushed from the bed, flung her arms around him, clung to him. In that moment, he'd been quite certain the woman was, indeed, insane.

He'd let her cling to him for what seemed an age. It reminded him of when she'd clung to him in the court, believing him her saviour.

He'd lifted her arms, guided her gently back to the bed. He'd sat on it beside her as, her mouth twisted in a perverse smile, she'd desperately searched his face, her own elated.

'I *have* come to release you, Lotta.'

She'd nodded, euphoric, still searching his eyes, gripping his hand.

'Lotta.' He'd spoken with measure, holding her eyes. 'I want you to understand that you will never be free. You will never leave this place, I will make sure of it. You will never see your child again. You will spend all your remaining days in this cell. You must be in no doubt about it.'

All rapture fled, she'd looked perplexed, eyes moving rapidly.

'But I *have* come to release you. I have brought you a gift. I want you to accept this gift from me.' He'd reached into his pocket as she'd watched, jaw twitching. 'Here.' He'd shown her the vials in his hand. The six brown vials.

'My medicine,' she said, feebly.

'Yes. Your medicine. I want you to take it, Lotta. But if you are to have one, you must have all. I want you to take it all. In this way you will be free.'

* * *

In this way I would be free. I knew what it was you offered me. Salvation. Salvation from this place, this pit, this life become for me worse, far worse, than death. For a moment I thought of Moll, but knew she was lost to me. My gaze steady, I surveyed you. My tormentor. My tormentor, at last, truly become my saviour. Our eyes locked in understanding. Silently, I nodded.

Yes.

* * *

He'd stayed with her as she drank. With a hand he'd supported her spine, lifted the vials to her lips when she began to flounder, her head nodding backwards, limply, as if she needed no more.

'Good girl,' he'd said, as she took it willingly from him. 'Good girl.'

* * *

I had a misty vision of you rising, laying me down, leaving my side. I moaned, my head rolling without agency from side to side. I felt a bliss come upon me. Mounting waves of bliss. A smile touched my lips.

At the warmest of rays upon my closed eyes, I opened them to see the iron bars at the window melted away in a glorious sun, a bird like a great golden eagle perched there. Eyes kind as he looked down upon me, he arched his wings, spread them wide, a wonderous weave of golden and ruby threads, before he swept down to scoop me within them, raise me onto his back. Together we flew, high, high above the earth, every field flourishing with great oak trees in lush leaf, flowers with petals bursting in vibrant red, yellow, blue. The wind rushed to meet my face and I laughed wildly as its speed stole my breath, the bird swooping, dancing, diving as if I rode a carousel.

With a sudden halt, the bird aimed its beak skywards to soar. I clung to it as, in a brilliant beam of sunlight, we rose into the heavens, like lightning shooting past the sun, high, higher, until I found myself floating on the carpet of wings in a blackness deeper than darkest night.

There, amongst an abundance of ice-white stars I glided, a peace like I had never known falling upon me. There, in the vastness, in the midst of countless spinning, yet deathly still planets, I looked at the earth below. A perfect circle in perfect silence.

And I wondered at the hush. Here, where the silence was so great, I could hear every beat of my heart, but no longer the thunder of a thousand guns. Where I could see the entirety of the world, yet no longer swathes of savaged lands, the barbed wire wilderness of war. The only sight before me a shimmering silver light binding the earth: a glorious halo of candles torching the darkness. That darkness chased away, bowing to the halo's haunting glow.

42

He'd left the hospital, feet as if not treading ground, reeling with a heady mix of elation and fear. He'd tried to master his nerves. Assure himself there was little chance of discovery, for he'd rehearsed the likely outcomes, in his mind, many times. With the peculiar sensation he did not inhabit his own body, he had hailed a cab, returned home to Gibson Square to wait.

The telephone had rung that evening, just before six o'clock. Lost to agitation in the drawing room, blind to his book, the maid had summoned him to a call from Doctor Adler. Margaret glancing anxiously at him, his stomach giving a sickening twist, he'd tried to raise his hand in reassurance, before walking unsteadily to his study. Preparing himself, he'd lifted the receiver to greet the doctor.

'I am so sorry,' Adler started. 'So sorry to have to inform you that your daughter-in-law, Charlotte, passed away late this afternoon. The nurses found her fitting on the bed. We did all we could, but we could not revive her. Her heart succumbed.'

It was done. Done. He spoke speedily, his genuine giddiness only making more credible his feigned shock:

'But I only saw her this afternoon.' Swiftly, in a tone of deep regret, he began his practised verse: 'It's my fault. I shouldn't have gone, I only distressed her. I went purely hoping to reason with her, to try to make her see sense. That I was not her enemy but one who cared greatly for her. It was useless. She became hysterical, was still hysterical when I left. I should have sought your advice before seeing her.'

'Yes,' Adler said. 'Unfortunately the strain of being confronted by one she saw only as a profound danger might have been too much for her. I have seen it before. But, please, do not blame yourself. You were simply doing what you thought best. As it is a sudden death, if you wish I can arrange an autopsy.'

'No, please.' He'd spoken quickly. 'The poor woman has suffered so much in life. Let us not subject her to any further indignity in death. Let her rest in peace.'

'As you wish,' Adler said. 'Again, I am so sorry.'

His hand shook as he replaced the receiver. He sat. *Dead.* The woman was dead. He'd allowed himself to absorb the enormity of it. How well his plan had worked. He'd taken care, of course, to remove the telling vials. Known her demise would take the form of something vague, a seizure or the like, an occurrence, he was certain, all too commonplace in an institution that housed the hysterical, epileptics. He'd been only too aware the authorities would not trouble with an autopsy for a lunatic unless he, himself, requested it. He'd searched himself for feeling, only finding numbness. A dazed numbness. But relief. Yes, relief. The woman was gone. Finally gone.

Readying himself, he'd returned to the drawing room to deliver the news to Margaret. At his sombre words, her face had crumpled. She'd leaped up, running to clutch at him, refusing believe it.

'But how? Why?' she'd pleaded.

Sitting her down, tenderly caressing her arms, he'd explained, just as he had to Adler, his visit that afternoon. Told her the encounter had been so disastrous, he had not mentioned it for fear of upsetting her. He'd told her how he had tried to assure the woman that he and Margaret only wished her well, for her recovery above all else. That they hoped, one happy day, for the four of them to be reunited, for her to be a mother to Moll again.

'But no matter what I said, she would not listen, only vilifying me just as before. I only meant to hearten her, to make her see she had all to live for. Instead I provoked a frenzy, she became overwrought. I did a great harm. I did wrong.' He lowered his head in lamentation.

'No, no.' Margaret's eyes welled as she lifted his face to hers. 'You did a good thing, only a good thing. Please. Do not berate yourself.' She'd stared stricken at him before sinking, sobbing into his shoulder.

It was then came a surge of guilt. At Margaret's distress, her comforting of him while he lied. But never again would he have to lie to his wife. Never again. Now there was an end to it. At last, an end.

Those next days he'd spent immersed in an other-worldly sense of disbelief at what had come to pass and euphoria. Margaret, driven by grief, had insisted on taking charge of the funeral, arranging that the woman be buried in the family cemetery in Finchley. The thought of her lying beside his mother and father had irked him, but as Raff's widow, Moll's mother, he'd had no choice but to agree. On that June day at the Islington Chapel, only Margaret, he and Ada had been in attendance, Moll, protected from her mother's passing, being cared for by the maid at home.

That day by the graveside, as they'd lowered her down, he'd searched the sky as if for a sign of the gods' displeasure. But the sun had shone instead as if to give its blessing. The birds had sung to him from the trees. All life in full bloom as he'd watched the heavy sod thud upon her.

* * *

It was a sorry end you gave me, William. Only Margaret, just one I loved, to stand watch, yet she cleaved to the one I loathed. No other I loved mourned me, for Mamma May, Patience and Annie could not know what had become of me. But Margaret, dear Margaret, she wept for me. Poor, dear Margaret. She who cast a spray of white lilies into my grave. She who did not suspect, that summer day, how swiftly she would become my companion.

* * *

'Old Jewry, sir.'

The carriage was stopped. Taking a slow breath, with his cane he pushed open the door. He climbed onto the street, handing up what coins the driver requested, the man tipping his hat in thanks, rousing the horse. He watched the carriage roll away, then turned, walking the passageway to the red-brick buildings towering over a small courtyard, a lamp burning there. He could see dim light beyond one of the black arched doors, open. He inhaled deeply before stepping inside.

Behind a wooden panelled desk, a young policeman looked up from his paperwork at his approach.

'William Linden. For the commissioner. I am expected.'

Margaret. Stiffly, he sat at the wall bench, awaiting the summons. *Darling Margaret.* She had lost her son, now his wife. She had clung to Moll those days, steeped her in love, but she had still more to give. The war grinding on, the country was no longer beguiled by tales of glory, but was growing fatigued. Legions of the wounded crammed in chaotic hospitals, they were crying out for volunteer nurses.

Margaret had been eager to play her part. She'd learned of a military hospital in Endell Street, Covent Garden, one run solely by suffragettes. She had gone to them, told them of her son and daughter-in-law's devotion to the cause, how she wished to serve in their memory. It seemed many there knew of their son, of the woman, and they had gratefully accepted her help.

She had found comfort in her work there, fulfilment, brimming with stories of her patients, her admiration for the founder doctors of the hospital. He'd been astounded when he'd heard it. Women doctors. One acting as doctor-in-charge, another as chief surgeon. A woman performing operations. He could hardly fathom it, but he'd held his tongue. He'd only been glad to see his wife so enthused. One evening she had returned home, delighted, telling him that word she was nursing at the hospital had reached Raff and the woman's old Hampstead friends, Annie and Patience, and, meeting her there, they'd gone to a tea-house. She said it had touched her how bereft they were at the woman's passing, how fondly, and with what regard they had spoken of their son.

Even if Raff's ghost lingered between them, those days had passed with more than a modicum of contentment. With Margaret nursing, Ada cared for Moll, beginning to tutor her in reading; the child at five showing a flair for it. Moll, often weepy those early months without her mother, thankfully now mentioned the woman less. They had told her what they could of her father. That he had fallen in noble service of his country, but it was hard to know how much the child understood.

But while they talked to her of Raff, kept alive in her his memory, at the shame of the woman dying in the madhouse, on her they remained silent. It suited him, that she was never spoken of. But sometimes, watching Moll playing, he'd feel the grip of guilt. He had been ruthless, truly ruthless in his pursuit of the child. He'd feel almost shock at his callousness. But he would allow himself to ponder this only for moments, quickly persuading himself it had all been for Moll's good. On the end he had brought her mother, he would never let himself dwell. Senses now restored, it seemed he'd been overtaken by a madness. As if he had emerged from a ghoulish nightmare in which he'd been merely the figment of imagination, cast in a role over which he had no agency. It had not been he but a character carved from insanity, one who had been made mad, who had performed that act. He would banish all thought of it, think instead of what harmony his family now enjoyed. With the woman unstirring beneath the sod.

It began in the spring. Spring 1918. The scourge that would come for Margaret. They said it had been spawned, festered in the trenches and like the fever of war would come to sweep the world. Within war-ravaged countries the press had been silenced, those powers reluctant to further lower morale, to confess this plague that would slay millions. It was only Spain, neutral, that had freely reported it. And so the curse had been named: Spanish Flu.

They had not known much of it then, that early May when Margaret had told he and Ada of it. An affliction so severe that soldiers who appeared well in the morning could be dead by nightfall. He'd been alarmed, anxious that Margaret remove herself from risk, but she'd been determined not to desert her post, insisting it might have been Raff sick, and every hand was needed, now more than ever.

She'd been in good spirits that late May morning. But returned from the hospital that afternoon, coughing, complaining of her limbs sore and heavy. Ada settled her in bed but by evening it was clear she had a fever. The doctor had diagnosed influenza, advised bed rest and fluids, but it was only when a fellow nurse from the hospital, Edith Power, had called to see how Margaret fared, that there was any mention of what deadly strain it might be.

'We are ravaged by it in the hospital,' Edith said. 'You must guard against infection. Keep your distance and keep the child away. I will care for Margaret if you will let me. Please, let me nurse her.'

He had accepted her offer as an experienced nurse gratefully. The woman was formidable, opening every window in Margaret's room and throughout the house. She ordered beef broth and copious jugs of water for Margaret to drink, instructing he and Ada to wash their hands often, allowing them sit with Margaret only briefly, masking and gloving them when by her side. She said they should not touch her hands, but with that command he could not comply.

Those first days, he would sit by Margaret's bed for short spells, placing a forbidden hand on hers, dismayed at her giant beads of sweat, the dire blueish cast of her skin. She was lucid only sometimes, by the third day appearing to struggle for breath. Edith had seen his distress.

'Please, try to take heart,' she said. 'She might recover.'

Sitting, on the fourth day, gloved hand on hers, at last, she seemed aware he was there. She turned her head weakly on the pillow, speaking to him with difficulty, through shallow breaths –

'Please.' The feebleness of her voice struck his heart, like a fist. 'Put Raff's name on my gravestone. Put our boy's precious name beside mine. Let his memory abide with mine there.'

Such talk crucified him. He lowered his mask. 'Don't speak so, my love. You will have no need yet of a gravestone. You will be here. Here with me, with Moll and Ada.' Tone bright, he willed that every dear name rally her.

She grew distressed. 'Please, William, promise me.'

'Of course, my love, of course.' Through his hated glove he gripped her fingers to assure her. Left to him he would rip off the gloves, but Edith had beseeched him to think of Moll.

She went on: 'And Lotta's – put Lotta's there – he would want her name near his.'

He was silent. He felt a stab, a darkness at the name he had not had to suffer in so long. Come with a bidding he was loath to obey.

'William, promise me,' she said, growing agitated.

'I promise,' he said.

It had been the fifth day he'd watched her, no longer lucid, but eyes rolling beneath her lids as if struggling with an unseen enemy. Labouring to breathe, she had lurched up suddenly with a ghastly rattling and whine. She coughed violently, a sickening spurt of blood splattering the sheet. He had looked alarmed at Edith who, rushing to Margaret's side, had ushered him from the room. Distraught, he'd paced the landing until Edith had come.

'I am so sorry, William. So sorry. She has pneumonia. I'm afraid it will not be long now.'

He had stared at Edith, his heart assailed by terror, a silent wail seizing his throat. Hurrying to Margaret's side, he had knelt by the bed, both his hands upon her one hanging limply, head buried in her arm.

'Please, my love, don't leave me.' He'd looked up to see her eyes closed, face stricken. He had tightened his hold. 'Please, my darling, forgive me. Forgive me for our son. For Raff.'

'Raff.' Voice choked, her eyes flitted open for seconds. 'Is he here?'

'Yes, my darling,' he'd whispered, stroking her fingertips. 'He is here. Here with you. Always here.'

Face at once serene, she closed her eyes, only for her body to jerk in obscene spasms. Edith urged him up, gently guiding him from the room.

For a day and a night he had watched his wife trying not to live, but to die. He had witnessed the convulsions, the thrashing, her choking, gasping for air, blood staining the corners of her mouth. It had only been at the end, the very end, when the battle between life and death had been won that she had known peace. As she took her last breaths and her life slipped away.

He looked up at approaching footsteps.

'Mr Linden, the commissioner is ready for you.'

43

It had been then. Then the haunting started. He thought of it now as he followed the policeman down the echoing corridor. It had been those evenings he'd sat by a fire he'd no desire to tend to, listening to Ada somewhere in the house, making special fuss of Moll after the loss of her grandmother. In those mornings he'd forced himself to a work he could no longer care about: a fraud in his chambers, sage hearer of opposing counsel, supposed authority on all deemed just. Weary at those fervent tongues, he'd wondered if the noble flame of truth and justice still lit those young hearts. If they, too, would come to meet their own Clarence Neville, betray their mistress, the Golden Lady, for status or reward. Just as he had all those years ago.

For now in his mournful silence he heard the darkest beats of his heart. Always he'd told himself it was purely for Margaret, Raff, he had walked that treacherous path. But had there not also been the allure of power, a desire to join the hallowed ranks? Had that not also made him willing? In his sleepless nights he taunted himself with it.

He grew certain Margaret's death had come as a punishment. A reckoning for his grievous wrongs. His sentence to be left to endure life without her. What else could it be? Why should he, a transgressor, be spared when she who had lived a lifetime of grace, compassion be taken?

But if he were to believe himself punished he must also believe there a supreme arbiter, a god. Yet if there were such a god, why did his darling wife have to suffer so? What loving god would conceive such scourges, inflict them on his creatures? Why divine a nature so cruel? And man's nature. If God had created man he had moulded then the entirety of his nature, whatever benevolent or malevolent. If all loving, why instil in him what was malign? Only to apparently lament that malignancy. It made no sense to him now.

He would remember, those nights, his son's words: *You do not even truly believe in God.* He'd been right. Whatever passed in his life as belief had simply been handed down like a coat to wear by his father. Yet, in the same instant, he now understood the veneration of saints. The adulation of the Beloved Soul. For his wife he had fashioned of a table an altar, laid across it her shawl, made a shrine of Margaret's treasured pictures, trinkets, a relic of a lock of her hair.

What do we leave behind, William? What are we now?

He followed the policeman through an imposing door, made a silent whisper to wherever Margaret and

Raff might listen: *What are you now? You are the Adored. The Beloved.*

Still, what little belief he'd held lay shattered in the wake of his wife's suffering. It had been in those torturous nights he had heard the beginnings of her voice. The woman's voice.

* * *

Yes, it was then I came to you, William. Then I found my pathway. Into that darkness in your mind, that void in your soul. It was there I rested from my wanderings. There I settled. There I made my home.

* * *

He had strived to maintain some normality for Moll. But the woman's presence had become so consuming, taunts so vicious at his absurd façade as a righteous man, he had neither the faculty nor inclination to carry on. He was fifty-eight years old. When he'd announced his decision to retire early, given his tragic losses, it had not been met with great surprise but much lauding of his achievements. At his farewell ceremony in the judges' dining hall at the Old Bailey, it was she who'd been his companion, who had observed scathingly every toast, her derisory laugh that echoed in his temples at every rapturous speech. He had thought retirement, more time with Moll, might bring him comfort, but it only stirred more her voice within. It was the child's eyes. The child had the woman's eyes.

Moll's trusting eyes had become goading. For he'd see in them the woman once again a girl, looking upon him with those same faithful eyes. He'd think how he had preyed on that faith. With slimy words of caring, had lured her onto his reptilian tongue, spat out her secrets like poison to destroy her, her mother and father. His own cunning repelled him. How then could he damn her for whatever cunning she had plied on Raff? There was no one to blame but himself for whatever had befallen his son. For all that had befallen his son. He'd had not the courage, the moral fibre to deny Neville, nor, deed done, the courage to confess his failings to his family. If he had so loved Raff, cared for him above all, he would have found that courage.

So long he had told himself he was not that man. Not the man who had so cruelly betrayed the woman. That that act had been an aberration. He'd excused his ruthlessness in stripping her of her child by assuring himself it was all for Moll. But it had not been. He had coveted the child. Wanted her to bring to him comfort, heal his marriage, wanted her mother dispatched. In those dark nights, he could no longer hide from that ruthlessness. And her end – the woman's end. It had been no madness overtaken him, he had known only too well what he did. *Mens rea. Actus Reas.* Guilty mind. Guilty act. He had had every wit about him. Had employed again the greatest cunning. Planned that final act, executed it to perfection. That cunning, that ruthlessness frightened him. Appalled him. For now he faced the truth. He was that man.

'Here we are, sir.'

The policeman ushered him into the plush room, mellow green, white-panelled walls, a leather chesterfield beside a mahogany table. His guide leaving, from behind the softly lit desk, the commissioner rose.

'William.' George Harden, one known to him of old, stepped forward to warmly greet him. They shook hands, Harden gesturing him to take a seat at the desk as he himself returned behind it. In silence, they surveyed one another for a moment. Harden placed a hand on some papers before him.

'Well, William, I asked you to meet me at this late hour so there'd be as little as possible to disturb us. I've given much thought to our telephone conversation and, without mentioning your name, have had a discreet word with one or two others. And I've briefed Charles. Made a note here on what he said.'

He nodded silently. Sir Charles Matthews. Director of Public Prosecutions. Now he would hear his fate.

* * *

Through your bleakest hours I was privy to your every thought. I knew myself to be your greatest torment. In death, as in life.

I watched you that November. The day the guns fell silent. There slumped in your study chair, I felt your stifled anguish. Raff. What had you done? You despaired of it: the carnage, devastation. The waste, the futility. For, suddenly, at the striking of a bell, it was over. The eleventh hour of the eleventh day of the eleventh month. Who had decreed the hour the slaughter would cease? What of those fallen on the tenth day? Felled at the ninth hour? For what did their deaths count? You thought of all those professed lucky; the maimed, shell-torn who would be carried, what was left of them, home. What had it all been for? You could not fathom it any longer. What had made you think that crusade so glorious? Honour seeming more vital than life itself.

You recalled your hallowed vision of God, King and Country. But what has become of your vision now? Tell me.

* * *

Harden rose. 'But first a drink, William, let's have a drink.'

He watched Harden walk to the corner cabinet. His once sacred credo of God, King, Country. What of it now? It had been ripped from its plinth, set aflame, ashes scattered over the putrefying flesh on No Man's Land. For, the common man and woman, once wooed by its glory, now saw in that summons only shame. They had lost faith. Now they derided the notion of Empire, their old masters who had wreaked upon them such desolation. Disdain had replaced deference. It was clear his day, the day of his ilk, was done. He sensed it in the brazen attitudes of his maids, the barely hidden scorn on the streets at his gentleman's attire. Some held it had not been military might but the people losing all stomach for it, turning on their governments, that had brought an end to war. A rebellion of hearts and minds but some grown bloody. The Irish taking advantage of sapped British forces to strike for freedom, disillusioned Russian deserters feeding the fire of revolution at home, the Tsar murdered, Bolsheviks ruling in his place. Now was the blight of Communism. Europe's map decimated, new and strange nations sprung from the mire. The menace of Marxism all around him. Workers no longer satisfied with their lot, demanding an end to the old world order. And women. From this hell they had seized their holy grail. He no longer recognised his country.

I can't wait till your world is no more, Papa.

No. This was not his world, nor any world he had ever known.

And he too had lost faith.

* * *

371

Yes. Like I long ago, you had lost faith. Faith in your masters, the creeds of old. Yet you could find no faith in the new.

In the dying days of the war, I watched. Roamed the French city streets of Verdun, tracing Raff's footsteps. In the square, amongst the rocks and rubble, children ran giddy around stray French and German soldiers, only days before sworn enemies, sitting together on broken crates. Stark ruins jutted angrily around them, seared, the city as if a scalded red desert. As if furious gods had torched the old world, leaving it dust smothered, gasping for breath at their feet.

The soldiers let the children play with their battered tobacco tins, dandling the younger ones on their knees. One had taken a harmonica from his holster to blow a merry tune, tapping out the rhythm with his mud-stained boots. Another had leaped up, madly laughing as he stomped over the rubble, his heavy coat flapping over his long black boots.

'*Dummkopf!*' his comrade had shouted to him as if he were crazed, the grinning soldier dancing on.

And I saw them: the minds of those shell-shattered boys in fetid uniforms, insignia made hollow by the gnaw of rats and trench-rot. I heard their silent prayer: that if only they danced wildly enough, long enough, they could dance away the ghosts. The memory of those who would no longer dance; those boys who lingered, like I, watching from the shadows, their impish smiles fading to whatever world they now belonged. And

I knew those left to this world would dance on. Ever longer, ever wilder to chase those dear, those damned away.

And the snow started to gently fall. Gently, gently upon an earth taking fledgling breaths from the fury. An earth shifted beneath us. All we have ever known swept away with the last of the gas on the wind, flickering out like the lone burning embers on the scorched battlefields of France. It was as if the snows had known they must come to cleanse the earth, to numb it, heal it of its pain.

So, your world is gone, William. But been reborn. For, every man who had sacrificed, suffered, demanded now a hand in his own destiny. He who'd been called to risk death for King and Country called in turn for reparation, the right to cast his vote. Dangerous now faithless, to that common man, the vote was granted. Britain no longer a land of lords and masters, but the land of every man. Every man who knew better now.

And women. We women. We who'd abandoned our pantries, our sculleries to serve. We who had proven our mettle, who refused to be tidily put back in place. We, too, were granted that treasured vote. Not like men. Not every woman. Only women of property. Only women beyond thirty years. But it is a beginning, William. A beginning.

And so our new world is come. And I whisper to Raff: *Do you see it, my love, can you see?* I wait, yearn for his answer, but am visited only by memory: *Do you feel it, Lotta? It is to us the new world belongs.* No, my love, no. It is not to you or I, nor Eddie or the Harries that this new world belongs but we that belong to another. For you and they that burned so brightly are lost to the dark. You that gave it breath, breathe no more but lie hushed. Still. Silent now.

And yet you hear our whispers, William. The whispers of the dead. Now you mourn for a world that is gone.

Just as I did.

* * *

Yes, he mourned a world gone. This deviant new world, barren without Margaret, Raff, the son he'd sent to his slaughter, was one in which he had no place. The man he now knew himself to be was one with whom he could not abide. He'd known what he must do. Over the last months he'd made the necessary arrangements, telling Ada only what he must: that he would be gone away, he would disclose more when all was settled. He requested, at his leaving, she close up the London house, take Moll to live with her in Edenbridge. The country, far from memories of her mother, her father, would be a happy place for the child.

Ada, although willing to comply, had been astonished when he informed her that all he had was now theirs, there was enough to keep she and Moll comfortable for their lifetimes. She implored him to tell her how it could be that he would require neither home nor income. He assured her he would have no need of them. He suspected she believed he intended to enter religious orders in Little Gidding. He did not disavow her of that notion.

During those months, he'd had a conversation with an old colleague, Thomas Finch, inviting Finch for a drink in Gibson Square. The man, Griffiths, he the spawn of each torrid event thereafter, played heavy on his mind. He'd wanted to know how the man fared after every sorrow he'd sown. He'd asked Finch, who moved in his circles, what had become of him. Finch had told him Griffiths was well, continuing successful in business, his arm suffered no lasting damage. He was still married to his unfortunate wife, parading about town, well known to be up to his old tricks with cocaine and women. Finch had been scathing of him and men like him.

'It's the power that crazes them, the almighty self, that makes them cruel,' Finch said. 'Allows them to believe they are above the moral and civil law. That the rules do not apply to them. They are cowed to. Lauded. And they become a god. A law unto themselves.' He took a sip of his gin. 'The laws of man may not apply. But the laws of the universe do.'

'You believe in a superior court?' he'd replied. 'In a type of Themis, the Goddess of Divine Justice? That they will be dealt their just deserts in a higher place?'

'I do.'

'I don't,' he'd said.

One week ago he'd made the telephone call. He'd known the likely consequence. The crime he would confess was punishable by death. Death itself no longer frightened him. In some ways he coveted it. Those he loved now dwelt in that other world. Even if he did not believe in Heaven it gave him some solace that he would go wherever they had gone. In this way, at least, they would be united.

Nevertheless, he'd forced himself to reveal all to Harden on the telephone, worried that through delay he might lose courage. After the call, in his study chair, he'd observed his feelings. Light-headed. Light-headed and lightened. But then he had been gripped by a sudden dread. He did not believe in Heaven but it seemed he feared Hell. Damnation. He steadied himself. No. For if he were damned, he must believe those God had abandoned in this life, somehow elevated in the next, in recompense for their suffering. He shook his head. There was no divine justice. So he must deliver his own.

Harden placed the whisky before him, taking his own to his seat, held his eyes before speaking.

'You see, William, we just don't think there's enough here to charge you with.'

He looked at him, astonished. He had admitted to murder. Committed murder.

'I murdered her.'

'No.' Harden gave a slight smile. 'The woman took the substance willingly. You didn't force her. And laudanum is perfectly legal. A totally legitimate purchase. You did nothing wrong, William.'

He knew and Harden knew he lied. He had knowingly supplied the woman with the means to kill herself, had coerced her to take it.

'She killed herself, William. And I'm sure your actions were purely benevolent. That you only wished to ease the woman's suffering. You had no way of knowing she would die.'

He opened his mouth to protest that he had been sure, certain she would die. That he had hoped for, intended it. That it would be her end.

Harden had spoken before him. 'William, Charles has made it clear that there is no charge to answer. No case to be brought.' His tone was firm. 'We want you to rest now and enjoy your retirement. Let that be an end to it.'

Harden did not wish him to say anything further. The custodians of justice wanted him to go away. Did not want the scandal of a judge convicted of a crime so heinous, such disgrace brought upon the office. Harden finished his drink and stood, extending his hand to bring the meeting to an end.

'Go home, William. To your grandchild.'

Leaving the untouched drink, he stood, did not shake Harden's hand but, stupefied, nodded his goodbye. Bewildered, he walked from the room to the harsh light of the corridor. There had been a crime but there was to be no punishment. He was at liberty but that liberty felt to him a curse. *Go home, William, to your grandchild.* He had no home. His home was no more. And his grandchild. Go to her. To the torture of her eyes.

* * *

Ah, William. You seem so cruelly disappointed. As if you had faith in those bastions of the law. In the justice you once held so dear. But it seems we do not live in a world where only the guilty are punished. The innocent, the blameless are hurt by Acts of God. Acts of Man. It seems there is no justice.

So I must deliver my own.

* * *

He stepped through the open door into the courtyard. He was free. Free to walk the streets, breathe the air. But he would never truly be free. *It seems there is no justice. So I must deliver my own.*

* * *

Yes, William, it seems I must stay close. That we have not reached the end of our story. For you have been granted freedom, but that will never be.

Your wound will ever weep with mine. Not only the wound of that cold, cold Halloween night and your every deed after. But the greatest wound. For you stole from me the very blessing of life. I remember now a fireside on another All Hallows' Eve so long ago. Of Pap holding me, a child, Mam chiding him as he scared me with his whispers of the Wandering Souls.

And I thought on why they should wander. But I know now what they crave: once more to sink their feet into the rich brown earth, to revel in the gusts of wind, the gentle rain upon their faces. I know of that yearning. And what I yearn most of all to feel but never will again: the tender touch of my child.

You will know my girl's touch, but it will not settle on you soft like feathers but harsh like thorns. For you, like I, are destined to wander, ever seeking peace but will know no rest.

And I see again Pap, holding me on that long ago All Hallows' Eve. But it is that child now abides in shadow and I that am spirit. I that have taken my place with the Wandering Souls. And I know all they seek.

Know they long, just as I, to be free.

* * *

He closed his eyes at her voice. Yes. There was justice. There was punishment. The punishment of her. The eternity of her. She and he forever bound by what wrong he had done her. By what had passed there in Chiswell Street so long ago. By all that had come of it. Truly, they were both haunted. By the ghost of Chiswell Street.

He opened his eyes. Each step through the passage-way brought him closer to the emptiness of home. To the child's eyes. Now he would have to watch her grow. He, for her sake, doomed to play the part of the contented grandfather, to hide from her the torment within. He would grow older, frailer, to watch her become stronger. Almost certainly to become a woman uncannily like her mother, in appearance, manner. The woman once again made flesh. He would be confronted, condemned by that vision every day. By the lie he lived and the truth of himself. Every hour of every day.

Standing on the wet paving, glistening under gaslight, he remembered. In September he had taken Moll to visit her grandmother's grave, given her a posy to lay there. He'd drawn his finger over Raff's beloved name by Margaret's to show it to her. As Moll had crouched by the graveside she'd spied a name at the foot of the grave-stone in fainter script. The name of one to whom he could not bear to give the title Linden. Could not bear to see etched beside that of his wife and son, but near enough that he kept a promise he had made to his wife.

Moll had peered up at him with those deep, inquiring eyes, and asked of him a question. The question he knew he must one day answer.

'Grandpa. Who's Lotta Rae?'

END

Acknowledgements

Acknowledgements are difficult for me to write because, although they serve mainly to acknowledge those who have played a part in the book, I want to include everyone from every time and place that has been dear to me, however impossible that may be.

So first, my agent, Sara O'Keeffe. Thank you, Sara, for your expert guidance and faith in my story. Thank you for being Lotta's champion, I will be eternally grateful. To Rosa Schierenberg for her calm and patience as we transported Lotta to these pages. To Cat Camacho for her keen eye, Alexandra Allden for her beautiful cover, and all the team at Welbeck for their tireless work. You have done a sterling job and I am so thankful to each of you. To Emma Dowson at ED P.R. and Simon and Declan at Gill Hess, thank you for your diligence twinned with gusto.

As this is my first book I will indulge my need to acknowledge people, times and places that have meant much to me. Although I can't name each person, if we shared those times I am thinking of you.

To my beloved father, thank you for the confidence you instilled in your children – the belief that anything we dreamed of was within our grasp. Dad, you and I walked the same City streets that Lotta walks with her own father: Chiswell Street, Whitecross Street, Liverpool Street. We did so, many times on Sunday mornings, along streets deserted and ghostly, allowing me to imagine who might have walked them in another time, long ago. To wonder if perhaps they walked them still. And to my brother: the King's Cross streets where Lotta abides we strode together, youthful and sprightly, serenading passersby with uninvited renditions of *Peggy Gordon*, pennies in scant supply but joy in abundance. To you, Victoria and all the boys and girls from those King's Cross and London days, you remain ever young in my memory.

To my bosom buddies, Shelley Harris and Sarah Capp, who have suffered my insistence to be a writer since I was a teenager. A writer I became, a novelist took a little longer. Luckily, you were patient. Thank you to you and all our friends – our cherished crew with whom we've shared so much fun.

To the many lads and lassies who danced the days away with me in Dublin town, and to the lasting friendships I formed there. To Billi Webster and Katell Keineg for their unending support, and Jadzia Kaminska whose house supplied the table for my early scribblings. To Marion McKeone who has been a stalwart, a crusader and a constant source of encouragement for me. Thank you.

To Lisa Hall in Tipperary, Lotta Rae's first reader, and our pal Mary Deane, who deserves a mention just for being herself but also for always having faith in me.

To my dear extended family. To the Mad Park clan: you all mean so much to me. To Catherine Leech, an avid reader who also advocated avid writing. To my Tipperary kin and Mary Taylor, who lent an ear to past publishing woes over tea and buns. To my Dublin cousins and wise elder of the MacGowans, Uncle Billy. To Rena and my husband's family. And my husband himself: Anthony Hayes.

Anthony, thank you for the belief you have shown in me since we met many moons ago. Thank you for your deep care, your loyalty and your love. It could well be impossible for you to know how much you are loved in return.

And to those who go unnamed but belong here, I am grateful for you all.

About the Author

© Anthony Hayes

Siobhan MacGowan is a journalist and musician who lived and worked in London for much of her life before returning to Ireland several years ago. She is from a family of great storytellers, the most prominent of which is her brother, Shane MacGowan, of *The Pogues*.

This is her debut novel.